Praise for *The Matters at Mansfield*

"A charming rogue, the kind of tongue-in-cheek humor that is perfectly at home in formal Regency language, and a nearly perfect murder hit the right note and will captivate readers in this nineteenth-century Nick and Nora Charles adventure."

—*RT Book Reviews* (4 stars)

"Lively plot, engaging characters, and a surprising finale."

—*Publishers Weekly*

"Combining elements of mystery and romance, the plot moves along quickly in immaculate, Austenesque prose." —*VOYA*

Praise for *North by Northanger*

Winner of the Daphne du Maurier Award and the
RT Book Reviews Award for Best Historical Mystery!

"An utter delight . . . every aspect is pitch-perfect."

—*RT Book Reviews* (top pick)

"Bebris provides another feast for Janeites in . . . this well-told tale."

—*Publishers Weekly* (starred review)

"Bebris captures Austen's style and the Regency period perfectly, drawing her characters with a sure hand. Her plot is poignant and gentle and will appeal to readers who prefer their mysteries without murder or violence." —*Library Journal* (starred review)

Other Mr. & Mrs. Darcy Mysteries by Carrie Bebris

Pride and Prescience (Or, A Truth Universally Acknowledged)
Suspense and Sensibility (Or, First Impressions Revisited)
North by Northanger (Or, The Shades of Pemberley)
The Intrigue at Highbury (Or, Emma's Match)

The Matters at Mansfield

(OR, THE CRAWFORD AFFAIR)

A Mr. & Mrs. Darcy Mystery

Carrie Bebris

A TOM DOHERTY ASSOCIATES BOOK

NEW YORK

This is a work of fiction. All of the characters, organizations, and events portrayed in this novel are either products of the author's imagination or are used fictitiously.

THE MATTERS AT MANSFIELD

A Forge Book
Published by Tom Doherty Associates, LLC
175 Fifth Avenue
New York, NY 10010

www.tor-forge.com

The Library of Congress has catalogued the hardcover edition as follows:

Bebris, Carrie.
The matters at Mansfield, or, the Crawford affair / Carrie Bebris.—1st ed.
p. cm.
"A Tom Doherty Associates book."
ISBN 978-0-7653-1847-3
1. Bennet, Elizabeth (Fictitious character)—Fiction. 2. Darcy, Fitzwilliam (Fictitious character)—Fiction. 3. Married people—Fiction. 4. England—Fiction. I. Title.

PS3602.E267 M38 2008
813'.6—dc22

2008030413

ISBN 978-0-7653-2383-5 (trade paperback)

First Edition: September 2008
First Trade Paperback Edition: September 2010

Printed in the United States of America

P1

For my brother

Acknowledgments

This novel began like all my others, with a faint whisper of an idea that developed over time into a fully realized story. As it evolved, many people lent their support, and in so doing contributed to the creation of the book you now hold in your hands.

My family probably feels sometimes as if I live in nineteenth-century England along with the Darcys. I am grateful to them for enabling and encouraging me to do so.

I appreciate my agent, Irene Goodman, for her advice and continued belief in me; my editor, Brian Thomsen, for trusting me when I said the Darcys next needed to visit Mansfield, and for his guidance on a number of matters during the writing of the novel; his assistant, Kristin Sevick, for her conscientious and prompt attention to endless details; Dot Lin for her promotional talents; and artist Teresa Fasolino for the beautiful paintings that grace the covers of the books in this series.

Fellow writers and friends Anne Klemm, Victoria Hinshaw, Mary Holmes, and Pamela Johnson served as sounding boards and critical readers at various stages in the book's development. Their input and ongoing support were invaluable.

For my education in dueling and the mechanics of flintlock pistols, I am indebted to Kristopher Shultz, a historical interpreter and weapons expert whose knowledge and enthusiasm brought to life these aspects of a nineteenth-century gentleman's existence. I am grateful to attorney Sheila Quigley for helping me navigate the complexities of Georgian marriage and estate laws, to Dr. Cheryl Kinney for her knowledge of Regency-era medicine, to Ann Voss Peterson for her horse expertise, and to dancing masters Lee Fuell, Patty Lindsay, and Joyce Lindsey for their patient instruction. I also thank the reference librarians of Woodbourne Library for so cheerfully and capably tracking down materials and answers to obscure research questions.

Others provided support in ways less direct, but no less appreciated. Many thanks to Sharon Short, Sarah Schwager, Karen Downey and the staff of Carousel House, members of JASNA-Dayton and JASNA-Wisconsin, and JASNA president Marsha Huff.

Finally, I thank Jane Austen for inspiring the Mr. & Mrs. Darcy mystery series, and my readers for inspiring me to continue it. A bookseller once told me, "You have the *nicest* fans!" and I quite agree. You help make writing a joy.

"There is not one in a hundred of either sex, who is not taken in when they marry. . . . It is, of all transactions, the one in which people expect the most from others, and are least honest themselves."

—*Mary Crawford,* Mansfield Park

The Matters at Mansfield

One

She was all surprise and embarrassment.

—Mansfield Park

It is a truth less frequently acknowledged, that a good mother in possession of a single child, must be in want of sleep.

Whatever the habits or inclinations of such a woman might have been prior to her first entering the maternal state, in very short order her feelings and thoughts are so well fixed on her progeny that at any given hour she is considered, at least in the young minds of the principals, as the rightful property of some one or other of her offspring.

Be she a woman of comfortable income, assistants may alleviate many of the demands imposed on her, and indeed there are ladies quite content to consign their little darlings entirely to the care of nurses and governesses until they reach a more independent age. But in most families, occasions arise when even the most competent, affectionate servant cannot replace a child's need for Mama, and when said Mama wants no proxy.

And so it was that Elizabeth Darcy, wife of Mr. Fitzwilliam Darcy, mistress of the great estate of Pemberley, and presently the houseguest of the Earl of Southwell, found herself the only conscious person in all of Riveton Hall during the predawn hours of an early August morning. Or rather, the only conscious adult, her daughter being so awake to the pain of cutting her first tooth that none but her mother's arms could comfort her.

"Hush now, Lily-Anne. Mama's here." Elizabeth offered the crooked knuckle of her forefinger to the child to gum. Having come to the nursery to check on Lily before retiring, she had found both baby and nurse so overwrought by hours of ceaseless crying (on the child's part, not the nurse's) that she had dismissed Mrs. Flaherty to capture a few hours' rest. The stubborn tooth had troubled Lily since their arrival and rendered futile every traditional remedy the veteran nurse had tried. If it did not break through this eve, the morrow would prove an even longer day for Mrs. Flaherty and her charge. Elizabeth herself would be unavailable to soothe her daughter, her time instead commanded by the event that had occasioned her and Darcy's visit to Riveton.

Darcy's cousin Roger Fitzwilliam, the earl, was hosting a ball to introduce his new fiancée to his family and neighbors. The Pemberley party—Elizabeth, Darcy, Lily-Anne, and Darcy's sister, Georgiana—had traveled to the groom's Buckinghamshire estate earlier in the week, as had the bride's family and numerous other guests. Darcy and Roger's aunt, Lady Catherine de Bourgh, had been the first to arrive, appearing a full fortnight earlier than anticipated to oversee her nephew's preparations. As the late earl's sister, her ladyship had grown up at Riveton Hall, and continued to generously dispense opinions regarding its management. That the present earl had little interest in hearing her advice did little to check its flow.

Having herself recently endured an extended visit by Lady Catherine, Elizabeth sympathized with her besieged host.

The earl, however, enjoyed one advantage that Elizabeth, in Derbyshire, had not: Lady Catherine yet maintained a large acquaintance in her former neighborhood, and had absented herself from Riveton for part of each day to call upon them. Her daughter, Miss Anne de Bourgh, joined her on most of these excursions. How Southwell's neighbors bore Lady Catherine's company eluded Elizabeth and Darcy, but they were grateful to be subjected to so little of it themselves. Their already inharmonious relationship with Darcy's aunt had been further fractured by the events of her prolonged residence at Pemberley, and the present house party at Riveton marked their first meeting since. Her daily absences had enabled them all to settle into a tacit, if tense, truce.

In contrast, Elizabeth had taken great pleasure in renewing her acquaintance with Roger's younger brother, Colonel James Fitzwilliam, whom she had met two years previous. The colonel's forthright manners and intelligent conversation united to make him the most amiable of Darcy's maternal relations, and she regretted that his military duties prevented more frequent opportunities to enjoy his society.

The only society Elizabeth coveted at the moment, however, were the inhabitants of her dreams. She paced the nursery, murmuring the sort of sibilant nonsense mothers have employed for millennia to calm distressed infants. Despite the stimulus of Lily's wails, her own eyelids burned with the urge to close. Yet even if she roused Mrs. Flaherty and returned to her own quiet chamber, she knew that maternal anxiety, or at a minimum, maternal guilt, would not allow her to sleep while her daughter suffered.

She sang. She rocked. She paced still more.

At last, exhaustion claimed Lily-Anne, and blessed silence settled upon the nursery. It was, however, a fitful slumber. Lily was still in discomfort, unconsciously rubbing her jaw against her mother's shoulder and squirming each time Elizabeth tried to lower her into the crib. Elizabeth sat with her awhile in a chair, but was so tired that she did not trust herself to retain a safe hold on Lily should she, too, succumb to sleep.

She decided to bring Lily back to her own chamber, in hopes that a shared bed would enable them both to rest. Darcy would not mind. There had been a few occasions at Pemberley when Lily, in need of extra comfort, had slept in their bed, and Darcy's presence often had a calming effect on the baby, awake or asleep.

She moved quietly as she carried Lily down the corridor where the earl's relations were quartered. The bride and her family occupied the floor above, and several gentleman friends of Roger's were in another wing altogether. She did not fear disturbing these more distant guests should Lily suddenly waken and complain at full volume, but Lady Catherine's room she passed with extra caution. Her ladyship's tenure at Pemberley had proven her a light sleeper, ever alert to everyone else's affairs.

She rounded a corner and stopped suddenly.

Anne de Bourgh appeared equally startled. They had very nearly collided. "Mrs. Darcy!"

"Miss de Bourgh?"

Both spoke in the lowest of whispers. Anne cast an alarmed glance in the direction of her mother's chamber. In the weak grey light just beginning to penetrate a nearby window, her face appeared pale as usual, but her features had lost some of their sharpness. The angles of her cheekbones had rounded, dissolving her typically haughty expression and softening her countenance. Instead of pinched, she looked almost pretty.

"I—I did not expect to—that is . . ."

"Nor I." Elizabeth shifted Lily to her other shoulder. The child had entered a deeper sleep as they walked and was becoming heavier by the minute. "I thought none but Lily and I was awake, and even she has finally decided the hour is grown quite late enough." She tried to formulate a polite query as to why Miss de Bourgh was wandering Riveton Hall fully dressed at half past four in the morning. She doubted that Anne, coddled since childhood for fragile health, routinely kept late hours. But her fatigued mind was not equal to the challenge of clever phrasing. "What draws you from your bed at this time of night?" she finally blurted.

"No one. I mean—"Anne nodded at Lily. "The child did not wake me, if that is your concern."

It had not been. In fact, the thought had not so much as entered Elizabeth's mind, which was primarily occupied with calculating how many hours' sleep she might yet manage to capture if she nodded off immediately upon reaching her pillow. Another part of her brain was attempting to determine whether Anne's improved appearance were indeed a trick of the light or a genuine transformation. Upon continued observation, the view afforded by their unusually close proximity suggested the latter.

Anne bristled under Elizabeth's scrutiny. Her gaze strayed to the window. "Actually, I am not up late, but very early. I woke and could not return to sleep, so I thought I would stroll in the rose garden whilst the sun rose."

Unlike herself, Elizabeth had never known Miss de Bourgh to take pleasure in walking or, for that matter, to walk any farther than necessity demanded. Lady Catherine had always kept her on a short tether, ostensibly to protect her weak constitution. The most vigorous exercise permitted was airings in a phaeton or immersions in the therapeutic waters at Bath.

Until now.

The change of practice might account for Miss de Bourgh's improved looks—Elizabeth had previously entertained the opinion that Anne's health would benefit from more, not less, exercise—though she wondered that her mother allowed it.

Or did she?

Miss de Bourgh's eyes again looked toward Lady Catherine's door. Pity moved Elizabeth as realization dawned along with the sun. To escape her ladyship's disapprobation, Anne had to take her exercise before anyone in the household—her mother, her chaperone, even the servants—awoke. Else an accidental slip of someone's tongue could betray her actions to Lady Catherine, who would bring them to a swift and decisive halt.

Elizabeth had never given much thought to Anne's life. She knew that living with Lady Catherine would be intolerable for herself, but she had never contemplated Anne's happiness. Anne had always seemed a mere appendage to the formidable entity that was Lady Catherine, existing to serve her mother's convenience. Now she wondered whether the "poor health" from which Anne had suffered all these years were the result of smothering—a slow suffocation of the soul.

How long had Anne been rising early to enjoy an hour's freedom before the shackles of life under Lady Catherine's domination closed upon her each day? From her appearance, she had been engaging in the practice for some time.

Good for her. Elizabeth wanted to praise the benign deception, but tact restrained her. She would, however, encourage it.

"I suspect what you are about," she whispered, offering a slight, knowing smile. "But do not be uneasy. Your secret is safe with me."

Anne's eyes widened. She stared at Elizabeth, struggling to formulate a reply.

Elizabeth spared her the trouble. "I wish you a pleasant morning," she said as Lily released an unfeminine snore that was a sweet lullaby to her mother's ears. "I intend to spend mine lying abed as long as my daughter permits me."

Two

There were more Dancers than the Room could conveniently hold, which is enough to constitute a good Ball at any time.

—Jane Austen, letter to her sister, Cassandra

"Miss de Bourgh has altered since we saw her in Bath last October."

Mr. Darcy regarded his wife curiously, then followed her gaze across the ballroom. It required a full three minutes to spy his cousin amid the scores of guests milling about, but at last he caught sight of her. Anne de Bourgh stood with her mother and Mrs. Jenkinson, her ever-present attendant, at the side of the dance floor. The de Bourghs were engaged in conversation with an older gentleman he recognized as one of Riveton's neighbors, the Viscount Sennex.

More accurately, Lady Catherine conversed. Anne listened silently, her attention straying to other parts of the busy room as her mother soliloquized unchecked. Wandering concentration, however, was endemic to participants in Lady Catherine's conversations. It was how one survived them.

"Altered?" he asked. "How so?"

"She only half attends her mother's discourse."

"After nearly three decades of constant exposure to it, she has likely heard the main theme before."

"But note how closely she observes the couples dancing. I believe she wants to join them."

Darcy doubted his cousin harbored any such desire. In fact, so restricted had been Miss de Bourgh's upbringing—her mother had forbidden even pianoforte lessons as unduly taxing on her health—that he was not entirely confident Anne so much as knew a waltz from a reel. "I have never seen my cousin dance."

"That is precisely my point. Do you not think it possible that she longs to engage in some of the same pursuits and pleasures as all the other young women of her acquaintance?"

Darcy looked at Anne again—truly looked at her, for perhaps the first time in twenty years. It is an easy thing to see one's longest acquaintances without actually seeing them—for familiarity to breed, if not contempt, incognizance—and to view people as they were, or as memory constructs them, rather than as they are. To Darcy, his cousin was merely a vassal in Lady Catherine's tightly controlled court. In all the years of their growing up, he had never thought of her as an independent being, and seldom thought of her at all. But now, forced by Elizabeth's conjecture to study Anne, he detected an air of wistfulness about her. The dancers indeed held more of her attention than did her own party.

"Perhaps she does wish to dance," he conceded.

Mrs. Jenkinson adjusted Anne's shawl, bringing it up round her shoulders. The heavy lavender fabric was more appropriate for winter wear, and appeared out of place amid the short sleeves and light wraps exhibited by all the other ladies of the assembly. The heat of the room rendered the garment entirely unnecessary—indeed, probably uncomfortable—but Mrs. Jenkinson persisted.

As soon as the attendant turned her head, Anne slipped it to her lower back.

Darcy approved the small display of spirit. He had never expended much thought on Miss de Bourgh's state of happiness as a permanent inmate of Lady Catherine's domestic circle. He had seen her only as the prim, emotionless person into which life under her mother's domination had formed her, and assumed that she had been content in that role. As babes yet in their cradles, Darcy and Anne had been the objects of an informal matchmaking scheme. Whensoever a boy and a girl of compatible age and station belong to families who share an acquaintance, the circumstance invites speculation from their mothers, if not the whole neighborhood, as to the possibility of a future wedding. The Fitzwilliam sisters had not been immune to this propensity, and had once indulged in an afternoon's fanciful supposition that perhaps one day the cousins would wed. Darcy's mother had died before he reached marriageable age, but in Lady Catherine's mind the idle "what-if" became an expectation—one that he had never intended to fulfill. He could by no means tolerate such a domineering woman as his mother-in-law, nor could he imagine her daughter capable of warming any man's bed, let alone heart. It would have been a marriage of misery, and from early adulthood he had tried to discourage all hope on the part of both his aunt and his cousin of its ever occurring.

Whether Miss de Bourgh had wished the match, he knew not, nor whether she harbored any other desires or dreams. If she did, he doubted Lady Catherine ever gave her opportunity to voice them. What a dreary existence his cousin must lead.

"This set will end soon," Elizabeth said. "Invite her to dance."

Darcy nodded, his eyes still on Anne.

"What is this I hear?" The familiar male voice behind him

prompted Darcy to turn round and meet the cheerful countenance of Colonel Fitzwilliam. "Not two summers wed, and already your wife encourages you to stand up with other women rather than endure your dancing herself?"

Two years older than Darcy, the colonel was his favorite relation, his friend as well as his cousin, and one of the few people from whom Darcy accepted jesting.

"I am afraid so," Darcy responded. "Are you now disillusioned about the longevity of nuptial bliss?"

"Not in the least. Rather, I am convinced that only true devotion could have blinded Mrs. Darcy this long to your rigid deportment on the ballroom floor." The colonel bowed to Elizabeth, who answered with a broad smile.

"Fortunately, Colonel, should you ever decide to enter the marital state yourself, your bride will have no such deficiency to overlook," she said. "You and Georgiana acquitted yourselves quite well earlier."

"A compliment more deserved by my partner than by me. Miss Darcy inherited all her mother's grace, leaving her brother bankrupt in that asset."

"You unjustly disparage your own talent along with my husband's. I grant you leave to exercise all the modesty you like, but if you continue to tease Darcy so, he will never again dance with anybody, let alone with Miss de Bourgh."

His eyebrows rose. "Our cousin is the lady in question?"

"Someone ought to invite her. Whether she accepts or not, a woman likes to be asked." She cast an arch glance at Darcy. "Though I have heard that my husband is not in the habit of giving consequence to young ladies who are slighted by other men."

The gently delivered rebuke echoed in Darcy's mind, pricking his conscience. "You are correct—Miss de Bourgh should at least receive the compliment of an invitation, though she is certain to decline. It would displease Lady Catherine if she exerted herself unnecessarily."

Colonel Fitzwilliam chuckled. "All the more reason to ask, I should think. It does our aunt good to have her will subverted on occasion."

"And as I have already earned her ladyship's censure for choosing my own wife, I might as well compound it?"

"Nay, you have proven your valor sufficiently. As a younger son, I have not nearly as many opportunities to demonstrate independence. Therefore, allow me to be the one who invites our cousin to dance."

"Very well. We will abet you by distracting Lady Catherine. During our aunt's visit to Pemberley this past winter, Mrs. Darcy developed quite an aptitude for it."

They joined Anne and her mother just as Lady Catherine paused for breath in the monologue she had been delivering. Lord Sennex nodded.

"Quite right, quite right." The white-haired sexagenarian leaned heavily on his cane, his own thin frame not much more substantial than the walking device. His clothes hung loose upon him, a contrast to the more close-fitting garments worn by all the other men in the room. "You are a sensible woman, Lady Catherine. I trust your daughter inherited that trait." He looked at Miss de Bourgh, but Anne was oblivious to the viscount's praise. The music had paused, and her attention was focused on the top of the room, where couples lined up to form a new set.

Colonel Fitzwilliam greeted the ladies and their companion. "Lord Sennex, have you met Mrs. Darcy?"

"Mrs. Darcy?" He regarded Elizabeth blankly. "I cannot say I have the pleasure of acquaintance with the lady, or her husband."

The denial took Darcy aback. He had dined with Lord Sennex

during previous visits to Riveton Hall, occasionally at the viscount's own home.

"Your lordship surely remembers Mr. Darcy," Lady Catherine said. "He is my nephew—my late sister's son."

Lord Sennex stared at Darcy, wrinkling his brow as he struggled for recollection. "Oh, yes," he finally said. "Of course." Though he nodded heartily, his eyes revealed no spark of recognition. "Pray, forgive my error."

It was a shame to see that the viscount had deteriorated so since Darcy last met him. He had always been a vigorous man, full of potency and fire. A second son, he had served as a major in His Majesty's army during the American Rebellion before inheriting the viscountcy upon the death of his elder brother. Though he had sold his military commission, he had never relinquished his commitment to the principles of honor and courage he had served. He was even rumored to have fought a duel or two in defense of them, and was their advocate in the House of Lords when debating with his peers. His had been a life of dignity and vitality.

And now he could not even recognize Darcy's face as he stooped over his cane.

"There is nothing to forgive, my lord. It has been several years since I last had the pleasure of seeing you."

"I suppose it has. Do you know Neville, as well, then?"

Ten years Darcy's senior, the Honorable Neville Sennex was the viscount's only son and heir. "Indeed. He included me in one of his hunting parties the last time I was in the neighborhood."

At the word "hunting," his lordship nodded enthusiastically. "Neville runs his pack five or six times a week during the season. This warm weather makes him restless as a treed fox—autumn can hardly come soon enough. I presume you caught your quarry that day?"

"The creature eluded us with a ticklish scent for two days, but the third morning we managed to capture it."

"Neville won the brush, no doubt. He is a passionate sportsman."

"So I recall." Too passionate, in Darcy's estimation. Neville Sennex kept a large, well-trained pack, but was himself a noisy hunter whose excessive shouts and tendency to override his hounds impeded their chase. Insensible of his own contribution to their failure, Mr. Sennex had been so angry after the second blank day that he had beaten not just the dogs but also one of his whippers-in. Darcy and Colonel Fitzwilliam had shifted uncomfortably in their saddles during the ungentlemanly display, and returned for the third day of the foxhunt only to avoid offending their neighbor.

Darcy glanced at his cousin to determine whether he, too, remembered the incident, but Fitzwilliam had engaged Miss de Bourgh in muted conversation. Just beyond Lady Catherine's peripheral vision, Anne nodded and took the colonel's proffered arm.

Elizabeth, standing opposite the couple, also noted the exchange. "Is your son here this evening?" she asked the viscount. Her query drew Lady Catherine's attention toward herself and thus even further away from Anne.

"He is in the card room. Neville does not care for dancing."

"Nor does my daughter," Lady Catherine declared. "If Anne chose to dance, she possesses so much natural poise that she would make a lovely figure. Indeed, she would be a credit to any partner. But Miss de Bourgh is a level-headed young woman who sympathizes with your son's disdain for frivolity. Is that not so, Anne?"

Anne, however, had escaped auditory range of her mother and was heading away with Colonel Fitzwilliam. Somehow, the couple had also managed to shed themselves of Mrs. Jenkinson, who remained behind.

"Wherever is she going?" Lady Catherine asked Mrs. Jenkinson.

"I am not certain, my lady. Miss de Bourgh merely said I was not needed."

"The room is rather warm," Elizabeth said. "No doubt Colonel Fitzwilliam escorts her to refreshment."

"The air is indeed close," her ladyship said. "I wonder that my nephew did not invite me as well. I could do with some lemonade. Riveton always serves excellent lemonade—not that tepid water they try to pass off as lemonade at Almack's. A good lemonade requires the proper proportion of tart and sweet to adequately stimulate the palate. You must sample Riveton's lemonade, my lord. Let us join Miss de Bourgh and the colonel."

"Actually, Aunt," Darcy interjected, "I was about to invite you to accompany me to the card room. Your lordship as well, if you are inclined. Perhaps we can find a game of whist." Darcy had no interest in cards this evening, let alone becoming trapped at a table with Lady Catherine for a period of time, but he hoped the temptation of a game would provide sufficient distraction to grant Anne a set or two on the dance floor.

"Quadrille," his aunt declared. "You know I favor quadrille."

"I believe Neville plays quadrille," said Lord Sennex. "Or is cassino his game of choice? No, no—I think it is quadrille. Yes, I am almost certain of it. Well, no matter. Whatever he plays, there may be an opening at his table. That would provide you an opportunity to renew your acquaintance with him, Mr. Darcy."

"I would be pleased to play cards with Mr. Sennex." In truth, Darcy had little desire to court the friendship of a man given to fits of temper, but he would tolerate his company if necessary to occupy his aunt. "However, should insufficient openings exist at his table, we can form our own."

"If your lordship plays, we would then require a fourth." Lady Catherine regarded Elizabeth appraisingly but without enthusiasm.

"Perhaps Mrs. Jenkinson could complete your table?" Elizabeth suggested. "She is the more experienced quadrille player."

As Anne's paid companion, Mrs. Jenkinson's primary responsibility was attending Miss de Bourgh. Her secondary duty was serving Lady Catherine's convenience, an obligation that commanded as much if not more time and exertion. Among other functions, Mrs. Jenkinson spent many an evening at Rosings rounding out her ladyship's card tables.

"Mrs. Jenkinson should see to Miss de Bourgh."

"Miss de Bourgh is well attended by her cousin at present," Elizabeth said. "I will inform her of your whereabouts upon their return."

"Tell her to come to me. She can take Mrs. Jenkinson's place at cards."

Darcy offered his arm to Lady Catherine. As they departed, Elizabeth caught his gaze with a smile.

"Enjoy your game."

Three

"Anne would have been a delightful performer, had her health allowed her to learn."

—Lady Catherine de Bourgh, Pride and Prejudice

Elizabeth watched Darcy steer Lady Catherine out of the room. No sooner had the small party crossed the threshold than the musicians struck the opening chord of the next tune. She scanned the arranged couples for Miss de Bourgh and Colonel Fitzwilliam, and discovered them not yet on the floor. They stood behind the gentlemen's side of the longways set, also waiting for Anne's mother to disappear from view. Once safe from her ladyship's surveillance, the couple hastily joined the bottom of the set.

Anne cast a final look over her shoulder toward the doorway. Apparently satisfied that her mother was not about to charge out and promenade her right off the floor, she indulged in a conspiratorial half-smile at her partner. The two made a charming couple. Colonel Fitzwilliam cut a striking figure in his formal dress uniform; the decorated red coat with blue facings, gold lace, and gold buttons created a presence that lent handsomeness to his otherwise unremarkable features. Anne held herself with all her customary dignity, but there was a lightness in her stance not ordinarily displayed. Her face reflected expectation and delight as she watched the top couples complete the dance's opening figures.

Elizabeth was not the only one to notice Anne's enjoyment. Lady Winthrop, a longtime friend of the Fitzwilliam family, also observed the cousins.

"I do not think I have ever seen Miss de Bourgh in such high spirits," Lady Winthrop said.

"Nor I, and the lower couples have not even joined the dance yet."

Anne watched the top dancers closely, no doubt committing to memory the order of figures and studying their execution. Lady Winthrop's eldest daughter led the dance, partnered with a gentleman Elizabeth did not recognize. Both were accomplished dancers, performing the figures flawlessly and with contagious enthusiasm.

"I am not acquainted with your daughter's partner," Elizabeth said.

"We were introduced only briefly, but my daughter and her friends were all information regarding the gentleman within ten minutes of his entering the room. He is Mr. Henry Crawford, and his catalogue of charms includes an income of four thousand a year and an estate named Everingham. He attends tonight as a friend of Admiral Davidson."

Elizabeth had met Admiral Davidson, one of Riveton's neighbors, earlier in the week, and recalled his having mentioned houseguests. "Mr. Crawford does not reside nearby?"

"His house is in Norfolk. He accompanies his uncle, Admiral Crawford, who visits on business with Admiral Davidson. My daughter tells me that Mr. Crawford and his sister were raised by the uncle in London."

"Is his sister also present tonight?"

"No. Miss Crawford is not part of the admiral's traveling party."

Miss Winthrop and Mr. Crawford cast off and moved to the bottom of the set, taking their new place immediately below Anne and Colonel Fitzwilliam. Their progression afforded Elizabeth a better view of Mr. Crawford. He was shorter than the colonel, perhaps five feet nine or ten, and had dark hair. His features were on the plainer side, but what nature did not provide he made up for with a genial expression that rendered his countenance pleasing to look upon.

As the music continued and the dance incorporated the set's formerly neutral couples, Elizabeth wondered how Miss de Bourgh would perform. Fortunately, the first three figures were simple ones. Anne completed them charmingly, exhibiting all the grace her mother had boasted. Her step was smooth and light; her expression reflected concentration but not anxiety.

The next figure was longer and more complex, involving Anne with not only her own partner but also their neighboring couple. Now temporarily partnered with Mr. Crawford, Anne moved with less assurance. She faltered, and a flush crept into her cheeks.

Mr. Crawford said something to her and offered a smile of encouragement. His kindness seemed to restore her confidence, and his superior dancing skill strengthened her fledgling efforts. She completed the figure without further error.

Whatever the gentleman had said, he apparently knew how to set a woman at ease. Perhaps it was his sister's influence. "Does Miss Crawford keep house for her brother now that he is of age?" Elizabeth asked.

"She lives with another relation," Lady Winthrop replied. "A half sister."

The colonel and Anne took right hands across with Miss Winthrop and Mr. Crawford. When her hand entered Mr. Crawford's grasp, Anne raised her eyes to meet his gaze. His eyes danced as merrily as he.

At the song's conclusion, he smiled at her once more before bowing to Miss Winthrop. Anne looked away quickly and honored her own partner with a curtsy. Colonel Fitzwilliam crossed the set and spoke to her, apparently encouraging her to remain with him on the floor for a second dance. She glanced toward the doorway through which her mother had disappeared, and shook her head.

Poor Miss de Bourgh. The risk of being caught enjoying herself was too great. The colonel escorted her back to Elizabeth.

"You dance beautifully, Miss de Bourgh," Lady Winthrop said. "I hope I have another opportunity to observe you this evening."

"I thank you for the compliment, but I fear I must disappoint your hopes. I rarely dance, and doubt even my cousin can persuade me to do so a second time tonight." She looked back at the dance floor, where Miss Winthrop and Mr. Crawford were among a dozen couples beginning a reel. Anne's expression suggested it was her own desire, rather than Lady Winthrop's, being thwarted by her abstinence.

"Perhaps some refreshment would revive your interest," Elizabeth suggested. "Colonel Fitzwilliam, I have it on good authority that Riveton serves exceptional lemonade. Is that so?"

"The finest. Would all of you ladies care to determine its quality for yourselves?"

Lady Winthrop declined, citing the need for a word with her daughter when the current dance concluded, but Elizabeth and Miss de Bourgh accompanied the colonel to the next room, where a table offered lemonade and rout cakes. The beverage was soon pronounced by all three to be without equal. Lady Catherine would have approved.

But her ladyship remained at cards, anticipating Anne's imminent participation. Elizabeth wondered how much longer she would play before sending Darcy to fetch her daughter.

The cessation of music in the ballroom heralded a break for the instrumentalists. Parched dancers took advantage of the lull and crowded the refreshment room. Anne having finished her lemonade, Colonel Fitzwilliam offered to refill her glass. When he returned, Mr. Crawford accompanied him.

"Mrs. Darcy, Miss de Bourgh, this gentleman has begged an introduction to my fair cousins. May I present Mr. Henry Crawford?"

"Indeed you may," Elizabeth said. "I am delighted to meet you, Mr. Crawford, particularly after witnessing your performance in the ballroom."

"I do like a good ball. Have you danced yet this evening?"

"I have not."

"By inclination or happenstance?"

"My husband is in the card room, and most of the other gentlemen present have engaged unattached ladies for their partners, as they should. A married woman such as myself has no business dancing when there are single ladies wishing to do so."

"You are noble to your sex, but even the most altruistic person cannot be expected to deny herself the pleasure of dancing for the entire length of a ball. You must stand up with me for the next set. Surely Mr. Darcy will not object to your enjoying a dance while he amuses himself at cards."

Elizabeth suspected "amusement" hardly described what Darcy experienced just now, but she kept that thought to herself. "He would not frown upon my dancing, though he would likely prefer that my partner be someone with whom he is acquainted, and the young ladies present might take exception to my monopolizing one of the most eligible bachelors in the room."

"Again, this concern for your unwed counterparts! What is it about marriage that makes people so eager for others to enter that state as soon as they cross the threshold themselves? Very well. I withdraw my invitation, but only if Colonel Fitzwilliam will take it up, for your husband can have no opposition to your dancing with his cousin. What say you, Colonel?"

"I would be honored to dance with Mrs. Darcy."

"There," Mr. Crawford declared. "I, meanwhile, will satisfy your anxiety for the plight of single ladies in attendance by beseeching Miss de Bourgh to stand up with me. Will you, Miss de Bourgh?"

Anne flushed. "I—I had not intended to dance again this evening."

"I beg you. Or at least, I beg your mercy. Will you not spare me the humiliation of being refused by two ladies in the space of two minutes?"

Anne glanced toward the doorway. "I do not think it a good idea."

Elizabeth resented Lady Catherine anew. Even from another room, she managed to stifle all gaiety in her daughter. Anne deserved a few more minutes of happiness at the ball before Lady Catherine turned her coach into a pumpkin.

Elizabeth touched Anne's arm. "Your mother is occupied," she said quietly. "Seize opportunity while you can."

Anne searched Elizabeth's face, her own eyes reflecting confusion. "I am not certain I understand your meaning."

"An amiable gentleman has made you an offer. If it will make you happy, accept him."

"I—" She looked at Mr. Crawford a long moment. "I must

beg you to excuse me, sir. When you approached, I had just been considering retiring to my chamber, which I now believe I will do."

"I hope naught is amiss. Have I offended you? If so—"

"You have given no offense. I feel a trifle unwell. A headache. I think perhaps from the exertion of dancing earlier."

"Would you like me to accompany you?" Elizabeth asked. "Or to summon Mrs. Jenkinson?"

"No, I simply need to rest, and that is better done in solitude."

"Is there nothing we can do for your comfort?" Colonel Fitzwilliam said.

"Please inform my mother and Mrs. Jenkinson that I have retired and wish not to be disturbed. But postpone the announcement if you can—my mother might insist on sending Mrs. Jenkinson to me, and I would rather be alone."

"Of course." Elizabeth could well understand Anne's desire for respite without—and from—Mrs. Jenkinson and her hovering. She herself would have found the constant presence of a companion intrusive and intolerable.

Anne turned back to Mr. Crawford. "Perhaps we will have an opportunity to dance together in the future, sir."

He bowed. "I look forward to it."

Colonel Fitzwilliam offered her his arm. "At least allow me to escort you out of this crowd and see you safely to your room."

As Anne scurried off, the clock struck midnight.

"Cinderella has left the ball," Mr. Crawford said. His gaze followed Anne and the colonel until the crowd swallowed them from view, then turned to Elizabeth. "At least she had a chance to dance with one prince."

"I believe she would have accepted your invitation, were it not for her headache. Perhaps, as she said, another opportunity will arise. How long do you remain in the neighborhood?"

"My uncle and I depart in the morning—he for London, I for Norfolk. Indeed, I intend to leave so early that we shall exchange farewells tonight."

"Do you return to Everingham?"

Her question appeared to amuse him. "I do, but as neither I nor Colonel Fitzwilliam mentioned Everingham, I must now puzzle out how you came to know of it. I presume myself the subject of a conversation that occurred before we met, but with whom? Hold! Allow me to guess. Are you acquainted with Admiral Davidson?"

"Only slightly. It was not he who revealed the name of your home."

"My uncle, then?"

She shook her head. "A much newer acquaintance of yours."

"Lady Winthrop? Yes—I see from your expression that I am correct."

"Indeed, you are. But how did you know?"

"I observed your earlier tête-à-tête. And why would I perceive such a thing while occupied on the dance floor? Either I could not help noticing a pretty woman, or I deliberately kept one eye on the mother of my partner. I shall leave it to your vanity to determine which."

"My vanity can have no influence on your motives, only on my perception of them."

Mr. Crawford had a charming manner, and after a few minutes' further conversation with him she found herself regretting for Anne's sake that her headache had forced her to retreat from his company. Conversation with him was easy, and Miss de Bourgh could benefit from greater confidence when interacting with those outside her most intimate circle.

They parted, and soon after, Colonel Fitzwilliam returned to the ballroom. He reported that by the time Anne had reached her room, she had already seemed improved.

Elizabeth was glad to hear it. "Perhaps Anne will yet return to the ball tonight."

"I hope she does," Colonel Fitzwilliam replied. "I found her a surprisingly delightful partner, and should like to dance with her again. But in the meantime, I believe you agreed to stand up with me." He extended his hand. "Unless you think we should go rescue your husband from the card room?"

"We ought to." She imagined to herself the conversation at Darcy's table, and could not quite suppress a smile. "After this dance."

Four

"I have more than once observed to Lady Catherine, that her charming daughter seemed born to be a duchess, and that the most elevated rank, instead of giving her consequence, would be adorned by her. These are the kind of little things which please her ladyship . . ."

Mr. Collins, Pride and Prejudice

Darcy shifted in his chair and stole what he hoped was a discreet glimpse at his pocketwatch. Midnight—a mere six minutes since his last covert glance. His suspicions were confirmed.

He would die at this card table.

Before evening's end, his hair would prematurely grey, his muscles would atrophy in his chair, and his mind would utterly collapse under the exertion of attending Lord Sennex's play as closely as his own. Quadrille had been the worst possible choice of game; the viscount was incapable of remembering not only the current trump suit for each hand, but also the resulting changes in card rankings. Indeed, his lordship, apparently unable to retain so much as which game they played, repeatedly attempted to capture tricks as if they competed at whist.

Darcy wished they *were* playing whist—at the next table, with the viscount's son. Not only was it a more straightforward game, but Mr. Sennex could have shared the responsibility of keeping his father focused. A son might more easily correct a member of the peerage without constant apprehension over inadvertently giving offense. However, their party had entered the card room while Mr. Sennex was in the middle of a rubber, and Lady Catherine had seized the opportunity to form the only table devoted to the outmoded game of her youth.

A self-satisfied smile crossed her ladyship's countenance as she led the final trick of the hand. Everyone waited for Lord Sennex, who sat on her right, to set down his sole remaining card. Play in quadrille, unlike whist, moved counterclockwise.

When it moved at all.

After eight hands, one would think Lord Sennex could retain at least that simple fact, but like most subjects, his grasp of it seemed to surface only at irregular intervals.

"My lord?" Darcy finally prompted.

"Oh—it is my turn! Of course." He dropped his card onto the table. "Remind me again—which tour is this?"

"We are just ending the second."

"Of how many?"

"Ten."

Ten tours. Forty hands. Though the players could have agreed upon a shorter game, Lady Catherine had insisted upon the customary number. By the time they finished this contest, Darcy would be hosting Lily-Anne's betrothal ball.

Miss Jenkinson played her own remaining card and Darcy quickly followed. He hoped his impatience did not show.

To compound the ordeal, it seemed Darcy's lot to repeatedly draw Lord Sennex as his partner. Darcy had been dealt fair hands, but none strong enough to take the minimum six tricks solo. So each time he won the bid, he called a king to form a temporary alliance with whoever held the named card. The unknown ally's identity was supposed to be revealed through play that supported the caller, but the instances in which the viscount helped Darcy capture tricks were entirely accidental. Lord Sennex's inattention had caused Darcy to lose three hands—and considerable additional stakes in penalty.

Lady Catherine and Miss Jenkinson, in contrast, somehow managed to call each other's kings each time either of them won the bid. Not only were the two ladies more practiced players of quadrille than the gentlemen, but their countless evenings thus spent at Rosings attuned them so precisely to each other's particular style of play that when partnered they formed an unstoppable alliance. They had declared and won the vole—taken all ten tricks—each time, collecting bonus winnings in addition to the hands' original pools.

While the secrecy and changing allegiances of quadrille utterly confused the viscount, Lady Catherine thrived on them.

Darcy understood why it was her favorite game.

Her ladyship collected the trick, adding it to the nine in front of her.

"We won another vole!" Lord Sennex exclaimed. "You may call my king again anytime."

"My lord, I named a king I held myself—the king of clubs."

"Did you now? I thought you called the king of diamonds."

"That was the previous hand, my lord."

"Oh, dear. Well, nothing to do about it now. So you called a king to make us think you had an ally, when in fact you secretly played solo? Very clever, I daresay. You are a formidable opponent, Lady Anne."

An awkward silence followed. Darcy was unsure whether Lord Sennex had confused Lady Catherine with her sister, the late

Lady Anne, or with Lady Catherine's daughter, Miss Anne de Bourgh.

His aunt's expression indicated similar uncertainty.

No one ventured to correct the viscount outright.

"You will no doubt find my daughter, Miss Anne de Bourgh, an able cardplayer. I cannot imagine what prevents her from joining us. I begin to suspect that Mrs. Darcy forgot to inform her that we await her here."

"Mrs. Darcy may be relied upon to deliver the message," Darcy said. Whether she delivered it in a fashion Lady Catherine would consider timely was another matter entirely.

"Anne is very fond of quadrille. We play at Rosings whenever we can make up a table."

"I cannot say that I care for it," said the viscount. "Never knowing who is one's ally and who is one's foe, the rules changing with each hand, and one's strength dependent upon the random collection of cards one is dealt. Now chess—chess is my game: a clear contest between two equally matched foes, facing each other across a defined battlefield where each man has his role and the challenge ends when one of the primaries falls. My favorite piece is the rook—the only one that can castle with the king. I do not suppose Miss de Bourgh plays chess?"

"No. But had she learned, I am sure she would be a skillful player."

His lordship sighed. "She knows only cards, I suppose. Does she play whist? Neville favors whist."

"She does. Mr. Sennex will find her a worthy partner in all respects."

Precisely *when* Mr. Sennex might have occasion to engage in a game of whist with Miss de Bourgh or anyone else in their party, Darcy could not speculate. A match certainly would not occur this evening. He was firmly entrenched at his own table and had not so much as glanced in his father's direction since they sat down.

Lady Catherine collected her winnings. While they had agreed to low stakes, bonuses for the vole and solo win had made this a relatively expensive hand. Miss Jenkinson's previous successes kept her well in the black, but the viscount remitted his fish wistfully, the sting of loss all the sharper for not collecting a partner's share of the win to which he thought he had contributed.

Darcy eyed his own dwindling stack of counters. His pocketbook could certainly afford the losses; for that matter, so could his self-respect. This was his aunt's game, and she had bested him many an evening in her own drawing room. Whatever he might think of Lady Catherine herself, her command of quadrille was without question, and in any contest there was no shame in losing to a superior opponent. He knew he should simply resign himself to an unsatisfying game, execute the motions of play without thoughts of victory. But for Darcy, playing at all meant playing to win. It was not in his character to perform at less than full measure in any endeavor, and he could no more underplay a hand and decline the challenge posed by each fresh round of cards than neglect any other test of intellect that presented itself.

His aunt placed a counter and fish into the basket and shuffled the cards for a new deal. Darcy and Miss Jenkinson also anted. Lord Sennex nodded and smiled.

"The opening stake, my lord?" Darcy prompted.

"What? Oh! Yes, yes." The viscount dropped his counter into the basket with the others and chuckled. "Cannot have anyone accuse me of being light."

Darcy collected his cards. It was a strong hand; if he took the bid he could probably win without a partner. Strategically, the other three players would form a tacit alliance, working together to prevent his success so that they could split the pool if he failed, but that was part of the challenge.

He waited for Lord Sennex to open the bidding.

And waited.

"Your lordship possesses the eldest hand," Darcy finally prompted.

Lord Sennex regarded him oddly, then glanced at his own wrinkled fingers. "I suppose I do."

"Do you care to bid?"

"Oh! No, I pass."

Darcy won the right to declare trump, and play proceeded to the accompaniment of Lady Catherine's unremitting discourse.

"Have you ever visited Kent, my lord?"

"I do not believe I have."

"You will find it beautiful country. I confess that I missed the northern landscapes when I first wed Sir Lewis and moved to Rosings, but now I feel equally at home in both settings. Anne will be the same, when she has been mistress of her own home for a while. A woman adjusts rapidly to new surroundings, provided she marries within her sphere."

Darcy heard this last statement as a deliberate slight to Elizabeth, whom Lady Catherine yet resented for her perceived usurpation of Anne's rightful place as his wife, but he ignored the remark rather than dignify it with the response she sought to provoke. He instead would exact reprisal in the form of a more direct blow to his aunt's overweening pride. A sound defeat in this hand, delivered while she rattled on about a hypothetical future home of which Anne was in no way of becoming mistress anytime soon, would constitute a fair requital.

Why his aunt had embarked upon the present subject eluded him. To Darcy's knowledge, Miss de Bourgh had no current marriage prospects, and at the age of eight-and-twenty stood in considerable danger of entering permanent spinsterhood. But he could devote no more thought to the matter if he wanted to win the hand, which he fully intended to do.

"My late wife never appreciated Hawthorn Manor," said Lord Sennex. "She was too attached to the home of her birth."

"Anne will not have that problem."

That, Darcy believed. He had always found Rosings to reflect the character of its mistress—all pomp and grandeur, with little warmth to solicit nostalgia or any other tender sentiment.

Darcy evaluated his remaining cards. He had taken the first six tricks and now faced a decision: whether to end the hand at this point and collect only the original pool, or attempt to take them all. If he continued the hand and succeeded, he would win a substantial bonus pool, but if he failed, his opponents would split the side stake.

He mentally reviewed the cards that had been used and who had played them. His opponents were out of trump, but two high cards remained unaccounted for. He believed Lady Catherine held them, though heaven only knew whether the viscount had been following suit throughout the hand. Continuing would require Darcy's full concentration.

He led a seventh card.

A noisy discussion erupted at Neville's table. Darcy did his best to bar it from his mind, but it soon reached a level that made it impossible to ignore. Neville addressed Sir John Trauth, one of his whist opponents, in a hot tone.

"You scratched your chin!" Neville's small eyes narrowed still more as his flaccid countenance distorted in resentment.

"It itches."

Neville rose to his feet. Short of stature, he gained the intimidation of height only when confronting a seated adversary, as Sir John remained. "You have scratched it twice whilst holding an ace."

Sir John, for fifty years known throughout the neighborhood as a forthright man, remained calm under Neville's ire. "Have I done so, I assure you the reflex was entirely coincidental. If losing the rubber disappoints you, examine your own play."

"At least I played an honest hand."

"Do you accuse me of cheating, Sennex?"

Silence claimed the room as all waited to hear Neville's response. To accuse a gentleman of dishonesty at cards was a grave matter: Settling the issue via pistols at dawn was not unheard of. Dueling might be illegal, but that did not prevent its practice.

"Eh, what was that?" Although the question had been directed to Mr. Sennex, it caught the attention of his father. The viscount, seated with his back to Neville's table, turned round in his chair. "Is that Neville? What is this commotion?"

No one, including Neville, ventured to answer him. Though his mind might have begun to fail him, the viscount still commanded the respect due a peer of the realm, and nobody wanted to disillusion a father about the poor sportsmanship of his son.

Lord Sennex gripped the table's edge and slowly pushed himself to his feet. "It sounds as if there is some sort of dispute. Neville, what is transpiring?"

"A minor disagreement, that is all."

"With Sir John? Why, he has been our friend since—since I do not know when. What can you possibly be arguing about with Sir John?"

Neville stared at Sir John a long time, his pique still evident. Finally, he said, "Nothing. It is over."

"Is it, Sir John?"

"Yes, my lord."

"Well, I am glad it is settled, whatever it was. What is everybody looking at? Have you not your own games to attend to?"

The silence was broken by the riffle of cards and clacking of fish as all returned to their games. All the players, that is, except those at two tables.

Sir John rose from his seat. "I believe I have done with cards for the night. I am returning to the ballroom." His partner made a similarly quick exit.

In the wake of their departure, Neville addressed his own partner, who was also leaving. "Surely you observed the same behavior as I?"

"Regrettably, I cannot say that I did."

Lord Sennex and his son both remained standing. Elder regarded younger with resignation; son regarded father with indignation.

"How dare Sir John humiliate me? He a mere knight? And you—you abetted him with your interference."

"A gentleman's honor is his most sacred possession. It should not be challenged lightly."

"I have had enough of your preaching about honor for a lifetime. And enough of your directing my affairs."

"Neville, rein in your anger. This is a night for celebration, after all." The viscount gestured toward Lady Catherine. "Join our table. Perhaps you would like to take my place at quadrille?"

"Perhaps not."

"Neville—"

Mr. Sennex clenched his jaw, struggling to check his ire. After a moment, he addressed Lady Catherine. "I beg your ladyship's pardon, but as you can see, I am in no mood for celebration at present. Tomorrow, however, I shall place myself at your disposal for quadrille or any other diversion in which you or Miss de Bourgh care to indulge."

"Very well, Mr. Sennex. I shall hold you to that promise."

He bowed. To his father, he said, "I am going home. I will send the carriage back to collect you."

The viscount watched him leave, then sank into his chair. He picked up his cards and played on Darcy's long-forgotten lead. "Lady Catherine, I apologize for my son's behavior. He is not generally ill-humored. You need have no misgivings about our earlier business."

Lady Catherine snapped down her card with such force she nearly bent it. "I hope not. Else I shall be sending an express to my solicitor countermanding this morning's documents—"

Miss Jenkinson having played, Darcy collected the trick and glanced at his cards, trying to recall what he had intended to lead next. After such an extended disruption, he could no longer remember with certainty which cards remained in play.

"—and another to Mr. Collins canceling the banns."

Darcy's head jerked up. His gaze shifted between his aunt and the viscount as if he watched a game of shuttlecock.

"I assure you," Lord Sennex said, "that is not necessary."

"All the same, perhaps we ought to postpone the date."

"There is no sense in postponing happiness. Besides, one month from today will have Neville home in time for the opening of fox-hunting season, which will put him in especially good temper."

"Miss de Bourgh is the granddaughter of an earl. Her wedding will not be scheduled around the pursuit of vermin."

"Of course not."

"Mr. Darcy, are you ever going to lead the next trick?"

Darcy stared at his aunt. Miss de Bourgh and Neville Sennex? He had never suspected such a partnership was forming. Lady Catherine was a craftier strategist than even he had realized.

"It seems that you and his lordship have effected an alliance that goes well beyond this game."

"Yes. Your cousin has just become engaged to Mr. Sennex."

"I shall be sure to wish her joy when I return to the ballroom." He withdrew the queen of spades from his hand.

"Kindly defer your congratulations until the morrow."

He dropped the card onto the table. "May I ask why?"

"Anne does not yet know."

With a triumphant flourish, Lady Catherine played the king of spades, overriding Darcy's queen and defeating his attempt at the vole.

"You should have called my king, Mr. Darcy. Have you not yet come to understand that you are far better off with me as an ally than as an opponent?" She collected the trick and placed it in front of her.

"That is, if you want to win."

Five

There certainly are not so many men of large fortune in the world as there are pretty women to deserve them.

—Mansfield Park

"You lost *how much* in a single hand?"

"Never mind. I was distracted."

Elizabeth nodded in passing to an acquaintance as Darcy adroitly maneuvered her away from Lady Catherine, who had been only too happy to declare her winnings when Elizabeth at last delivered Anne's message. "Was not the entire purpose for *you* to distract *her*? Whatever turned things round?"

"News you will no doubt find quite diverting." Darcy glanced back at the card table from which he had just escaped. Though the room was clearing, Lady Catherine and Lord Sennex remained, deep in conversation. "This, however, is not an appropriate venue in which to reveal it."

"Apparently we are fortunate that the summons to supper terminated your game, or you might have lost Pemberley by evening's end. Lady Catherine's fondest dreams would have been realized as she ousted me from its premises."

"My aunt has other matters on her mind this week."

"Oh, more cryptic talk! You know how it delights me when you speak mysteriously. I suppose I shall have to wait until we are safely alone in our chamber before you explain further?"

"I am afraid so."

"Very well. I can spend supper regaling you with Miss de Bourgh's adventures in the ballroom."

"Did she enjoy her dances with Colonel Fitzwilliam?"

"*Dance*—she stood up with him for only one before the fear of being caught by her mother forced her from the floor. But yes, from all appearances she enjoyed it very much. Another gentleman in their set afterwards invited her to dance with him, but having turned down Colonel Fitzwilliam's offer of a second dance she declined his invitation, too. Which is a shame, for I believe she would have liked to accept them both."

"Was the gentleman someone we know?"

"Colonel Fitzwilliam introduced us. He is Mr. Henry Crawford, a guest of Admiral Davidson." She scanned the dining room, but could not readily locate Mr. Crawford. "I do not see him in this crowd or I would identify him to you. He seems an affable gentleman, with a friendly countenance and engaging manners. Too, merely the fact that he invited Miss de Bourgh to dance earns him a place in my esteem."

"You have suddenly developed an intense interest in my cousin's social intercourse."

"We do have a stake in it."

"How so?"

"I doubt the Miss de Bourgh we knew a twelvemonth ago would have defied her mother and danced tonight. For all the vexation Lady Catherine's prolonged visit to Pemberley caused us, I daresay it benefited Anne. The separation from her mother allowed her to think for herself—and of herself—for what was undoubtedly the first time in her life. She needs more such opportunities."

"You are not suggesting that we invite my aunt for a return visit?"

"I want her to stay for six months this time, and to bring Miss Jenkinson with her."

At Darcy's horrified expression, she laughed.

"Set your mind at ease—nothing could induce me to feel *that* charitable. Though now that I think on it, we should invite Miss de Bourgh to visit us at Pemberley for a while—without her mother or companion. Miss Jenkinson could use the hiatus to take an extended holiday. Surely she has family somewhere that she has not seen in a decade or two."

"Your plan assumes Lady Catherine would be willing to spare either of them."

"Provided she has someone to nod mutely at appropriate intervals in her soliloquies, the particular company she keeps is entirely interchangeable. There are others in the neighborhood, such as Mr. and Mrs. Collins, who can serve her purpose just as well. Mr. Collins, you know, is only too willing to drop everything whenever his patroness issues a summons to Rosings. I do scruple to subject Charlotte to an increase in her ladyship's attention, but as a clergyman's wife she understands the need to sacrifice for a good cause."

"Their party would number only three—how will Lady Catherine play quadrille?"

"Oh, dear. I suppose Miss Jenkinson must stay behind after all. Well, we shall have to plot her liberation for a later date. I can allot attention to only one charitable enterprise at a time, and Miss de Bourgh inspires more of my sympathy."

They found their place cards. Although Lady Catherine had been assigned to a different table, the presence of others prevented Elizabeth and Darcy from continuing the discussion. They spent the meal engaged with their fellow diners in the sort of idle chatter that Elizabeth tolerated and Darcy abhorred.

Afterward, they danced a set together, then mutually decided they had experienced enough of the ball. Elizabeth departed to look in on Lily-Anne while Darcy took leave of their host. She found the baby sleeping contentedly, a tiny sliver of white peeking through her lower gum, and walked to her chamber with a lighter heart. Passing Miss de Bourgh's room, she considered looking in on her as well to enquire whether her headache had improved. No sounds came from within. As she did not wish to disturb her if Miss de Bourgh had indeed found rest, she continued without stopping, but a scheme began to form in her mind. She quickened her step, eager to share the idea with Darcy.

Upon opening the door to her own chamber, she discovered that Darcy had not yet returned. A note, however, lay on the floor with her name written across the front. She picked it up and saw that it bore the de Bourgh seal. Before she had a chance to open it, Darcy entered.

She momentarily set the letter aside on a small table near the door. Whatever Lady Catherine had to say could wait.

"I have been thinking, Darcy. Let us suggest that your cousin Anne return with us to Pemberley from here. If she accompanies us, Lady Catherine cannot use the inconvenience or rigors of travel as an excuse to deny the invitation. Miss de Bourgh will conduct her journey under our protection, enabling you to personally ensure her every comfort, and Pemberley is closer than Rosings, so the length of the trip will prove less taxing on her 'fragile constitution' than returning to Kent. The scheme also provides the advantage of immediacy. If we plan the visit for some future date, once Anne is back at home her mother has leisure to devise any number of excuses to prevent its ever actually occurring."

"She cannot just as easily invent pretexts in person?"

"Evasion and equivocation are more easily achieved from a distance."

Darcy removed his coat and folded it over the back of a chair. "While that may be true, it seems Miss de Bourgh has another engagement that will prevent her coming to us as you propose. Lady Catherine informed me this evening that my cousin is about to become affianced to Neville Sennex."

"Lord Sennex's son?" Elizabeth allowed herself a few moments to absorb the information. She had observed no hint in Anne's manners that a betrothal had been contracted, though hindsight now suggested that perhaps the engagement, not a headache, had caused her to decline Mr. Crawford's invitation to dance. "I am all astonishment."

"Miss de Bourgh might be as well, when my aunt informs her of the marriage. Lady Catherine has been negotiating the entire agreement without her knowledge."

"But Anne is of age; she should have been consulted. After all, she does not have to give her consent."

"My aunt is confident she will acquiesce, as she has no other prospects at present."

Elizabeth pitied Miss de Bourgh. Ladies in society's upper ranks often had little say in the selection of their own husbands; marriages amongst the *ton* were foremost business transactions designed to forge alliances, merge estates, build fortunes, and enhance pedigrees. Even among less exalted ranks, affection was often a secondary, negligible consideration, and Elizabeth was thankful anew that it governed her own marriage.

"Knowing Lady Catherine, I am hardly surprised that Miss de

Bourgh's inclinations were not considered. The marriage is quite a coup for your aunt."

"Indeed, yes. It allies the de Bourghs with an old, established family and restores Lady Catherine's line to the rank of peers after having married a mere baronet herself. Miss de Bourgh will immediately become the Honorable Anne Sennex, and rise to still higher precedence when the viscount dies and his son inherits the title. As the present Lord Sennex is a widower, even while he lives Anne will be mistress of Hawthorn Manor, one of the finest estates in this part of the country, and enjoy greater wealth than she knew at Rosings."

"It sounds like a good establishment for your cousin, particularly as she has reached an age where many women must settle for less, if they marry at all. In exchange, Mr. Sennex acquires Lady Catherine as his mother-in-law. Miss de Bourgh certainly must have charmed him, for it would seem that most of the advantages of this bargain fall on her side."

"Mr. Sennex will be amply compensated for any pain and suffering he endures as a result of his relationship to my aunt. Anne brings a substantial portion—the settlement Lady Catherine brought to her own marriage—and eventually will inherit the entire estate of Rosings." He paused. "It is, by all appearances, a good match for them both."

The hesitation, though so slight as to be almost imperceptible, suggested he had left something unsaid.

"However advantageous the marriage may be in worldly considerations, I cannot help but hope that Anne and her husband might also share affection—if not immediately, at least over time," she said. "I have not met Mr. Sennex. What sort of man is he?"

"Unfortunately, I cannot say that I care for his society. Though my intercourse with him has been limited, in nearly every instance he has shown himself to be a man of short temper and unpleasant disposition. If fact, just this evening, rather than graciously accept defeat, he all but accused his whist opponent of cheating, though his own partner could not support the allegation. And despite invitations whenever I visit Riveton, I will not hunt with the gentleman, nor will Colonel Fitzwilliam." Darcy went on to explain their aversion.

Elizabeth was sorry to hear the character of Anne's fiancé so described. "For Miss de Bourgh's sake, I had wished him to be a more amenable gentleman, but one can hope he might improve under her influence. Too, your cousin is used to living with someone of difficult temperament. Perhaps as mistress of her own house she will be able to better manage Mr. Sennex than she can her own mother. Or at least minimize the time she spends in his company. At present, she is constantly at Lady Catherine's command."

A sharp rap on the door so startled Elizabeth that she jumped.

"Darcy! I must speak with you immediately!" The voice was unmistakable.

Darcy glanced at the door, rattling in its frame with the force of repeated knocks, then back at Elizabeth. "Apparently, so are we all."

Elizabeth scowled. "Does not Lady Catherine understand that we have retired for the night?" Faint strains of music and laughter indicated that the ball continued below. Whatever her ladyship required, could she not apply to Lord Southwell? This was his house, after all. "I suppose she will not go away until we answer."

Darcy had scarcely depressed the latch when Lady Catherine burst into the room. Colonel Fitzwilliam followed, his entrance less dramatic, but his countenance bore a gravity that Elizabeth had never before witnessed in him. Clearly, the matter that brought them was no trifle.

"I have just come from my daughter's chamber," Lady Catherine said. "Anne is missing."

Six

"An engaged woman is always more agreeable than a disengaged . . . All is safe with a lady engaged; no harm can be done."

—Henry Crawford, Mansfield Park

"Likely Miss de Bourgh has recovered from her headache and returned to the ball," Elizabeth said. "Have you sought her there?"

"Of course I have!" Lady Catherine replied. "What do you think I have been doing for above an hour?"

"Perhaps you might tell us, instead of abusing Mrs. Darcy for a perfectly reasonable question," Darcy said.

Lady Catherine expelled an exasperated breath. "I sent Mrs. Jenkinson to Anne directly after supper to enquire after her headache. When she reported to me that Anne was not in her chamber, I looked for her in the ballroom. No one had seen her recently, but Lady Winthrop mentioned that earlier in the evening she had witnessed Anne dancing." She cast a stern look at Colonel Fitzwilliam. "I thought surely Lady Winthrop had mistaken some other young lady for my daughter, but the colonel has admitted his guilt in the matter. I do not know what you were thinking, Fitzwilliam, to risk Anne's health by exhausting her."

"I did not believe any harm would derive from a single dance."

"No harm? Look what your rash action has come to. Anne developed her headache as a result of overexertion, and now cannot be found."

As Lady Catherine did not include the Darcys in her indictment, Elizabeth inferred that Colonel Fitzwilliam had omitted their involvement from his confession. She would have to thank him later for his discretion.

Recalling the previous night, when she had encountered Anne headed for a walk, she asked, "Have you looked in the gardens? It is a warm night, and I noticed numerous guests strolling outside earlier. Perhaps she decided to take some air."

"Anne knows better than to expose herself to the night air," Lady Catherine declared. "She never so much as sleeps with a window open."

"Nevertheless," Colonel Fitzwilliam said, "after searching all the rooms where company is assembled, I indeed circled the gardens, and sent two servants through the hedge maze. They startled more than a few couples, but Anne was not amongst them."

"I should hope not!" Lady Catherine snapped.

"Has Southwell been informed?" Darcy asked.

"The earl is occupied with his guests," Lady Catherine said. "He is a useless creature anyway when it comes to serious matters, and therefore performs greater service by distracting others from this crisis rather than taking the situation in hand himself. That is why I must rely upon Colonel Fitzwilliam and you."

While concerned for Anne's well-being, Elizabeth thought this situation hardly constituted a crisis. "Miss de Bourgh is a grown woman in familiar surroundings. Surely she is somewhere in the house, perfectly safe and unaware she has even been missed. In fact, she might have even returned to her chamber by now."

"As I told you, we just came from there, after searching the ball. She is not in her room. And before you suggest that she has returned whilst we have been in conference, Mrs. Jenkinson waits for her there and would have informed me. Her chamber is only round the corner."

Darcy reached for his coat. "Then let us search the remainder of the house. I agree with Elizabeth—Anne cannot have gone far. In the time we have spent discussing this, we could have found her and all of us returned to our own affairs."

As he thrust one arm into the garment, the other sleeve disturbed the note Elizabeth had set aside upon his entrance. She had quite forgotten it. The sheet drifted to the floor and landed at Lady Catherine's feet.

Her ladyship looked at Elizabeth sharply and took it up. "What is this?"

"I discovered it upon returning from the ball, but had not yet found opportunity to read it," Elizabeth said. "It bears the de Bourgh seal. Is it not from you?"

"This is Anne's handwriting."

"Let us open it directly, then." Elizabeth reached for the letter.

Lady Catherine broke the seal herself. "Yes, let us."

"I beg your pardon, but that note is addressed to me."

"I beg no one's pardon. It is from my daughter. She can have nothing to say to you that I may not read. I am privy to all her communications."

Elizabeth extended her hand. "You are not privy to mine."

Lady Catherine ignored her and unfolded the letter. In the interest of finding Anne, Elizabeth allowed her to continue rather than descend into argument. Darcy's aunt kept them all in suspense as she read the lines silently, but the rapid transformation of her expression from one of self-righteousness to one of fury revealed that the letter held news of some import.

Lady Catherine turned to Elizabeth. Her complexion mottled, she crushed the edge of the paper in her hand as she held it to Elizabeth's face. "What, in heaven's name, is the meaning of this?"

"How can I possibly answer you while I remain ignorant of the letter's content?"

"Ignorant! That you are, without doubt! In countless subjects. But apparently you are perfectly well informed of the news this letter contains."

Dear Mrs. Darcy,

Forgive my burdening you with the responsibility of imparting news to my mother which it will distress her to hear, but you alone understand the decision I now make. I have taken your counsel: Tonight I leave for Gretna Green with Mr. Crawford. You advised me to accept his offer if it would make me happy, and it does. Though the grief that I am conscious of causing others, particularly a parent who has been ever mindful of my welfare, burdens my heart, it is lightened by hope that my transgression may in time be forgiven, and that my mother will come to accept the gentleman I have chosen as my husband.

I am indebted to you for the courage to act in the manner that will constitute my own happiness, and repent the difficult position in which I leave you. Consider me ever—

Your most grateful and obliged servant,
Anne de Bourgh

Colonel Fitzwilliam regarded Elizabeth with shock. Even Darcy beheld her with astonishment. But the most bewildered person in the room was Elizabeth herself. When had she encouraged Miss de Bourgh to run off to Scotland with a man she just met?

"Who on earth is this Mr. Crawford?" Lady Catherine demanded.

Elizabeth could scarcely order her thoughts enough to speak. "A gentleman we met tonight—a friend of Admiral Davidson."

"And you urged her to *elope* with him?"

"No! He invited her to dance and I—"

"You stupid, common baggage! How dare you presume to offer my daughter advice on any matter, let alone one so critical? Do you think because of your sister's elopement that this is an acceptable way for a young lady of Miss de Bourgh's station to wed? Do you think at all? Are you capable of intelligent thought?"

The force of Lady Catherine's rage struck Elizabeth almost as a physical blow. She was not one to cower in the face of conflict, and had stood up to Darcy's aunt on previous occasions, but she had never in her life been the object of such wrath.

"I did not encourage Miss de Bourgh to elope with Mr. Crawford or anyone else. Indeed, I cannot imagine what led her to believe I had, nor the circumstances which brought the opportunity about. When last I saw her, Colonel Fitzwilliam was escorting her out of the ballroom, while Mr. Crawford remained behind with me—"

"Plotting this caper?"

"No! We exchanged a few pleasantries and then parted."

"Whereupon with your blessing he abducted my daughter. You have ruined her future, utterly ruined it! Do you so much as begin to comprehend the damage you have wrought with your heedless counsel? How, on the eve of a betrothal that would have merged the de Bourgh line with an ancient, worthy family, you have jeopardized the union I labored hard to achieve? Or was that your goal? You were not satisfied with usurping Anne's intended place as Darcy's wife, so you sabotaged her chance at a superior match?"

"The marriage may yet be prevented," Darcy said. "Surely they travel the Great North Road. If I leave directly and pursue them on horseback, perhaps I can overtake them before they reach Scotland."

"I will accompany you," Colonel Fitzwilliam offered.

Darcy nodded. "Let us find Mr. Crawford's uncle and Admiral Davidson, if they are still here at Riveton. If we can confirm what time the couple departed and their means of conveyance, we can seek them more effectively."

"The two admirals have already gone home," Colonel Fitzwilliam said. "I saw them leave as we searched for Anne. Should we stop at Admiral Davidson's house on our way?"

Darcy glanced toward the window. Black had shifted to dark grey. "I hesitate to take the time. Dawn will break soon, and with the daylight their carriage can increase its pace. You are familiar with Mr. Crawford's appearance, and so can provide a description when we enquire after him along the road?"

"I can."

"Then let us not lose another minute. Tell a servant to ready our horses. I will meet you in the stables, so that our own departure will be less apparent to the other guests." He turned to Lady Catherine. "What would you have me do when I find them?"

"Wed or unwed, bring them both back here directly. I will deal with Mr. Crawford myself."

Seven

"I answer no such irrelevant and insidious questions."

—Henry Crawford, Mansfield Park

Darcy rapped on the battered chamber door. The wood appeared to have suffered a great deal of abuse over time, forced open by countless outraged fathers and others who, like Darcy and Colonel Fitzwilliam, had pursued eloping couples to this inn and arrived too late. The border village of Gretna Green, with its lax Scottish marriage laws, did such a considerable business in hasty weddings that several local inns offered one-stop convenience to expedite the process. Within minutes of their arrival, English couples could wed and bed at a single location, heading straight from the marriage room to an adjacent bedroom, thus thwarting the efforts of anyone who might arrive too late to insist upon a more prudent approach to matrimony.

Whatever had his cousin been thinking, to consent to such vulgar nuptials? Anne had not even been wed by a proper clergyman, but the innkeeper himself—unfortunately, a perfectly legal union under Scottish law. Darcy dreaded having to report to Lady Catherine that her daughter had been married by one of the village's infamous "anvil priests," with the innkeeper's wife and an ostler as witnesses. At least the couple had not wed at the blacksmith's shop itself; the cottage at the village's main crossroads was the first building travelers encountered, and as such, Gretna Green's most notorious wedding venue.

A second knock elicited sounds of movement from within the chamber.

"Who calls?" asked a male voice.

"Fitzwilliam Darcy."

His answer received no immediate response, making Darcy grateful that Colonel Fitzwilliam stood sentinel outside the window, ready to detain Mr. Crawford if the scoundrel attempted to avoid them. Darcy was glad his cousin had accompanied him—not only for the companionship on what had been a long, hard ride, but also for his impressive regimental uniform that had elicited ready cooperation from all they questioned as they traced the couple's route. If Mr. Crawford tried anything underhanded, Colonel Fitzwilliam could manage him.

A minute later the door opened, and a short, dark gentleman greeted him with a smile far too self-assured for the circumstances.

"Mr. Darcy! It is a pleasure to make your acquaintance at last. We have been expecting you, or some emissary of Anne's family, since the wedding."

"Is Miss de Bourgh within?"

"No, but Mrs. Crawford is."

"I would speak with her."

"By all means."

Mr. Crawford opened the door wider and stepped aside. Anne

sat perched on the edge of the bed, but upon Darcy's entrance stood and drew her dressing gown more closely around her. Darcy noted the self-conscious gesture and averted his gaze, which, as there was little else to behold in the tiny room, landed first on the rumpled coverings of the hastily made bed and then bounced back to Mr. Crawford, whose own limited attire comprised breeches and an untucked shirt. When he looked at Anne once more, her face was scarlet.

Any hope he had harbored of having reached Anne before the couple consummated their marriage evaporated. There was no undoing the union now; all that remained was repairing as much damage as possible.

With obvious effort, she raised her eyes to meet his and regarded him anxiously. "Is my mother with you?"

"No."

Her expression relaxed ever so slightly.

"Colonel Fitzwilliam, however, waits outside."

She flushed again and looked away.

"And here, Anne, you worried about how news of our nuptials would be received by your relations. Why, we have nearly enough guests to host a wedding breakfast. Do invite the good colonel in, Mr. Darcy. It looks about to rain again."

Mr. Crawford's lightness sounded forced; perhaps the bridegroom was not so confident after all. Regardless, Darcy had little patience for levity at present, particularly from that quarter. He was weary and sore from days of travel, and frustrated by his failure to prevent the marriage.

He crossed to the window and signaled Colonel Fitzwilliam to join them, not because Mr. Crawford had suggested it, or because of the cursed rain that had delayed them just enough to thwart their mission, but for motives of his own.

Anne pulled her dressing gown so tightly about her that she

strained the fabric. "Darcy, I would rather our cousin not see me in this state."

"He need not." Darcy felt awkward enough witnessing her dishabille, and he was a married man. Colonel Fitzwilliam was a bachelor. "He can keep your new husband company while you and I converse in private."

"Keep me company, or be my keeper? Come, Mr. Darcy. Surely you do not think I would abandon my bride after going to such lengths to secure her?"

Darcy leveled the groom with an impassive stare. "I do not know what to think of you, Mr. Crawford, for I do not know what kind of gentleman prevails upon a lady to abandon her family, her principles, her caution, and her duty to enter into an irrevocable union in a manner that can only engender sorrow and ill will amongst all who know her, and gossip amongst those who do not."

Actually, Darcy knew exactly what kind of man would do so. His brother-in-law Mr. Wickham was such a man. Several years ago, the fortune hunter had nearly enticed Darcy's sister into eloping, but Georgiana's conscience had compelled her to confess their plan to Darcy before it could be enacted. Wickham later succeeded in seducing Elizabeth's youngest sister, Lydia, a girl of lesser fortune and, regrettably, fewer scruples.

Yes, Darcy indeed had experience with men who allowed selfishness to govern their matrimonial tactics. Mr. Crawford, however, was by Elizabeth and Colonel Fitzwilliam's accounts wealthy enough to have courted Anne honorably, which made his motives more difficult to comprehend. So, too, were Anne's. Georgiana and Lydia had each been but fifteen when Wickham preyed upon them, and in Georgiana's instance her would-be seducer was a man she had known all her life, as much a part of the landscape of Pemberley as its woods. Anne de Bourgh was nearly twice that age, more mature, more cognizant of the consequences of elopement. And far less familiar with her suitor.

Colonel Fitzwilliam's tread signaled his approach. Darcy greeted him at the door, closing it behind him to shield Anne from view. He spoke in a low tone. "It is as we feared. We are too late."

Fitzwilliam's countenance, already strained from their arduous journey, deflated. He likewise muted his voice. "Is Anne well?"

"I believe her welfare might be better determined without Mr. Crawford in attendance."

"I will escort him downstairs to settle his account with the innkeeper. If Anne's health can support further travel, shall we depart as soon as the postilions can provide horses?"

Though they were all in need of rest, remaining in Gretna Green was insupportable. "Make the arrangements, but let us journey no farther than Carlisle today." Carlisle was not ten miles distant; there they could overnight at a proper inn. "Assuming Mr. Crawford's post-chaise accommodates four, we require horses for only one carriage. He is hardly in a position to object to conveying us."

"On the contrary, he needs to court our goodwill. Surely they both realize Lady Catherine will not receive them kindly—if she receives them at all."

"You know our aunt. She will be waiting with her solicitor to attempt to settle some sort of marriage articles with Mr. Crawford the moment we produce the couple at Riveton."

"Shall I send word to her that we have discovered them?"

"I will write her from Carlisle. Riding in a closed carriage with Mr. Crawford might expose additional information we ought to include."

"Riding in a closed carriage with Mr. Crawford might reveal more about him than we care to know. This escapade has hardly disposed me well toward him."

Mr. Crawford called from within. "Mr. Darcy, if you and the colonel have finished talking about us, we have finished dressing."

"He is unrepentant?" Colonel Fitzwilliam asked.

"Utterly."

"That will change."

Mr. Crawford departed with the colonel, whose military bearing clearly communicated no tolerance for brash behavior. The pistols he carried at his side brooked no foolishness, either.

Left to themselves, Anne regarded Darcy like a convicted felon awaiting sentencing, or a child anticipating a thorough scolding. Were Lady Catherine here, she would deliver both with vehemence, and he could see Anne bracing herself for a tirade rehearsed over several hundred miles. Rather than face him, she crossed to the window and drew aside its cheap, tattered curtain. A light rain indeed began to fall.

Despite his impatience, he spoke gently. "Did Mr. Crawford coerce you?"

Several raindrops struck the glass. "I expect that is the only explanation that could possibly make sense to you."

"One of few. You are not a silly young girl. I cannot believe you were so overcome by infatuation that you ran away with a stranger on impulse."

"It was no impulse, and he is not a stranger. I have known Mr. Crawford nearly a year."

"How?"

"We met last autumn in Bath."

"Why, then, was your mother unacquainted with him when we discovered your note?"

"We were introduced after she departed Bath for Pemberley."

Anne had wintered in Bath while Lady Catherine assisted the Darcys with fraudulent legal charges that had taken five months to resolve. He recalled that she had written her mother several times during that period requesting permission to extend her stay in the city, citing its steady benefit to her health. Lady Catherine had consented, congratulating herself on selecting Bath as the most salubrious of England's spa towns, and believing her daughter safe under Mrs. Jenkinson's supervision.

"Did Mrs. Jenkinson approve the acquaintance?"

"Yes, though she did not realize its extent. Mr. Crawford was in and out of town, and when we did encounter each other he seldom paid me particular attention in her presence. He never called at our lodgings, and when we saw him in public he would include Mrs. Jenkinson equally in our exchange of pleasantries. He and I conversed more freely on occasions when other matters, such as retrieving my shawl or procuring a glass of water, occupied her. At assemblies, we sometimes danced whilst she played at cards. She could not have foreseen this turn of events—pray, do not blame her for it."

"So Mr. Crawford courted you surreptitiously. And you were a willing party to the deception?"

"For most of our time in Bath, I did not think of his attention as courtship, though I confess that as our acquaintance improved I occasionally indulged in the daydream that one might develop. I was simply gratified that a gentleman as charming as Mr. Crawford desired my conversation."

"Did you never question why?"

She turned. Something like spirit lit her expression. "Is there a reason he should not? Because you never showed interest, am I unworthy of any gentleman's notice?"

The question so startled Darcy that he could not respond.

"There I was, in Bath, for the first time since your wedding. Can you comprehend the humiliation of returning to a scene where my mother had, since my coming-out, discouraged suitors with the explanation that I was reserved for my cousin by an 'understanding'? A cousin who had just married someone of significantly lesser status in the eyes of Society? Not only did I bear the stigma of having been rejected by my own kin as a desirable wife, but I was essentially entering the marriage market for the first time at eight-and-twenty: a decade older than most of the girls around me. I was painfully aware that my inheritance constituted my primary, if not sole, attraction to any suitor.

"Believe it or not, there *were* other suitors, once my mother left Bath. Not many, but a handful of gentlemen, all of whom wooed me only for my dowry and the promise of Rosings to come. The impoverished peers who had squandered their own wealth did not even attempt to disguise their motives. Other gentlemen were more bold and less honest. In fact, Mr. Crawford earned my gratitude, and that of Mrs. Jenkinson, for revealing to us the histories of more than one fortune hunter."

"While Mr. Crawford was protecting you from the avaricious addresses of other gentlemen, did you or Mrs. Jenkinson enquire into his own reputation?"

"Upon his initial arrival in town, word circulated that he had recently ended an affair with a married lady who had pursued him most shamefully. Early in our acquaintance, he acknowledged the truth of the reports, as well as sincere regret at ever having entered into the liaison. That was the only ill I ever heard spoken of him. Details about his estate and income were easily verified, which put to rest any misgivings I might have harbored about his motives for cultivating my regard. His situation is quite secure without need of my inheritance.

"In addressing me, he courted my friendship, not my fortune. We engaged in agreeable discourse on any number of subjects. Always, when he spoke, I felt he spoke to me—Anne de Bourgh, not Lady Catherine's daughter or Sir Lewis de Bourgh's heir. It was the first time in my life that someone took genuine interest in anything I had to say. When his interest developed into something more, I am uncertain. Any hint of partiality I ascribed to my own vanity, for he never declared himself whilst I remained in Bath. For my own part, by the time my mother summoned me home in March, my affections were engaged. I mourned the loss of his companionship, for he had brought diversion to a very dull existence."

"How was this 'friendship' sustained after you returned to Rosings?"

"It was not; communication between us ceased. I was in Kent, he was at Everingham or in any number of other places—York, London, Richmond—he delights in travel and is never in one place for long. We could not correspond; even had propriety permitted it, my mother would not have. To this day, I do not know what transpired during her time at Pemberley, but she returned absolutely determined to arrange a marriage for me with a man of the highest consequence possible. Nothing short of a future lord would do, better if the gentleman already possessed a title. I was to be bound over to the highest bidder as soon as an impressive enough bridegroom could be procured and the marriage articles drawn up."

"And you rebelled at her plan?"

"Quite the contrary. I am conscious of my duty, Darcy, and I had no reason to hope for better situation than what my mother sought for me. I never expected to marry for affection, and at this point in my life, I realized that was an unlikely luxury."

"Then how came you to elope with Mr. Crawford?"

"I would have borne a *mariage de convenance* if it were to a gentleman I could respect, or even a fool who would treat me kindly. But my mother appeared to have settled upon Neville Sennex, and that is a match to which I could not submit."

"Why not?"

"I am troubled by his character. Indeed, after my observations this se'nnight past, I believe him not just an unpleasant man, but one of violent temper.

"We called at Hawthorn Manor each day after our arrival at Riveton, and both my mother and his father seemed determined to put us in each other's company. I endured the awkward conversations and tried to make myself agreeable, but Mr. Sennex clearly resented the interviews. As a host, he was not solicitous of my comfort or interests; it was only at his father's behest that he partook in even the most cursory exchange. His treatment of Lord Sennex fell far short of the respect any father, let alone a viscount, deserves. He displayed such impatience with his lordship's befuddlement in our presence that I cannot imagine his conduct when they are alone.

"Our third visit saw slight improvement in his manners toward me, but I am afraid the servants suffered as a consequence. He exploded at a housemaid for a trivial oversight, threatening to dismiss her if it happened again. I noticed, as he did so, that she rubbed a faded bruise on her forearm. Twice more that afternoon he berated servants mercilessly for minor infractions.

"The day before the ball, the viscount and my mother—who seemed to desire a private tête-à-tête—insisted that Mr. Sennex lead me on a tour of the house and grounds. He obviously despised the task. We walked through perhaps half a dozen rooms, he barely uttering a word except to enquire how Rosings compared. He could not seem to resolve in his own mind whether he wanted Rosings to be of inferior significance or extraordinary worth. He was quizzing me about the rents—as if I have any knowledge of such business—when he abruptly cut me off.

"We had entered a chamber that contained so many weapons it could have been an armory: rifles, muskets, a set of dueling pistols, a fusil from his father's military days. There were swords that had been passed down through the family for generations, and I do not know what else—the room could not have held less interest for me, and I wondered that of all the places in the house, he should have brought me there. But he was more animated than I had ever seen him, rattling on and on about the power of the various weapons, as if the information ought to impress me.

"Finally, to my immense relief, a servant entered to announce the arrival of a gentleman whom Mr. Sennex had been expecting. I was quite surprised when, a moment later, Mr. Crawford entered. My presence took him equally by surprise. He'd had no idea of my being in the neighborhood; he himself had arrived only that morning, and called at Hawthorn to collect a horse he was acquiring from Mr. Sennex. The two gentlemen had met at one of their London clubs, and had arranged the matter during a recent visit there.

"Mr. Sennex would have deposited me back with my mother and the viscount, but Mr. Crawford invited me to view the horse along with him. As we walked toward the stables, Mr. Crawford displayed all the congeniality I remembered. Upon close inspection of the horse, however, his demeanor changed. The animal, which Mr. Sennex had represented as a fine hunter, was head shy and scarred from an injury near its left eye that had damaged its vision. The mount was not worth nearly as much as Mr. Sennex had claimed, and from the terse argument that ensued I inferred that the horse had originally been offered to Mr. Crawford as payment for a gambling loss. Mr. Crawford said he would take the horse, but did not consider the debt fully discharged. Mr. Sennex stormed off to the house to retrieve banknotes to make up the difference, leaving us with the horse.

"As we awaited his return, Mr. Crawford asked what had brought me to Hawthorn Manor. I explained that I visited with my mother. Though I did not intend to share my suspicion that she and the viscount plotted a betrothal, he knew me well enough to perceive my discomfort, and I found myself revealing my apprehensions. Mr. Crawford became grave. He said he did not know Mr. Sennex well, but that he had a reputation at the club for a quick temper. He also said that given the behavior of Mr. Sennex's horse and the look of the injury, he suspected the mare's scar to be the result of having been struck with the horn hook of a hunting crop, rather than the accident Mr. Sennex had claimed. 'A man who could injure so valuable an animal . . .' He left the sentence unfinished, but I understood him. Striking a wife—also a man's legal property—is not so very great a leap.

"Mr. Crawford urged me to avoid an engagement with Mr. Sennex. I told him that my mother seemed determined, but that I would speak with her. He extracted a promise from me to meet him in Riveton's rose garden at dawn to tell him the result."

"Later, when I attempted to convey to my mother my uneasiness about Mr. Sennex, she would not hear. An obedient wife had nothing to fear, she said, and implied that a betrothal agreement was indeed imminent. My cooperation was not only expected, it was demanded.

"I spent the night recalling the bursts of anger I had witnessed in Mr. Sennex and imagining the force that had caused the horse's scar applied to me. Early the next morning, en route to my assignation with Mr. Crawford, I encountered Mrs. Darcy and thought for certain that she suspected the rendezvous. By the time I reached the rose garden and Mr. Crawford, agitation so overcame me that it is only by some miracle that he made any sense at all of my utterances.

"Mr. Crawford revealed his partiality for me and declared that he could not stand by whilst I sacrificed myself to Mr. Sennex. He offered himself as a husband and asked whether my mother would consider him an acceptable substitute. When I doubted her accord—he possesses no title, and negotiations with the viscount were so far along—he proposed a desperate solution: an elopement. I could not conceive of such disobedience, but he urged me to consider it for my own welfare. I was to give him my answer at the ball. We would underplay our acquaintance to avoid suspicion, but he would contrive a few minutes' conversation in which I could indicate my decision by some sign. He would come prepared; if I accepted, we would depart from there, with the distraction of the festivities to mask our disappearance.

"I tried to speak to my mother a final time before the ball, but she cut me off in her haste to meet yet again with Lord Sennex. As I watched her carriage depart for Hawthorn Manor, I knew that I had to act that night, for I would not have the courage to disobey her in person when she put a finalized betrothal agreement in front of me to sign. Now it is done, and I can only imagine the extent of her displeasure. Will she ever receive us at Rosings, do you think?"

"She wants to see you posthaste. Colonel Fitzwilliam and I are to return you and Mr. Crawford to Riveton as quickly as the miles can be traveled."

Anne sighed and glanced round the shabby room that had been her bridechamber. Her entire posture bespoke resignation. "We can depart whenever you wish. Delaying the reunion will not make it easier."

Eight

"I have not been in the habit of brooking disappointment."
—*Lady Catherine de Bourgh,* Pride and Prejudice

It is a pity Miss de Bourgh cannot join us this afternoon." Lord Sennex lifted his teacup but did not sip, instead returning it to the saucer as if he could not quite remember what he had been about to do with it. Elizabeth itched to brush away the stray cake crumbs that had collected in the folds of his neckcloth. 'Twas unfortunate enough that advanced age deprived the viscount of his full faculties. Must it also compromise his dignity?

"Forgive me, your ladyship," he continued, "but where did you say your daughter is?"

Lady Catherine had not said. Indeed, Lady Catherine had not said much over the past several days to Lord Sennex or his son about Anne's sudden absence, even though the viscount had called each day since the ball. Darcy had sent word to his aunt that Miss de Bourgh had now become Mrs. Henry Crawford, but her ladyship refused to accept the news. Until Mr. Crawford presented himself to stand trial in the court of Lady Catherine, she would not speak of the matter.

Except to Elizabeth. In private, Lady Catherine harangued Elizabeth ceaselessly for her role in the elopement—a role Elizabeth herself yet struggled to comprehend. Culpability for the entire affair was deposited squarely on her shoulders, despite her protests of innocence. Not only did Elizabeth stand accused of all but personally conducting the couple to Gretna Green, she also bore responsibility for their ever having met in the first place. Had Lady Catherine not been forced to abandon Anne in Bath to aid the Darcys the previous autumn, her daughter would not have fallen prey to that fortune-hunting Mr. Crawford. Had Elizabeth not enticed Darcy to betray his duty, Anne would be safely married to her cousin by now. Had Elizabeth's sister Lydia not eloped, the notion never would have entered Anne's mind.

Were Mrs. Jenkinson still at Riveton, Anne's former attendant could have shared Elizabeth's accommodations in the doghouse. But the longtime servant, after disclosing all she knew about Mr. Crawford (relatively little) and the elopement (nothing at all), was summarily dismissed without references or her final month's pay. She was expelled from Riveton with instructions to inform Lady Catherine's solicitor of her new direction so that her belongings at Rosings might be forwarded. The poor woman had been utterly bewildered as she departed for the cottage of a sister she had not seen in five-and-twenty years. Elizabeth had given her ten pounds and assigned one of her own footmen to escort her safely to Sussex. Why she felt responsible for Mrs. Jenkinson's predicament, she could not say. Perhaps Lady Catherine's reproaches were beginning to find root.

Her ladyship's prevarications with the viscount, however,

clearly were not. What little information she had conveyed, Lord Sennex seemed unable to retain.

"My daughter attends to wedding-related business." It was the same equivocation Lady Catherine had used with Lord Sennex since Anne's disappearance, but delivered with more defensiveness—and less patience—than previously. They anticipated the return of the newlyweds sometime this day, and her ladyship grew more impatient each hour. Though she had received Lord Sennex with civility, she wanted him gone before the Crawfords appeared. She did not want any outsiders, particularly Lord Sennex or his son, to witness the reunion. They were not to know of Anne's clandestine marriage until Lady Catherine had satisfied herself that it was incontrovertible.

Elizabeth saw little point in postponing the inevitable admission to Anne's erstwhile fiancé. Darcy's letter had affirmed that her marriage to Mr. Crawford was valid, and even were it not, Mr. Sennex could hardly be expected to accept Anne on the same terms as before the affair. If he accepted her at all.

"Ah, yes—gone down to London to order her wedding clothes, I imagine." Lord Sennex nodded knowingly. "Young ladies are always so excited about that aspect of the nuptials. But why did you not accompany her? Surely Miss de Bourgh would appreciate her mother's counsel in selecting her trousseau."

"Anne knows my opinion of her arrangements. And if she does not, she should. Would your lordship care for more cake?"

The viscount's eyes brightened at the invitation. As he tasted his second slice with the unreserved delight of a five-year-old, Elizabeth reflected that perhaps senility had its advantages. While others dwelt on guilt and misery, Lord Sennex found joy in cake.

A servant entered with a letter. "Mrs. Darcy, this just arrived."

Elizabeth recognized the hand at once. She rose. "Pray excuse me, my lord. This comes from my husband, and I would read it immediately."

He looked up from his cake long enough to nod. "Of course."

She left the drawing room but had no sooner closed the door behind her than it opened.

"Where are you going with that?" Lady Catherine joined her in the hallway, leaving the door slightly ajar. "That letter contains news of Anne, and I will not be kept waiting to learn it."

"What about his lordship? Would you leave your guest sitting by himself?"

"The old fool is too occupied with his cake to miss me. What does it say?"

Elizabeth broke the seal and read the opening sentences. Mr. and Mrs. Crawford would not arrive at Riveton today. Or tomorrow. Or next week.

"There has been an accident."

"An accident?" Lady Catherine attempted to take the letter for herself. "Let me see that! What sort of accident? Is Anne injured?"

Elizabeth scanned the lines as best she could while fending off Darcy's aunt. "A carriage accident . . . The mishap occurred when they stopped at an inn. Just as Anne was alighting, one of the horses suddenly reared and so jostled the chaise that she lost her balance. She fell to the ground and the carriage wheel rolled over her leg. . . . The apothecary advises she not be moved."

"Was no one handing her out? Where was that husband of hers? Does he neglect her already?"

She scanned further. "Mr. Crawford was indeed assisting her from the vehicle, and blames himself for not having been able to somehow prevent the accident."

"The scoundrel could have prevented it by not abducting her to Gretna Green in the first place. That gentleman now has even more to answer for. And an apothecary? Has no one summoned a real physician? Where is this inn?"

"Mansfield."

"Nottinghamshire? Whatever are they doing there?"

"No, a small village in Northamptonshire. According to Darcy, rain forced a detour from the main road. They lodge at the Ox and Bull."

"This whole situation is cock and bull. It is time—long past time—that Mr. Henry Crawford was held accountable for it. I will brook no further delay."

"You would have him leave his wife in her present condition to continue here?"

"No, I want him to remain precisely where he is. I am going to Mansfield. Today."

Today suited Elizabeth just fine. The sooner Lady Catherine departed, the sooner Elizabeth would be left in peace. "Would you like me to convey your excuses to Lord Sennex?" she offered.

"No, I want you to oversee your own preparations for departure. You are accompanying me."

Nine

To anything like a permanence of abode, or limitation of society, Henry Crawford had, unluckily, a great dislike.

—Mansfield Park

The Ox and Bull had served as Mansfield's only inn for seven generations. What began as a small public house had over the years expanded into a conglomerate of rooms haphazardly added as demand justified and profit allowed. The dining room had been twice enlarged to accommodate the numerous villagers who dined there; in addition, the inn now boasted eight private bedchambers, a small parlor, a communal sleeping room for servants, and stables that also functioned as the local livery. The Bull, as its regular patrons called it, sprawled rather than sat on the main road of the modest village, across the green from the church, whose tall, straight spire chided its neighbor for undisciplined deportment.

Despite the inn's rogue architecture, it was a respectable establishment. So its proprietors, Mr. and Mrs. Gower, informed Darcy and his companions. Thrice.

Anne's accident upon their arrival brought the innkeeper and his wife outside immediately. All attention was on the injured lady. Henry bent over Anne, attempting to calm her in a quiet voice as Darcy, Colonel Fitzwilliam, and Mr. Gower worked with the postilion and the ostler to remove the carriage wheel from atop Anne's leg without causing her further harm. Mrs. Gower hurried off to fetch the apothecary.

By the time Anne was freed, a small audience had gathered. Mr. Gower sent a servant to open one of the bedrooms so that Anne might be brought inside. Mr. Crawford, who yet bent over Anne, lifted her into his arms and stood, providing onlookers their first true glimpse at his countenance since the ordeal began. The innkeeper stiffened.

"Here, now. This is a respectable inn."

"I should hope so," Henry said evenly. "Mrs. Crawford is a respectable lady."

"Mrs. Crawford, is she?"

Several spectators repeated the name in low tones. Henry ignored the murmurs; Anne was oblivious to them, her countenance overcome with pain.

"My wife is in agony. Are you going to show us to the room, or not?"

"Aye, as she is injured."

Mr. Gower led them to a room at the top of the stairs. As Henry settled Anne on the bed, Mrs. Gower returned with the apothecary. The sight of Mr. Crawford made them both stop in surprise.

"Mr. Crawford—I did not recognize you earlier in the commotion." She cast an appraising look at Anne. "Your injured friend is welcome, but I must remind you that this is a respectable inn."

"I shall bear that in mind."

Darcy and Colonel Fitzwilliam withdrew while the apothecary

examined Anne. In the dining room, they found that several patrons who had witnessed the accident were gathered in one corner, already relating the tale to newcomers at a nearby table. Upon their entrance, the conversation hushed.

They approached the innkeeper. "Have you three rooms available?" asked Darcy. "I am uncertain how long we will require them."

The innkeeper assessed the two of them, then opened his register. "What names shall I record?"

"Mr. Fitzwilliam Darcy of Derbyshire, and Colonel James Fitzwilliam of Buckinghamshire. The third gentleman is Mr. Henry Crawford, but it seems you are already acquainted with him."

"Mr. Crawford is well known in Mansfield."

"I was not aware of his possessing any connection to Northamptonshire," Darcy said.

"None that any gentleman ought to boast of."

"Might I entreat you to explain?"

"Your companion can provide his own account, and a glib one I am sure it will be. Meanwhile, if whatever business brought you here involves Sir Thomas Bertram, you would do well to leave Mr. Crawford behind should you go to Mansfield Park. I do not expect your friend is welcome at that house."

Darcy hardly considered Mr. Crawford his friend, and after the reception Henry had met in Mansfield, was still less inclined to cultivate a stronger association with him than the one forced by the gentleman's marriage to Anne. He would not, however, betray to a stranger how little he knew about his newest relation.

"We have no business in Mansfield," Colonel Fitzwilliam said. "We stopped here only to change horses and refresh ourselves."

"Mr. Crawford is a bold one, passing through this village at all." Mr. Gower called over a boy of about ten. "This is my son, Nat. If you will identify which luggage belongs to you and which belongs to the Crawfords, he will see that it gets to the proper rooms."

"We have only portmanteaus." Leaving in haste and journeying by horseback, Darcy had carried little more than a spare shirt. Henry and Anne had also fled relatively unencumbered. "The Crawfords each have a small valise."

The absence of baggage earned a censorious look from the innkeeper. "Well, Nat, you should have an easy time of it. The Crawfords are in room one, and Mr. Darcy's and the colonel's rooms are across the hall." The boy set off.

"I run a respectable inn, Mr. Darcy."

"So I understand."

"I will not tolerate immoral behavior going on beneath its roof for my children to see, nor will the decent folk of this village countenance such. Is that lady upstairs truly Mr. Crawford's wife?"

"I can produce proof if you require it." Darcy had procured a copy of the marriage certificate for Lady Catherine, but his tone discouraged any such request from the innkeeper. "She is also our cousin, the daughter of Lady Catherine de Bourgh, and the niece of the Earl of Southwell. As this is a 'respectable inn,' I trust she will be treated with due consideration."

As a rule, Darcy deplored invoking the names of his titled relations. But Anne was experiencing enough distress without also enduring condemnation from her hosts. She would no doubt receive an ample quantity of that from her own mother in short order.

The names produced the desired effect. Part of Mr. Gower's glower diminished. "Mrs. Crawford shall receive proper attention while she is a guest of the Bull. Though what sort of reception her husband finds in Mansfield, I cannot guarantee."

Darcy and the colonel inspected their rooms. Darcy's was

small and simply appointed, but clean. The bed occupied most of the chamber, leaving insufficient space for a table or other writing surface on which to execute his most pressing obligation, that of sending word to Riveton Hall of the accident.

He asked his host where he might procure writing supplies, and was directed to Hardwick's on the main lane through town. While Colonel Fitzwilliam remained behind at the inn on the chance that he might be needed, Darcy proceeded to Hardwick's. He found the shop to be an all-purpose establishment, serving as the local linendrapers, haberdasher, jeweler, stationer, and so on. He purchased a quill, paper, ink, and wax, and returned to the inn.

The group of villagers he had noted earlier yet lingered in the dining room, and he chose a seat near them. Normally he would have distanced himself from the talkative party to better compose his thoughts—indeed, anxiety for Anne disordered them enough without the added distraction of boisterous conversation—but he hoped to learn more about the apparently notorious Mr. Crawford without the indignity of actually having to enquire. With half his mind focused on the neighboring table, he addressed his letter to Elizabeth. It was easier to write to her than to Lady Catherine, and she could break the distressing news to Anne's mother in person.

At first, Darcy's presence stifled the very discussion he wished to overhear. Upon his sitting down, the group's most vocal member, a middle-aged man with bushy grey hair and a bulbous nose, self-consciously initiated a new topic, and for a time one would have imagined that the world turned upon the issue of whether Abe Tucker's dairy cow would calve this week or next. Were Mr. Tucker himself present, he doubtless would have been pleased to learn that, by consensus, the calf would arrive no later than Thursday. Also, that the thief who had stolen a hen from Mrs. Norris's poultry house had been discovered by his mother and promptly marched over to offer a stammering apology, which had been accepted in a manner certain to deter the eight-year-old felon from embarking on a permanent criminal career. And that it would surely rain again this se'nnight. Unless it did not.

However, human nature being what it is—especially when augmented by successive pints of small beer—the villagers could not long suppress their curiosity regarding the gentleman upstairs, the lady he claimed was his wife, and what business could have brought them to Mansfield. Darcy felt their gazes upon him as he penned his letter; it was only a matter of time before the bushy-haired fellow, whom the others called Hobson, finally addressed him.

"Begging your pardon, sir, but I saw the accident earlier. I hope that Mrs. Crawford will recover?"

Darcy had to give the man credit. He wondered how long the laborer had been formulating an acceptable way to initiate conversation with a gentleman on whom he had no claim. He looked up from his letter. "Are you acquainted with the Crawfords?"

"Not directly, sir. But for a time, Mr. Crawford was often seen about the village."

"A guest of our minister, Dr. Grant," interjected another member of the party, a young scrawny fellow with a friendly but pockmarked countenance. The others called him Spriggs.

"Yes, Dr. Grant," Hobson said. "Mrs. Grant is Mr. Crawford's sister—"

"Half sister," Spriggs corrected.

"—so Mr. Crawford is known around the neighborhood. He didn't spend much time in the village—he was mostly up at

Mansfield Park—but he'd offer a nod as he rode through, which is more than we ever received from Miss Crawford."

"Mary Crawford—that's Mr. Crawford's full sister," Spriggs, apparently the Crawford family's official genealogist, clarified for Darcy's benefit. "Have you met her?"

"I have not had the pleasure."

"Quite a beauty, Miss Crawford."

Hobson scowled. "Trouble is, she knows it."

"She lives with the Grants, but they all moved to London nearly a twelvemonth ago. Dr. Grant got himself a stall in Westminster."

"He ought to give up the living here if you ask me." Hobson drained his glass. "Damned selfish, I say, collecting his salary while the rectory sits empty and Mr. Bertram covers the Mansfield parish duties in addition to his own at Thornton Lacey. Especially after the scandal with Mr. Bertram's sister."

"Miss Bertram was no innocent," muttered a man at a nearby table.

"Mrs. Rushworth, you mean. When she gave up the name Bertram, Mr. Crawford should have given up her. No gentleman has any business running off with another man's wife."

"No proper lady, married or not, would have gone."

Darcy signaled the serving girl to bring the men another round.

"Well, don't let Mrs. Norris hear you saying such about her niece, or she'll make your ears burn."

"Let her rail. What does anyone care about that old busybody's opinion? Even Sir Thomas doesn't. Won't receive his own daughter, and I say good riddance. If my Nellie ever brought such shame on my house, I'd cast her out—and castrate the dog she ran off with."

"I'd leave that satisfaction to her cuckolded husband."

"Rushworth is outraged enough to do it. He won't take her back, and I hear he's actually going to divorce her."

"Put her and Mr. Crawford on trial?"

Just then the apothecary descended the staircase. Though Darcy regretted his timing—he wanted to learn more about Mr. Crawford—anxiety for Anne propelled him away from Hobson's conversation.

"Mrs. Crawford is fortunate," said Mr. Dawson. "Though her leg is terribly bruised and swollen, it appears to be unbroken. I believe the recent rain softened the ground enough that her limb sank into the earth when the carriage wheel rolled over it. She is in a great deal of pain, however, and I recommend she not travel for at least a fortnight."

Darcy added the essentials of Mr. Dawson's report to his letter and arranged for it to be dispatched to Riveton posthaste. By the time he completed his task, Hobson and his comrades had disbanded, taking their elucidating discussion with them.

He went upstairs. Mr. Crawford answered his knock and admitted him. Mrs. Gower had departed, leaving Henry alone with Anne, who lay sleeping. Someone had helped her out of her muddy clothes and into a nightdress, barely visible beneath the quilt tucked around her. Darcy could not see the injured leg at all.

"Mr. Dawson gave her laudanum." Mr. Crawford pushed a stray lock of hair away from Anne's eyes. "Her sleep was fitful at first, but I believe she rests more comfortably now."

"I have sent word to Riveton of the accident."

"Thank you. That was a duty to which I did not look forward."

"Do not thank me yet. While I composed the letter, several other patrons in the dining room engaged in a most intriguing conversation. Do you care to speculate as to its subject?"

Mr. Crawford had the decency to appear uncomfortable. "Henry Crawford?"

"Indeed. And one Mrs. Rushworth."

"There are many other villages in which I would rather find myself."

"Anne confided to me that you had recently ended an affair with a married lady. I now presume she referred to Mrs. Rushworth—unless you maintain a succession of mistresses?"

"No, only the one. Though lately I have contemplated starting a harem."

Darcy's lack of amusement eradicated Mr. Crawford's attempt at wit. His grin faded.

"Trust me, one such as Maria Rushworth is enough," Mr. Crawford said more soberly. "She is willful and vain and selfish, and I believe I felt more regret at her disloyalty toward her husband than she did. Believe it or not, it was *she* who persuaded *me* to elope. I had not lived with her above a month before I realized my error, and prolonged the affair only in the failed hope that my feelings would rekindle to what they ought to be after the misery our liaison had caused all her family. I felt an obligation to remain with her, but finally I could not live the falsehood any longer."

"I am to understand that *honesty* led you to sever the association?"

"Ironic, is it not? That a relationship born in deception should end with the belated emergence of integrity? But so it did. I am a reformed man, Mr. Darcy. From this day forward, the only wives I seduce will be my own."

With Anne asleep, Mr. Crawford went downstairs to face Mr. Gower. He either ignored or was oblivious to the innkeeper's ill will as he signed the register, his right hand sweeping across the page as he formed a flourish at the end of his name. His autograph dominated the folio, nearly eclipsing the more restrained signature of a Mr. Lautus whose name appeared above.

Mr. Crawford seemed to move through the world with a dramatic flair that spilled out onto everything he touched. Darcy hoped for Anne's sake it would not overrun her.

Ten

"You can be at no loss . . . to understand the reason of my journey hither. . . . you ought to know, that I am not to be trifled with."

—*Lady Catherine,* Pride and Prejudice

In the space of four-and-twenty hours, the Ox and Bull shrank. Somehow the inn that had lounged on the village green spreading its cobbled-together wings in lazy imitation of more formal guesthouses now seemed to stand at attention, its walls constricting as it labored to contain the company within.

It was the wind, some said. A summer gale had ruffled the village the full length of that unseasonably stormy day. By dusk, it had blown in a force of nature stronger than any Mansfield had previously known.

Lady Catherine de Bourgh.

Her ladyship came accompanied by Elizabeth, who nearly tumbled out of the chaise in her haste to escape after the longest ride of her life—measured not by distance, but by the perceived movement of time. Though Lady Catherine had ordered a grueling pace, so fractious had been the atmosphere within the carriage that Elizabeth felt no horses in the world could convey them to Mansfield quickly enough. Her ladyship's indignation over the elopement, now nursed for more than a se'nnight, teamed with anxiety for Anne's health and conviction of Mr. Crawford's negligence to render Darcy's aunt the most cross passenger with whom Elizabeth had ever had the misfortune of being trapped in an enclosed vehicle.

Directly they arrived, her ladyship strode into the inn, cast an appraising look about her that pronounced the surroundings altogether inferior, and demanded the whereabouts of Mr. and Mrs. Crawford.

"They are in their room, ma'am," said the innkeeper. "If you give me your name, I will send one of the girls to announce you."

"I am Lady Catherine de Bourgh, Mrs. Crawford's mother. Merely identify which chamber is theirs—on this occasion, I prefer to announce myself."

The innkeeper complied. Lady Catherine marched up the stairs while Elizabeth lingered behind.

"My husband, Mr. Darcy, has also taken lodging here. Where might I find him?"

"I believe he, too, is presently in his room, across the hall from the Crawfords. Will you be staying?"

"Yes." She hoped their stay would not prove long. She had sent Lily-Anne home to Pemberley with Mrs. Flaherty and Georgiana, and did not want to be separated from her daughter for an extended period.

He glanced up the staircase. "And her ladyship?"

"She requires accommodations as well—the best available. Have you enough rooms for us all?"

"Certainly. We have only one other guest, a single gentleman, besides your party."

Elizabeth was pleased to hear that with the exception of a lone gentleman, they had the inn to themselves. Though surely Lady Catherine would exercise discretion in her dealings with Mr. Crawford, the general mood of all their party was not sociable.

She went in search of Darcy and found him standing in the hall, along with Mr. Crawford and Colonel Fitzwilliam.

"Lady Catherine desires a few minutes' private conversation with her daughter," Darcy explained. "She also suggested that you see to her room arrangements."

Elizabeth released a heavy sigh, but it was inadequate to expel the week's worth of vexation that threatened to well over. She doubted her ladyship's "suggestion" had been issued as anything resembling a request. Since Mrs. Jenkinson's dismissal, Lady Catherine had treated her as a replacement attendant, and Elizabeth had acquiesced more often than she was proud to admit—a sinner doing penance for aiding and abetting Anne's elopement, though within her own mind she yet defended herself against the charge.

"I have already done so on my own initiative," she said. "Mr. Crawford, how is Anne's health today?"

"She was feeling much better—"

Lady Catherine's muffled voice carried through the closed door. Though her words were indistinguishable, her tone clearly communicated the delight she felt upon being reunited with her newlywed daughter.

"—at least, until a few minutes ago."

Elizabeth pitied Anne. Standing up to Lady Catherine was difficult enough when one could—well, physically stand up. Anne was unused to directly defying her mother, and her injury rendered her all the more defenseless against Lady Catherine's verbal assault. As much as Elizabeth wished only to enjoy the exclusive company of her husband and the quiet of her own chamber, she felt compelled to lend Anne her support.

"I believe her ladyship has had sufficient time to wish the bride joy." She rapped on the door.

"You would divert my aunt's displeasure toward yourself?" Darcy asked. He appeared fatigued, and Elizabeth recalled that, however unpleasant had been her previous se'nnight, his had been worse.

"I merely return it to its natural course. The new Mrs. Crawford may consider the correction her bridal gift." She knocked a second time, then opened the door without waiting for a response.

Darcy raised his brows at the presumptive tactic.

"It is impossible for me to sink any further in her ladyship's esteem," Elizabeth said before entering. "Join me if you dare."

Anne greeted her arrival with an expression of relief and gratitude; Lady Catherine, with her usual condemning countenance.

"Is there something you require, Mrs. Darcy?"

"If you have done monopolizing her, I would greet the new Mrs. Crawford."

Before the startled Lady Catherine could intercept her, Elizabeth went to Anne's bedside. "I understand congratulations are in order. I hope your marriage brings you much felicity, though I was surprised as anybody to learn of it."

Anne's face bespoke confusion. "Truly? But you said you knew what I was about. And that I should accept Henry's offer if it made me happy."

"I meant his offer to escort you to the dance floor, not to Gretna Green. I had no presentiment of your eloping. But now you are wed, and we"— she looked meaningfully at Lady Catherine, observing as she did so that Darcy and the other gentlemen had also entered the chamber—"*all* of us—ought to look forward, not back."

Lady Catherine's gaze moved from Elizabeth to Mr. Crawford. It was difficult to determine which of them she held in greater contempt at the moment. "Indeed we must," she finally declared. "So I would know, Mr. Crawford, how you intend to provide for my daughter. I demand a full reckoning of your worth, because our first order of business will be drawing up the marriage articles your elopement so conveniently avoided. I sincerely hope you did not intend to enhance your income with a bridal settlement from me, for there will be none after the utterly objectionable manner in which you brought about this union."

Mr. Crawford stepped toward Anne, so as to enter this battle with a united front. Lady Catherine, however, interposed herself. The tactic disconcerted him. For a moment he looked as if he might make a second attempt to reach his wife's side, but upon further evaluation of his opponent, the errant bridegroom settled for holding his ground.

"I assure you, I am well able to provide for Mrs. Crawford."

"Anne is accustomed to a certain style of living which must be maintained, both during your lifetime and in the event of your untimely demise." Her tone suggested that such an event would be considered untimely to only one party of the conversation. "My solicitor has been investigating you and your financial affairs. He will arrive here within a few days' time to draw up the agreement. Everything from pin money to her widow's jointure will be specified. I understand you are independent, with property in Norfolk?"

"Indeed. Everingham is a fine estate, and upon coming into possession I made many improvements—"

"It is unencumbered? No entail will prevent Anne or her daughters from inheriting should she bear no sons?"

"Mother!"

"Anne, we must address these matters. They should have been delineated before you wed this man, or any man. You have a fragile constitution. If you predecease your husband, would you have your children left penniless while the son of a second wife inherits everything? If Mr. Crawford dies before you, would you lose your home whilst some remote relation seizes all?"

Though Lady Catherine's delivery was dramatic, Elizabeth knew all too well that she did not exaggerate the threat that entails posed to women's security. As Elizabeth had no brothers, upon her father's death the Bennet family home would go to a distant cousin, leaving her mother and unmarried sister dependent upon the generosity of Mrs. Bennet's sons-in-law.

"Everingham is unentailed. I may leave it to whomever I wish."

"What of your spinster sister? Are you responsible for her maintenance?"

Mr. Crawford chuckled. "I would hardly call Mary a spinster. She is still young and I fully expect she will wed, and quite well. But should she not, she inherited a fortune of her own upon our father's death and can live quite comfortably upon it."

"Have you other dependents? The estate is not burdened by annuities?"

Mr. Crawford's expression hardened. "A few superannuated servants receive pensions, but they amount to an insignificant sum. With all due respect, I believe that I have answered enough of these queries at present to satisfy your concerns about Anne's welfare, and that further discussion of the subject is more appropriately postponed until our solicitors arrive."

"Due respect? Your decision to elope rather than secure my blessing for my daughter's hand demonstrates your regard for propriety. As does your infamous affair of last summer. Oh, yes—I know of your liaison with Mrs. Rushworth. Did you think I would not hear of it the moment my solicitor began his enquiries?"

"I anticipated it would come out."

"It was never hidden! Had you exercised discretion, the affair might be ignored by Polite Society. But you lived together for months, flouting every convention of morality and respectability. You are not a significant enough personage to have been on the lips of every member of the *ton*, but those who know you, know of the scandal. And now you have mired my daughter in it as well. For centuries the de Bourgh name stood untarnished, until it became allied with yours. Had you not interfered, Anne was to have married a future viscount. A viscount! The only title you bear is that of adulterer—and, Mr. Crawford, I give you notice right now that *that* appellation had better be obsolete. Your days of philandering are over."

"I assure you, they were so the moment I met Anne."

"Your liaison with Mrs. Rushworth is indeed ended?"

"Most certainly. I have not seen her since we parted last autumn."

"It is entirely by coincidence, then, that of all places you could contrive an accident that requires your continuance in a remote village, the event occurred in this neighborhood—the seat of Mrs. Rushworth's family?"

"Mother! You cannot possibly think—Henry, do not even answer that accusation. It is most unjust."

Mr. Crawford regarded Lady Catherine with indignation. "If you believe me to have orchestrated this mishap, to have intentionally caused Anne harm so that I might be near my mistress, you entirely misjudge my character. Even were I capable of such treachery, Mrs. Rushworth and I did not separate on cordial terms. I would be anywhere in England but Mansfield."

A knock sounded on the door. Mr. Crawford appeared grateful for the interruption. Indeed, Elizabeth, having endured her share of Lady Catherine's foul mood, welcomed it herself. Henry opened the door to find Mr. Gower.

"Mr. Crawford, your horse and the other belongings you sent for have arrived."

"Is Magellan settled in the stables?"

The innkeeper appeared confused. "I'm sorry, sir?"

"My horse?"

"I beg your pardon, sir—I thought the servant called it by another name. Charleybane."

"A bay?"

"With a white blaze, and a scar."

Mr. Crawford issued an exasperated gasp. "Admiral Davidson sent the wrong mount."

"I don't know anything about it, sir, only that your horse is in the stable and a visitor waits for you below."

"I am not expecting anybody. Who wishes to see me?"

"Mrs. Rushworth."

Eleven

"He is the most horrible flirt that can be imagined. If your Miss Bertrams do not like to have their hearts broke, let them avoid Henry."

—*Mary Crawford,* Mansfield Park

"You need not trouble yourself," Mr. Crawford said to Darcy as they descended the stairs.

"Lady Catherine requested that I accompany you."

"Ah. From my initial encounter with my new mother-in-law, I apprehend that it would cost you more trouble to refuse. Tell me, so that on future occasions I might better perform the role of a model son, do the members of this family always obey her ladyship's orders?"

"I comply when it suits my interests to do so."

"And at present, it suits your interests to play nursemaid? If you offer me a sweet, I promise not to misbehave."

"At present, I wish to see my cousin restored to her mother's good will, which is more easily accomplished if Lady Catherine can be assured of your reliability."

"That suits my interests also. Very well, monitor this meeting with Mrs. Rushworth if doing so will prove my devotion to Anne, though I hardly require a chaperone. I have no idea what motivates Maria's call, but I can state with certainty that we will not be arranging any sort of tryst."

Darcy was not quite so certain. His faith in Mr. Crawford was provisional, the elopement having prejudiced him to a degree not easily mitigated. Upon reaching the parlor, however, he was more inclined to accept Crawford's pledge on the likelihood of renewing an *affaire de coeur* with Mrs. Rushworth.

The room was empty save for one well-dressed couple. The lady wore a tall hat, short gloves, and one of the most forbidding countenances Darcy had ever beheld. Flinty eyes penetrated the creases of a visage which had looked upon the world for at least threescore years. Was this truly the face that had launched a thousand ships? At nine-and-twenty, Anne must have seemed a debutante by comparison.

"Your friend is more . . . mature . . . than I anticipated," Darcy said.

"That is not Maria. It is her mother-in-law."

The much younger gentleman, whom Darcy took to be Maria's husband, was tall and broad, and might have cut an impressive figure were his frame not weighted by evidence of an abundant table. Darcy guessed him to be of similar years to himself, but the unnatural roundness of his features made his age difficult to judge with greater precision.

Mrs. Rushworth regarded Henry with disdain. "So it is true. You had the effrontery to return to Mansfield."

"Believe me, madam, I find myself here entirely by accident."

"I have seen how you conduct yourself, Mr. Crawford. Nothing you do occurs by accident."

Her gaze shifted to Darcy. She silently assessed him, betraying no hint of the opinion she formed. "Whoever your companion is," she said to Crawford, "I would caution him against continuing to associate with a gentleman who repays trust with treachery."

"And if he is married, I hope he knows to keep you away from his wife," Mr. Rushworth added.

"Mr. Darcy, I am sure, appreciates your caveats, but he need have no anxiety on either of those points. Have you additional advice to offer him, or is the remainder of your business with me?"

"Most assuredly with you. Perhaps he could withdraw whilst the three of us discuss respect for what belongs to others."

"I look forward to hearing your thoughts on the subject." Henry turned to Darcy. "Pray excuse us."

Darcy welcomed the dismissal. He had just endured one conversation between Henry Crawford and an incensed mother-in-law, and did not care to witness another, let alone one with the added fuel of a betrayed husband. He could predict the course of their dialogue. They wanted the satisfaction of voicing their indignation, and it would matter little whether Mr. Crawford attempted to placate them or silently subjected himself to the tirade. Darcy left them to air their grievances and sought out the far more desirable company of his wife.

He found Elizabeth in their room. Though he wished he were coming upon her in their chamber at Pemberley, after a week of exhausting travel under even more exhausting circumstances, he was glad she was in Mansfield. He never liked to be separated from her for long. He drew her toward him.

"Now that we are alone I can greet you properly."

She smiled. "Or improperly."

At present he would settle for a kiss. "You left Lily-Anne well?"

"Yes. Her new tooth is growing in quite nicely. She should give

Mrs. Flaherty no trouble now that they are home, and I expect we will be able to join them there soon."

"Meanwhile, you have abandoned Anne to Lady Catherine?"

"Your cousin pleaded a headache and asked everybody to leave so that she might sleep. Had she not, I myself might have pleaded a headache."

"Did my aunt submit to Anne's request?"

"Knowing her to be ever protective of Anne's health, what do you suppose?"

"I expect she chased you and Colonel Fitzwilliam from the chamber, then remained to dull Anne's pain with heavy remonstrances."

"Such seemed her plan, but it was thwarted by the colonel, who suggested she remove to her own chamber to make notes in preparation for the solicitors' arrival. She is now, I believe, happily occupied in planning the best means by which Anne's children can eventually inherit Rosings without its ever falling under Mr. Crawford's control, while at the same time ensuring that Anne and her descendents are irrevocably established as the sole heirs to Everingham."

"The latter may require some persuasion. One cannot know the future, and while no bridegroom wants to contemplate the possibility of becoming a widower, a gentleman of integrity and foresight would wish to provide for all of his children, including those of a second wife should he marry more than once. The matter of Rosings, on the other hand, should prove a fairly ordinary arrangement for Lady Catherine's solicitor to draw up. It is already held in trust for Anne, with her ladyship and two of Sir Lewis's brothers as trustees."

"But will her solicitor draft the documents with the proper spirit of contempt for Anne's husband? Infuse her last will and testament with sufficient invectives to enable her ladyship to continue chastising Mr. Crawford from beyond the grave? These finer points require her direct oversight." She opened her reticule, which had been lying on the bed, and withdrew a fan. "This room is stifling. The recent rain did nothing to banish the summer heat."

The day was indeed hot. Darcy opened the window to admit a light breeze. He had closed it earlier because it overlooked the inn's main entrance, and the sounds of coaches and patrons' voices carried. A fine carriage that he presumed belonged to the Rushworths yet waited below.

"Tell me more of Mr. Crawford," Elizabeth said. "By now you have spent sufficient time with the gentleman to have formed an opinion of him."

He came away from the window. "Actually, I do not know that I have. He is intelligent and amiable, and seems to genuinely care for Anne. Yet he is also unrepentant about the elopement, and I cannot decide whether that attitude represents an admirable strength of conviction in the face of opposition, or ungentlemanly arrogance and selfishness."

"I understand he gained his independence early. Therefore he likely has become accustomed to doing as he pleases."

"I inherited Pemberley almost as young, and I like to think that I inherited a sense of responsibility along with it. A true gentleman considers the welfare of those who depend upon him. In persuading Anne to elope, he has put his wife in an untenable position with her mother."

"He bears the greatest portion of her ladyship's wrath himself. Indeed, one could argue that when they fled to Scotland, Mr. Crawford thought *only* of Anne's welfare. I spoke with Anne after Lady Catherine left her chamber, and she revealed her reservations about Mr. Sennex. Both she and Mr. Crawford believe the elopement rescued her from an evil far greater than her mother's censure. Lady Catherine may, in time, forgive Mr. Crawford, whereas once a marriage took place between Anne and Mr. Sennex, she would have become his legal property and no one would have been able to protect her."

"What of Mr. Crawford's affair with Mrs. Rushworth, and the position in which it has left her? Can that be construed as anything but selfish?"

"Adultery is hard to defend, and as I am unacquainted with the particulars, Mr. Crawford will have to provide his own justification if he can. How did he behave toward her just now?"

"The Mrs. Rushworth awaiting him was not his former paramour, but an irate mother accompanied by her wronged son. I suspect that any justification Mr. Crawford attempted to offer was not well received."

"Mr. Rushworth's resentment no doubt runs deep."

"I think his mother's might run even deeper, and she is not a woman one would want to cross. If Henry Crawford found dealing with his own mother-in-law unpleasant, Maria Rushworth's is worse. Today has been enough to make me grateful for my own."

"Indeed? My mother will be in such transport over your admission that she might require a visit of several months to sufficiently vocalize her felicity. Shall we invite her to Pemberley as soon as we return ourselves?"

"I am not *that* grateful."

"Just as well. I do not think the bachelors in the neighborhood have quite recovered from her previous stay."

"Perhaps, then, her next visit ought to be postponed until she has succeeded in her quest to find a husband for your remaining unattached sister."

"I think that endeavor will gain momentum when she no longer has Kitty's imminent wedding to distract her."

"The wedding is not until next spring. I would hardly define that as 'imminent.' "

"It is a wedding, and we are speaking of my mother. By the time our nuptial day arrived, you could have persuaded *me* to elope." She fanned herself. "The air is still close. Does the window open farther?" She rose and crossed to the window. Something in the courtyard below caught her attention. "Mr. Crawford appears to have moved his conference outside. I must say, Mrs. Rushworth looks terribly young to have an adult son."

"Young? The sun must be in your eyes."

"You can see that the sky is overcast. No, the woman Mr. Crawford argues with is definitely no older than I."

Darcy approached the window to see for himself. A young woman in high dudgeon carried on an animated quarrel with Mr. Crawford. The Rushworths were nowhere in sight. In the distance, a carriage climbed the rise of the road that led out of the village.

"That is not Mrs. Rushworth. At least, not the Mrs. Rushworth I met."

The woman might have been pretty, were her features not contorted in fury. As she stomped and waved a paper in her hand, the words "humiliation," "divorce," and "ruined" drifted through the window, followed by something not fit for a lady's ears, let alone lips, which cast aspersions on Mr. Crawford's parentage.

Her outburst drew the notice of several passers-by. Two women heading toward the church paused to observe the drama.

"Maria, get command of yourself." Though Mr. Crawford remained calm, he spoke loudly enough for the Darcys to hear. His words only incited Maria to greater hysteria.

"I do have command of myself! I know exactly what I am about. Would that I had possessed such clarity of mind when I first had the misfortune of meeting you!"

The two female spectators divided. One continued toward the

church, while the other hurried down the lane toward a white house. Maria and Henry did not want for observers, however. Mr. Gower, the ostler, and two more villagers from a nearby shop found their way to the courtyard.

Mr. Crawford glanced at the gathering crowd. "Perhaps we could discuss this matter in a more private location?"

"So we can be accused of further criminal conversation? Is one trial not sufficient? No, I will not subject myself to more gossip."

"Arguing about this in front of the entire village will not create gossip?"

"Since your arrival they already talk about nothing but you—you and your *wife*." She choked out the final word.

"Maria—" He stepped toward her and said something in a voice too low for others to hear. She regarded him with fresh scorn and shook her head. He spoke again.

She responded with a slap to his face.

"You stay away from her, Mr. Crawford!" cried a lady hurrying down the lane. She had apparently been summoned by the woman who had raced off to the white house and who now trotted in her wake. "Stay away from my poor niece!"

"Mrs. Norris." Henry rubbed his cheek. "How delightful to see you again."

"You despicable rake! Have you not caused my dear Maria enough grief?"

"Indeed, madam, I—"

"How dare you show your face in this village? How dare you flaunt your new wife before Maria, before us all—a family who treated you so well? Maria was content with Mr. Rushworth until you led her astray. And now that she has been cast from her father's home, with no one in the world but me to treat her kindly, you arrive in Mansfield with your bridal entourage to humiliate her further."

"I assure you, that is not my purpose in—"

"Sir Thomas knows you are here. Your presence is an insult not only to Maria, but to all her family, especially her father. And to me, who took her in, thinking nothing of myself or my own reputation. I performed my duty as a Christian and as an aunt, despite the burden of supporting us both on a poor widow's income. And whilst I sacrifice and Maria suffers, you blithely parade through the village with no conscience or shame. I have never seen the like in all my days . . ."

She excoriated him in this manner for several minutes more. Henry Crawford was a rogue, a knave, a scoundrel, a libertine. He was evil incarnate, and apparently entirely to blame for the falls of Maria, someone named Julia, and the Holy Roman Empire.

"She left out Adam and Eve," Elizabeth said to Darcy.

"I think she simply has not gotten to them yet." Darcy closed the window against the sound of Mrs. Norris's voice rising to another fevered pitch. Overhearing the scene below caused him greater discomfort than the temperature in the room. Though the actors insisted on a public performance, observing it nonetheless felt like eavesdropping. He moved away from the window, no easy feat in the tiny chamber.

Elizabeth, too, turned her back on the display. "Do you suppose we ought to rescue him?"

"Mr. Crawford is responsible for himself and must make whatever amends he can with the people he has wronged."

Mrs. Norris's euphonic tones carried through the glass. Darcy winced.

"But perhaps we can contain the spectacle."

Twelve

"I cannot think well of a man who sports with any woman's feelings; and there may often be a great deal more suffered than a stander-by can judge of."

—*Fanny Price,* Mansfield Park

By the time Elizabeth and Darcy reached the courtyard, another gentleman had ventured into the fracas. He was a tall, serious-looking man perhaps a year or two younger than Darcy, and wore the black coat of a clergyman. Despite his sober mien, he had a kind face, though Elizabeth privately admitted that her assessment might be influenced by the fact that he had somehow induced Mrs. Norris to stop talking—a kindness to them all.

He was speaking to Maria's champion as they approached.

"Aunt Norris, if Mr. Crawford is capable of contrition, I am sure he feels it now. Let us leave him to the reflections of his own conscience."

Mr. Crawford cleared his throat. "Edmund, I—"

He stopped at a look from Edmund. It was the clergyman whose expression seemed to hold the most regret.

"We are no longer on such intimate terms of friendship. You may address me as Mr. Bertram."

"Of course." A look of remorse indeed seemed to overcome him. "Mr. Bertram, I *am* sorry for my part in the events of last year."

Mr. Bertram regarded him in silence for a long minute. "Maria, this man is not worth your anguish. Return home with our aunt."

"One moment." She removed her ear-bobs, large sapphires that had set off her eyes to advantage. "Here," she said, holding them out to Henry.

He shook his head. "Keep them. They were a gift."

"I no longer want them." When he did not take them, she overturned her hand and let them fall onto the ground. "Give them to your wife, bury them right there in the dirt—it matters not to me, so long as they are forever gone from my sight. As I wish you to be."

As she and Mrs. Norris departed, a shaft of sunlight broke through the clouds. Henry bent to retrieve the earrings. Anne appeared in the doorway of the inn, supported by Colonel Fitzwilliam.

"Henry?"

"Anne? Good heavens! What are you doing out of bed?" Henry hastily shoved the ear-bobs into his coat pocket as she took tentative steps forward to meet him. When they were reunited, Anne traded her cousin's arm for her husband's. He glared at Colonel Fitzwilliam. "I cannot believe you brought her down here!"

"I agree entirely—she ought not to have left her bed. She heard the uproar and insisted on coming to see you," the colonel explained. "I attempted to dissuade her, but she threatened to descend the stairs by herself if I would not aid her. And her mother—"

"Heard the disturbance as well," Lady Catherine announced

from behind them. She shouldered her way through. "I expected you to possess enough consciousness of basic propriety to avoid so public an exhibition. I suggest you assist your wife back to your chamber." Her eyes swept the assembled villagers. "And I suggest all of you return to your own business."

Her command, coupled with the arrival of a coach, dispersed the idle onlookers. The first passenger to alight caused Lady Catherine's countenance to reflect the closest thing to satisfaction that Elizabeth had seen on it since the ball.

"Mr. Archer," her ladyship greeted him.

Elizabeth recognized the name of Lady Catherine's solicitor. His lean frame nearly bent in half, so deep was the bow he offered his employer. His fob chain caught the afternoon sunlight and gleamed against his black suit. When he uprighted himself, large eyes set in a thin, unsmiling face rapidly assessed his environs.

Before approaching Lady Catherine, Mr. Archer paused to assist a female passenger emerging from the coach. Henry wheeled Anne toward the door of the inn.

"Your mother is absolutely correct," he said in a low voice. "You should be resting inside."

"But—"

"Do not protest."

He guided her forward, but she moved with such excruciating slowness that witnessing her struggle made Elizabeth's own leg hurt.

"Mr. Crawford," said Lady Catherine, "Mr. Archer will want to see you later this afternoon."

Henry nodded without turning around.

Mr. Archer, meanwhile, had dispatched his chivalrous duty for the day. The moment his fellow passenger was safely on the ground, he abandoned her to glide over to Lady Catherine.

The young woman he had assisted looked around, absorbing her new surroundings. She was a slip of a girl, possessing one of those faces and figures that might pass for sixteen or six-and-twenty with equal credibility. She wore a simple calico gown that had seen better days, a similarly exhausted bonnet, and no gloves. Her sole adornment was an amber cross on a gold chain that hung round her neck. A lock of red hair had come loose from her bonnet and hung behind her like a fox's brush. She clutched in her hands a small card.

For all her waiflike appearance, her eyes reflected intelligence and purpose as she scanned the retreating spectators. Her gaze lit on a dark-haired gentleman in a brown coat who was walking toward the livery.

"John!"

The gentleman, his back to her, apparently did not hear her call and continued walking. She ran toward him and stopped him with a hand on his arm. "John!"

When he turned around to face her, the woman's own countenance fell. "You are not John."

"No, madam. I am sorry to disappoint you."

The woman released his arm and he continued toward the livery. Meanwhile, the woman turned toward Elizabeth and the others. "I'm looking for a man named John Garrick. Do any of you know him?"

No one acknowledged familiarity. She turned a hopeful face to Elizabeth, who shrugged sympathetically and shook her head.

The woman addressed Edmund. "A handsome man, he is. Dark, though not very tall. A merchant marine. He might not be in Mansfield presently, but I believe he has family here, or has at least visited. Have you ever seen such a man here, Reverend?"

"All sorts of travelers pass through on the coach, but no seamen have lingered here in recent memory," Edmund said. "Being so far from any port, Mansfield does not often host sailors." He cast a confirming glance at the innkeeper. "Correct me if I am in error, Mr. Gower. You see far more visitors than do I."

"Last sailor I recall in Mansfield was your wife's brother, when Mr. Price came for your wedding."

The woman's expression deflated. "Are you certain? Do none of you know him, or anyone named Garrick?" She fingered her necklace, looking as if she might break into tears. "I need to find him. I've come so far, and I've nothing to return to."

"Perhaps you have not traveled quite far enough," Darcy said. "There is a larger Mansfield in Nottinghamshire. Might you have mistaken his direction?"

She shook her head. "He gave me no direction at all. I came here because of this." She held out the card in her hand. It was a trade card from Hardwick's shop, advertising its address and selection of goods for sale. "John gave me this necklace the last time I saw him. I assumed he bought it during his travels, but after he left again, I discovered this card under the lining of the box. He sometimes spoke of a sister, used to visit her now and again, but never said where she lived. I hoped maybe his family came from Mansfield, and he found the chain while visiting her."

Elizabeth pitied the woman and wished she could do something to help her. Mr. Crawford knew numerous sailors through his uncle. Was it possible he had at some time met this John Garrick? Such a coincidence was improbable, but not impossible. However, Mr. Crawford, concentrating on Anne's progress toward the inn, had not so much as looked over his shoulder in response to the woman's entreaties.

"Mr. Crawford," Elizabeth called.

He murmured something to Anne and kept moving toward the door.

"Mr. Crawford," she repeated more loudly. "Do stay a moment. Perhaps you can aid this woman."

The hail caught not only his attention, but that of the woman. "Oh! Can you, sir?" She went over, coming round his side to stand before him. And gasped as a look of pure joy overtook her countenance.

"John!"

Mr. Crawford stiffened and halted his advance.

"Daft girl!" Lady Catherine growled. "That is Mr. Crawford. Mr. Henry Crawford of Everingham—a gentleman, not some vagabond marine."

Her ladyship's less-than-gracious introduction seemed to go unheard. The woman had ears, and eyes, only for Henry. "John, thank heavens I've found you! Mama's gone—so is the house—there was a fire. I didn't know how soon your ship would return or where else to go, so I thought I'd try to find your sister—"

Henry regarded her wordlessly.

"Are you deaf?" Lady Catherine bellowed. "This man is not John Garrick!"

The woman stared at Lady Catherine in confusion.

"John Garrick, indeed!" her ladyship continued, so agitated that one of her facial muscles twitched. "Crawford! His name is Crawford!"

The woman blinked. Then her countenance suddenly cleared. "Ah! I understand." She leaned toward Henry and spoke in a muted voice. "She's a little touched, isn't she? Like old Mrs. Carter." She nodded knowingly, then addressed Lady Catherine.

"It's . . . all . . . right . . . ma'am." She pronounced each word slowly and deliberately, as if addressing a young child. "I know his name."

She then turned her attention back to Henry. "I must say, John, you do look the gentleman in those fancy clothes. That is a fine brown coat—as nice as that other gentleman's." She regarded Anne with curiosity. "Is this your sister?"

"No!" Lady Catherine thundered. "She is his wife!"

The woman smiled at Lady Catherine indulgently. "Of course she is."

"Do not adopt that tone with me, you baggage!"

"Oh, dear," she said to Henry. "Just like Mrs. Carter. They become so cross in old age."

"I am not old!"

"I believe she needs a cordial."

Lady Catherine pounded her walking stick with vehemence. "What I *need* is for you, Mr. Crawford, to properly identify yourself to this deluded chit so that we can attend to business of far greater consequence."

The woman gently patted Lady Catherine's hand. Her ladyship regarded her skin as if an insect had landed on it.

"I am not deluded, ma'am. Though I haven't seen him for two years, I should think I know my own husband."

"Husband? I should think not!"

Anne, who had been listening in bewilderment, now addressed Mr. Crawford with impatience. "Henry, why do you not speak?" She leaned heavily on his arm. Her injury was clearly troubling her, the laudanum was not helping, and the desperate Mrs. Garrick's determination to see her husband's face in every stranger, though pitiable, exacerbated Anne's suffering.

"John, why *are* you so silent?" The happiness that had illuminated the woman's face since first spotting Henry faded as doubt began to manifest. "Aren't you pleased to see me?"

"This is not to be borne," Lady Catherine declared. "Tell her, Mr. Crawford! Tell her that you have no idea who she is—that you have never laid eyes on her until this moment."

Henry glanced from his indignant mother-in-law, to his

distressed wife, to the apprehensive stranger. His own expression was inscrutable.

"My name is indeed Henry Crawford."

Lady Catherine chortled in triumph. Henry ignored her, his gaze entirely on the crestfallen Mrs. Garrick.

"Forgive me, Meg."

Thirteen

Henry Crawford . . . longed to have been at sea, and seen and done and suffered as much. . . . The glory of heroism, of usefulness, of exertion, of endurance, made his own habits of selfish indulgence appear in shameful contrast; and he wished he had been a William Price, distinguishing himself and working his way to fortune and consequence with so much self-respect and happy ardour, instead of what he was!

—Mansfield Park

I—I don't understand," Mrs. Garrick said.

"Nor do I," said Anne. "Henry, you truly *know* this woman?"

"I met Meg while I was a student at Cambridge. She knows me as John Garrick."

"She claims to be your wife."

"The particulars of the situation are . . . complicated."

"I *am* his wife! We married five years ago—in my parish church, before witnesses!"

Anne dropped Henry's arm like a thing diseased. She swayed, but when he reached for her she rejected him. Colonel Fitzwilliam stepped forward to steady her.

"Mr. Crawford, explain this outrageous assertion," Lady Catherine hissed. "Who is John Garrick?"

"It is a name I invented."

"And you married this—this Meg person—under that name?"

"I did."

Anne fainted.

Henry tried to prevent her from falling, but Colonel Fitzwilliam caught her. Henry reached for her. "Allow me to—"

"Do not touch her. Not ever again."

Darcy had never seen such cold fury in his cousin. At that moment, he looked every inch the military officer facing a sworn enemy on the battlefield. "Would that I could have saved her from your grasp before today," the colonel said. He lifted Anne into his arms and carried her into the inn, away from the faithless Mr. Crawford.

A hand on Darcy's own arm drew his attention to Elizabeth. The briefest look between them communicated her intention to follow and offer Anne whatever succor she could. He watched her go, grateful for the constancy of his own spouse.

There remained the minister, Mr. Crawford, Meg, Darcy, Lady Catherine, and Mr. Archer.

Meg gestured toward the entrance through which Colonel Fitzwilliam had whisked Anne. "Will anybody tell me who that lady was?"

"That is Mr. Crawford's other wife," Darcy said.

"His *what*?"

Darcy fixed Mr. Crawford with a glare. "I cannot comprehend such deceit, let alone any possible justification for it. Do you think yourself the Prince of Wales?"

"His dishonesty does not end with these two ladies," said Edmund. "What were you about, making an offer to Miss Price last spring?"

Meg kicked Henry's shin. "You snake! You married me with a false name and then roamed England making love to other women while I waited for you at home? How many wives do you have?"

"Only two."

She kicked his other shin. "That's one too many!"

Henry doubled over, rubbing one of his injured limbs. Darcy was of the opinion that Mr. Crawford deserved to be kicked elsewhere; he judged from Mr. Bertram's expression that even the clergyman concurred.

"Actually, Mr. Crawford has but one legal wife," declared Mr. Archer.

"The question is," Darcy said, "which one?" The woman he had married first, or the woman he had married under his legal name? Darcy himself did not know the answer.

"If he married under a false name, that constitutes fraud. The marriage is voidable," Mr. Archer said.

"Unless it is a name under which he is commonly known," Mr. Bertram responded, "in which case the ecclesiastical court may rule in favor of preserving the marriage."

"Everyone in my village knew him as John Garrick!" Meg said.

"Everyone in London, Bath, and a host of other cities knows him as Henry Crawford—his legal name," Mr. Archer replied.

"The courts will have to sort this out," Darcy said. Unfortunately, no matter which way they ruled, the scandal would disastrously compromise Anne's position in society—if it left her with any at all. "Who is the local magistrate?" he asked the minister.

"My father, Sir Thomas Bertram. I would suggest moving this discussion to his home, but given Mr. Crawford's previous association with my family, my father could not tolerate the man's presence at Mansfield Park even for the satisfaction of committing him to gaol."

"Gaol?" Mr. Crawford appeared stunned by the very notion.

"Bigamy is a capital offense."

"But surely, as I am a gentleman, he would release me on my own recognizance pending trial?"

"Perhaps he might do so for another gentleman," said Edmund, "but as you have proven yourself no gentleman in any meaningful sense of the word, I doubt your plight will engage his sympathy. I shall summon my father here directly."

"No." Lady Catherine, who to this point had been in a state of contemplation, pronounced the word with such force that it held the weight of a full speech. "Postpone that summons, Reverend, if you would. Prior to Mr. Crawford's appearance before the magistrate, I wish to confer with my solicitor to ensure that my daughter's interest in the case is properly represented."

"Once Mr. Crawford enters custody, you will have ample time to engage a barrister and otherwise prepare for the trial."

"Even so, I wish to be present at Mr. Archer's initial interview with Mr. Crawford, and I would not subject myself to the indignity, or the noisomeness, of entering a gaol to speak with him."

"Very well. He can remain here until you have had enough of him. As it happens, my father conducts much of his magisterial business at the inn. When you have done with Mr. Crawford, simply send word to Mansfield Park that you have need of Sir Thomas."

"I shall. In the meantime, Mr. Bertram, I request that you hold the subject of Mr. Crawford's alleged marriage to Mrs. Garrick in strict confidence. This is a delicate matter, and I would not have it become a topic of public discourse. Nor, I expect, would you, given not only your sister's circumstances, but the Miss Price you mentioned. Doubtless, you wish to protect her reputation from association with this affair."

"She is now my wife, so indeed, yes—I assure you of my discretion."

Mr. Crawford turned to the bewildered Mrs. Garrick. "Meg—"

"Don't even speak to me, John. Or whatever your name is."

"Meg, I understand you are angry, but—"

"Angry? *Angry?*" She laughed maniacally. "Do I have something to be angry about?"

"Meg—"

"Did I ever mean anything to you? Or was it all playacting? When my mother died and the fire took our cottage, the one thing that helped me survive was the belief that I still had you. And now I learn that I never had you at all. I might not even be married! Where am I to go, John? I cannot go back to the village and resume my life as 'Mrs. Garrick.' Mrs. Garrick doesn't exist. And I have no money to go anywhere else."

"For now, go inside and take a room. Explain to Mr. Gower that I will pay for it."

"You have a great deal to pay for."

"Meg—"

She turned her back on him and went within. Lady Catherine and Mr. Archer followed, withdrawing for their tête-à-tête.

Henry stared at the door through which Meg had passed. Then he turned to face Darcy's glare.

"It began as playacting." He seemed to be speaking as much for his own benefit as for Darcy's or Edmund's. "One spring I was a guest at a house party where endless rain confined us indoors, and we entertained ourselves by engaging in impromptu theatricals. My friends were particularly diverted by my portrayal of a seafarer named John Garrick, a character I created from stories I recalled hearing from my uncle and his fellow naval officers. While traveling back to Cambridge, washed-out roads detained me in a small village for several days, and I amused myself by continuing the role among the simple folk I encountered there. For the duration of my stay, I was John Garrick, merchant marine, regaling the villagers with my adventures on the high seas.

"It was there that I met Meg," he continued. "She worked at the inn, and would often draw near as I told my tales. When the weather cleared and I prepared to leave, I knew from her crestfallen countenance that I had won her. 'She lov'd me for the dangers I had pass'd, and I lov'd her that she did pity them.' "

"All the world's a stage with you, is it?" Edmund said bitterly.

"No. When I returned after Easter and Michaelmas terms solely to see her again, that was genuine."

"I do not believe you know the meaning of that word." Edmund shook his head in disgust and turned to Darcy. "I cannot listen to more. Should you have need of me, I can be found at my father's house or the parsonage in Thornton Lacey." He departed.

Henry watched Edmund walk off, then turned to Darcy. "I am not a cad. When Meg's father suddenly died, leaving her and her bedridden mother destitute, my desire to rescue her was also genuine. So I married her."

"Under false pretenses," Darcy said. "How very noble of you."

"I was overtaken by the romance of it. I did not dwell upon the consequences."

"That appears to be a theme of your courtships."

"I realize I have acted badly, but if my attempt to explain is going to elicit naught but hostility I must beg leave to postpone further discussion of the matter. This has already been a day of vituperation from so many quarters that I cannot begin to absorb it all." He started to enter the inn.

Darcy was not finished with him. "Why did you never confess your true identity to Mrs. Garrick and install her at Everingham?"

"A former servant as mistress of a large estate? You know as well as I do that she would have been ostracized by the entire neighborhood. Still worse would have been her reception in London. She would have been isolated, lonely, and miserable. Meg was better off in her native village, among her own people."

There was a degree of truth in Mr. Crawford's assertion. The social gulf between Meg's world and the Polite World was indeed great—so great that it would have acutely restricted Mr. Crawford's own connections. Usually it was bridegrooms who dropped the acquaintance of inappropriate associates from their bachelor days, not the other way round, but Mr. Crawford's visiting card tray would have accumulated naught but dust in the weeks following Meg's introduction. His wife would have been a social liability, and Henry Crawford craved society.

"So you relegated your wife to a cottage with her crippled mother while you enjoyed a carefree gentleman's life in London and Bath?"

"I provided well for Meg—she wanted for nothing. She no longer needed to work at the inn. She had a household servant and a nurse to help with her mother."

"On a merchant marine's pay?"

Henry shrugged. "John Garrick sailed on profitable ships."

"And what of my cousin Miss de Bourgh? How can you justify your treatment of her?"

"I rescued Anne as well—from bondage to the deplorable Neville Sennex. But whereas my marriage to Meg was unequal, a youthful indiscretion regretted in hindsight, Anne is a lady of my own station, worthy to assume the role of Everingham's mistress and mother to my heirs. Had I more time, I would have extricated myself from Meg before wedding Anne—it would have been far tidier—but eloping to Scotland was the decision of a moment, necessitated by Anne's imminent betrothal. Even so, I had contrived a plan to terminate my obligation to Meg. Had she not traveled here, she would this week have received a letter informing her that John Garrick had died at sea. She would have inherited a sum large enough to attract a decent husband if she chose to remarry, or to maintain her comfortably for the rest of her life if she did not. Anne and I would have lived happily ever after, and no one would have suffered any injury."

"No one but the grieving widow, the deceived wife, and anyone who values honesty in the world."

"I can see you are unmoved. Very well. I am grown quite parched from all this talk and am going inside in search of a draught that will quench my thirst and fortify me for the forthcoming interviews with Lady Catherine and Sir Thomas that I anticipate with so much pleasure. You may join me if you like; otherwise, should anyone else materialize to condemn me for a past wrong, tell him to return within a few hours, at which time he may abuse me at his leisure. By then my ears should be able to accommodate fresh rancor."

Darcy was so thoroughly sick of Mr. Crawford—his smoothness, his excuses—that it was with relief that he watched the door close behind him. He wandered out of the courtyard to the village green, where a stone bench offered a view of the inn's entrance. From here he could remain alert to Mr. Crawford's movements while achieving deliverance from the rake's proximity.

Shortly, Elizabeth emerged. A minute's scan revealed his position to her, and she joined him on the bench.

"I saw Mr. Crawford as I passed through the dining room. You have done with him?"

"For the present. How is Mrs.—" He had been about to call his cousin "Mrs. Crawford," an appellation which now elicited such feelings of abhorrence that he shuddered to pronounce it even in his own mind. "How is Anne?"

"Conscious, though I do not know how long she will maintain that state. The apothecary administered more laudanum. She was quite agitated by today's revelations, as anyone would expect. Colonel Fitzwilliam remains with her. In his own mind he stands guard against any attempt Mr. Crawford might make to gain admittance, but I believe he also provides Anne a calming influence. His presence when she regained her senses seemed to offer steadiness on a day on which her life has been utterly upended."

"Where is my aunt?"

"Closeted with Mr. Archer."

"That conference will likely continue through the evening." Lady Catherine must be desperate to mitigate the damage Mr. Crawford had wrought upon Anne, and was fortunate that Mr. Archer had arrived when he did. The solicitor was his aunt's most trusted advisor—or henchman, depending upon one's perspective. Whatever Lady Catherine bade, Mr. Archer undertook with alacrity. He obviated difficulties and made problems go away. Whether a matter was titanic or trifling, her ladyship had only to say, "Mr. Archer will handle it," and whatever "it" was, was done.

How even Mr. Archer could meliorate the crisis at hand, however, Darcy could not imagine. As if voicing his thoughts, Elizabeth asked whether the situation could possibly end well for Anne.

They both knew the answer. "Once word of this circulates—and I do not see how exposure can be avoided—Anne is ruined," he said. "Even should her marriage be ruled valid, the scandal of bigamy, compounded by the elopement, will forever taint it. And if she is in fact not married at all—"

"She never will be, to anybody," Elizabeth finished. "Her virtue has been compromised. Though it happened through no fault of her own, no respectable gentleman will have her." It was a sad statement of fact.

"While my allegiance of course rests with Anne," Elizabeth continued, "I cannot help but also pity Mrs. Garrick. She, too, is an innocent victim of Mr. Crawford's duplicity. What an awful discovery, to learn that not only might she have been living in a conjugal state with a man to whom she is not truly wed, but that the man himself is entirely a fiction. Even should the court determine that they *are* indeed married, she is married to a stranger. She does not know her own husband."

"The more I learn about him, the more I believe no one knows the real Mr. Crawford. He is another George Wickham, only with the financial wherewithal to indulge his vanity's every whim. He is a player of roles, a chameleon, cold-blooded and able to present himself as anything necessary to protect his interests."

"I wonder whether Mr. Crawford himself knows the real Henry Crawford."

The coach upon which Meg had arrived prepared to leave. Passengers who had been waiting inside the inn now came out and boarded. It sped away, its team's hooves thundering.

Darcy and Elizabeth returned to the inn. Darcy had expected to find Mr. Crawford still quenching his thirst, but he was not in the dining room. Mrs. Gower said that he had taken a new chamber for himself and retreated.

As the dining room was nearly empty, they decided to take their own meal while they could enjoy it in relative peace. Afterward, they stopped by Anne's room.

Colonel Fitzwilliam opened the door. "She is sleeping," he said quietly. "Though not well."

"Is there aught we can do for her?" Darcy enquired.

He stepped to one side and reappeared with a valise. "Return this to Mr. Crawford, if you will. I do not want the sight of it to further distress Anne when she wakens."

They took the bag and knocked at Mr. Crawford's chamber. After a minute elapsed with no response, Darcy and Elizabeth exchanged uneasy glances.

"Perhaps your aunt summoned him?"

He did not reply, but knocked again more forcefully. There was no sound of movement within. He tested the door and found it locked.

They enlisted the aid of Mrs. Gower and her key ring, but they hardly need have. By the time she opened the door, Darcy knew what he would find.

An empty room.

Fourteen

Could he have been satisfied with the conquest of one amiable woman's affections . . . there would have been every probability of success and happiness for him.

—Mansfield Park

A search of the inn turned up no Henry Crawford. Or John Garrick. Or a gentleman by any name who resembled the master of Everingham. The pleasure of his company had not yet been requested by Lady Catherine and Mr. Archer, nor had he attempted to see either of his wives.

The hunt led to the livery, where a young stable hand reported that Mr. Crawford had ridden off about the same time the coach departed.

"Thought for a second I saddled the wrong horse for him, in all the hubbub," the boy said.

"Was there some crisis?" Darcy asked.

"Oh, no, sir—nothin' dire. Just a busy few minutes, what with puttin' the fresh team on the coach, and Mr. Lautus wanting his horse right away, too, and both of 'em being bays, and Mr.

Crawford wantin' his mount brought round the back of the stable for some reason. Plus, Mr. Crawford's horse weren't his usual one—the chestnut he used to stable here when he stayed with Dr. Grant—so I had to ask the ostler which horse was his. When it shied from Mr. Crawford I thought maybe I'd got it wrong and the scarred bay belonged to the other man. But Mr. Crawford said no, the animal was his, and it was time he tested it."

"In other words, he fled," said Elizabeth when Darcy repeated the conversation to her and the rest of the party that had gathered in the dining room. Colonel Fitzwilliam and Mr. Archer had joined her as soon as she and Darcy enquired whether they knew Mr. Crawford's whereabouts. By the time they rapped on Meg's door, they had formed a determined corps. Meg, upon hearing that Mr. Crawford was missing, waited as impatiently as they for news.

"Of course he fled," said Meg. "He cannot stay in any one place for long."

"I should never have allowed him to leave my sight." Darcy's whole bearing evinced self-reproach.

"No, you should not have," Lady Catherine declared.

Elizabeth wished Darcy would not assume the entire blame for Mr. Crawford's disappearance. The man himself bore responsibility. "Darcy is too honorable a gentleman to have predicted that another would so degrade himself as to flee rather than face the consequences of his actions."

"Mr. Crawford is a despicable coward," said Colonel Fitzwilliam.

"A coward," said Mr. Archer, "and an accused felon who faces hanging if convicted."

The colonel made a sound of disgust. "Let him face me on a field of honor, and I will save the courts their trouble."

This was a side of the colonel unfamiliar to Elizabeth. "You would duel with Anne's husband?"

"No one knows whose husband he is at present, not that he is a prize any woman should covet. A pistol shot would decide the matter cleanly. Both his wives would be free of him."

"I would rather win that satisfaction myself," muttered Meg.

Despite Mr. Crawford's head start, the men resolved to ride out in search of him. With only a few hours' daylight remaining, they left directly and took separate paths.

Meg was agitated as she watched them depart. As they crested the hill out of the village, she headed toward the stable. "I'm going, too."

Lady Catherine snorted in derision. "I hardly believe that necessary."

"I think it is," she said.

"Can you even ride?"

"If someone will hire me a horse. It seems I can no longer rely on my husband to assume my debts."

Elizabeth attempted to dissuade her. No woman ought ride about unfamiliar countryside on a strange horse unaccompanied, particularly as dusk approached. She could meet rough terrain, or even rougher highwaymen. What if she encountered a wild animal, or a band of gypsies?

"I can take care of myself," Meg assured her. "With my husband gone for months at a time, I have had to learn. What I cannot do, is sit idle."

As Elizabeth silently debated the wisdom of hiring a mount for Meg, Lady Catherine declared she would do so. The offer stunned Elizabeth.

"Thank you, ma'am!" Meg exclaimed. She patted Lady Catherine's arm. "I will be quite safe. Don't you worry."

"I am not at all concerned for your safety."

As Meg rode off, Elizabeth turned to Darcy's aunt. "You have been surprisingly generous toward Anne's rival."

"It is not generosity; it is an investment."

Elizabeth raised a brow.

"Should Mrs. Garrick actually find Mr. Crawford, she does me a service." Lady Catherine produced a handkerchief and wiped her arm where Meg had touched it.

"And if misfortune finds her first, *that* does me a service."

Meg was the first to make her way back to the inn, entering the courtyard at dusk. Elizabeth observed her arrival from the window of her chamber and met her as she reached the top of the stairs. "Did you find any sign of him?"

Meg shook her head. The wind and exercise had loosened her hair, and a large red lock hung down one side of her face. "I expect he is halfway to wherever he's going by now."

"Have you any notion where that might be?"

"A day ago I would have said the sea. Now I wish him at the bottom of it." She pushed the hair behind her ear, revealing a long, fresh gash on the back of her hand.

"Mrs. Garrick, are you all right?"

"I cannot answer to that name anymore. Call me Meg. As for my hand, it's merely scratched. I passed a stray hedge branch too closely."

"Surely it hurts. The apothecary is presently with Mrs. Crawford. Perhaps he can provide a salve to ease the sting."

"Don't trouble him. I can manage."

"It is no trouble." Elizabeth moved to rap on Anne's door, but Meg stayed her hand.

"Please don't." Anxiety creased her expression. "I haven't any money to pay for such things. I spent all I had just getting here in hopes of finding John, and he is not coming back."

"The men have not yet returned. They may find him."

"Even if they do, a scratch is the least of my troubles."

She withdrew to her own room. Elizabeth stood staring at her closed door for several minutes, debating whether to make a gift of the salve or let the matter drop. Meg was right: Her difficulties far exceeded anything an ointment could heal. Deceived by the person she should most have been able to trust, she now found herself alone in a strange village with no friends and no funds—precarious circumstances indeed.

Precarious enough to make a person desperate.

Darcy returned after the grey light of dusk had faded to black.

The moment he entered their chamber, Elizabeth knew that his hunt had proven futile. His countenance—nay, his entire demeanor—declared the news more loudly than could any town crier. He sagged into a chair, rested his head against its back, and closed his eyes.

"You are slumping," she said.

"I am."

"You must be my other husband, then. Fitzwilliam Darcy never slumps."

"He does today." He remained thus another minute, looking worn out from the day's events in a way that went beyond physical. Just as Elizabeth began to wonder if he were going to speak again or fall asleep in that position, he sighed and opened his eyes. "If this 'other husband' of yours is Mr. Crawford, I entreat you to produce him, as I had no luck locating him myself."

"Mr. Crawford has not leisure to slump. His trips to the altar consume all his time."

"I begin to think they must. It would not surprise me if that is where he is now—in another village, with another woman."

"For a man who only pretended to be a sailor, he does seem to have a girl in every port. I believe, however, that he will not be mooring again in this particular harbor. Anne has not asked for him, and Meg is so angry that she set off in pursuit of him after you departed."

"On horseback?"

"She rides fairly well, actually—not that I am the most discriminating judge of horsemanship. I believe Lady Catherine was unpleasantly surprised by her competence, as she furnished the mount in partial hope that Meg would meet with some accident."

"That is a severe indictment of my aunt."

"I merely repeat her own admission. She resents Meg's existence almost as much as she does Mr. Crawford's. Meg, however, had the effrontery to return unharmed."

"And the others?"

"Neither Colonel Fitzwilliam nor Mr. Archer have yet come back." A knock sounded on their door. "Though perhaps I spoke too soon."

It was not one of the gentlemen, but Lady Catherine.

"Mr. Darcy, I knew I heard your voice." She attempted to maneuver her way into the room without invitation, but Elizabeth prevented her from fully entering. Though Elizabeth's tolerance for Lady Catherine's arrogant behavior had by necessity increased during her ladyship's residence at Pemberley, that tolerance fast approached its limit. Darcy's aunt would have to settle for speaking to him from just within the doorway.

Darcy rose and came to stand behind his wife. "How is Anne?"

"Resting. She was so overwrought when she awakened that I asked the apothecary to administer more laudanum. How long did you intend to lounge in here before reporting to me?"

"Until I finished speaking with my wife."

"What has she to do with the matter of Mr. Crawford's disappearance? Any news you have is of far greater import to me. I should have been apprised of it first."

"Had I found Mr. Crawford, I would have informed you directly I returned. As it happens, I did not."

"Let us hope, then, that Colonel Fitzwilliam or Mr. Archer completed their mission with better results. You gave up prematurely, in my opinion. Apparently, I must rely upon my other nephew or my agent to protect our family's interests."

"It grew dark, and I saw little point in continuing my course when none of the occupants of any house I passed had observed a gentleman who met Mr. Crawford's description. Obviously, he took a different route. I fervently hope my cousin or Mr. Archer did achieve more success, for I am as anxious as you are to see Mr. Crawford answer for his crimes."

"Surely you comprehend the gravity of Anne's circumstances. It is imperative that we act quickly to—"

Lady Catherine fell silent at the sound of the inn's door opening below. A moment later, Mr. Archer mounted the stairs.

"Did you apprehend the scoundrel?" her ladyship asked.

"I did not. He is gone. But despite his absence, we may initiate some of the legal matters we discussed."

"Then let us proceed posthaste." She turned to Elizabeth and Darcy. "You will excuse us while we confer. Mrs. Darcy, I would consider it a favor if you would sit with Anne and administer more laudanum if she should wake. Do not allow her to cry or indulge in hysteria—as I have told her myself, such emotions are unnecessary, not to mention unbecoming."

Elizabeth went to Anne's room not in deference to Lady Catherine, but out of her own desire to comfort the unfortunate Mrs. Crawford. When Anne awakened, Elizabeth offered not laudanum but compassion. Anne did not need sedation, she needed a chance to grieve, whether by giving voice to her feelings or experiencing them in the privacy of her own heart. Her anguish was deep, but its expression hardly constituted hysteria. They conversed a little, Anne's pain and humiliation still too raw to fully articulate. Afterward, she settled into a natural sleep that Elizabeth believed would do far more to restore her strength and spirits than drug-induced lethe.

By the time Elizabeth heard Colonel Fitzwilliam's tread on the stair, the hour had grown late. He was already talking with Darcy in their chamber as Elizabeth emerged from Anne's room to join them. The colonel immediately interrupted the conversation to enquire after Anne. His expression was grave, but eased slightly at her report.

"I am relieved that she has found peace for the moment," he said. "It is that blackguard who deserves to suffer."

"You did not overtake him, I presume?"

"No one has seen him. It is as if the devil passed invisible through the countryside on his journey back to hell. Pardon me for speaking so strongly, Mrs. Darcy. I wish I could aim more than words at Mr. Crawford."

"You merely voice what we are all thinking."

"Do you think it would be permissible if I stood watch in Anne's chamber through the night? I doubt Mr. Crawford will dare show his face here again, but if he does, I do not trust him."

Elizabeth admired Colonel Fitzwilliam's protective instincts toward his cousin. "I think Anne needs the support of all her family right now."

After bidding them good night, Colonel Fitzwilliam remained at Anne's side until relieved by Lady Catherine herself, who chased him out of Anne's room upon discovering him there. It was improper, her ladyship insisted, for any man to spend time unchaperoned with Anne in her bedchamber, let alone at such a late hour. She would superintend Anne's comfort and safety herself.

The supervision had amounted to rousting Elizabeth from her own bed to pass the night beside Anne's, where Elizabeth alternated between dozing lightly and reflecting on whether the solicitude of an honorable male cousin could truly cause Anne's reputation any greater damage than it had already suffered. She determined that it could not, that Anne deserved consolation from whatever quarter and at whatever hour it was tendered, and that the chair in Anne's room was the most uncomfortable piece of furniture ever fashioned.

As it turned out, the vigil proved unnecessary. Though Anne had wakened during part of the colonel's watch, she slept through Elizabeth's entirely, and Henry Crawford did not return.

But his horse did.

Riderless.

Fifteen

You express so little anxiety about my being murdered under Ash Park Copse by Mrs. Hulbert's servant, that I have a great mind not to tell you whether I was or not.

—Jane Austen, letter to Cassandra

The restless night gave way to an equally restless morning. Anne, it seemed, had been the only member of their party to capture more than intermittent sleep. Elizabeth had returned to her chamber to find Darcy dressed, and when they went down to breakfast they found Colonel Fitzwilliam already at table.

"I could not lie still," he confessed. "I am near mad for useful employment, but I know not what action to take."

"At present there is little to be done beyond turning the affair over to the magistrate," Darcy said.

"I offered to call upon Sir Thomas, but Lady Catherine bade me wait. She said Mr. Archer would handle it."

A minute later, the inn door opened to admit the solicitor, a dark silhouette against the pale daylight behind him. Mr. Archer was dressed in the same black suit he had worn the day before, or perhaps an identical one; he did not project the impression of a gentleman wont to enliven his wardrobe with variety. Such as color.

He appeared surprised to find their small party assembled, and consulted his pocketwatch. "Half past eight already? Still, rather early for breakfast."

"Perhaps in London," said Mrs. Gower, bringing out additional tea, toast, rolls, and rashers. Elizabeth hungrily reached for a roll and spread it with strawberry jam. The long night had left her famished, and she expected this day to prove still longer.

As Mr. Archer moved farther into the room, Elizabeth noted that his suit indeed sported a bit of color—a stripe of yellowish sheen near his left knee. He crossed to the staircase, where the descent of Lady Catherine halted his progress. A look passed between them, her brows rising in question. He responded with a nod so slight as to be almost imperceptible. After she passed, he proceeded to his own chamber.

Her ladyship settled into a chair at the head of the table. "Mrs. Darcy, who attends Anne presently?"

"She woke and desired solitude in which to order her thoughts. She said she would call for one of us or your maid if she required anything."

The room darkened as more clouds passed over the sun. Her ladyship's countenance darkened as well.

"Someone ought to sit with her and engage her in constructive discourse, else she might indulge in melancholy." There was little doubt who the "someone" was that Lady Catherine had in mind.

Much as Elizabeth sympathized with Anne's plight—both her recent marital mess and the lifelong misfortune of fate having assigned Lady Catherine as her mother—she had maternal matters of her own occupying her attention this morning. She anticipated that today would bring confirmation from Georgiana or Lily-Anne's nurse of their safe arrival at Pemberley, and until she received it, thoughts of her daughter would command the majority of her consciousness. Though she trusted that all went well, she had never before been separated from the child for such a long period of time, nor by so great a distance, and she missed the little person who had in so few months wrought such significant changes in her life.

"You are well attuned to Anne's needs." Elizabeth tried not to choke on her roll along with the words. "What comfort her mother's presence would bring her."

"I will see her following breakfast."

"Perhaps your ladyship might breakfast with your daughter. I wish I could breakfast with mine this morning."

"Lily-Anne is an infant. Of what possible interest could her presence be to you or any of us? Children are best left to their nurses until they not only have learned to speak, but have attained sufficient years and experience to have something worthwhile to say."

"Surely by now your own daughter has acquired both."

"The events of recent weeks prove that my daughter's maturity does not include enough sense to act in her own interest. Therefore, she can have nothing to say at present that would concern me. And even if she did, the guest rooms of this establishment are far too cramped to dine in comfortably, otherwise I would have ordered a tray to my own chamber. I shall breakfast right here."

A serving maid brought an empty teacup and plate to Lady Catherine and lit a candle on the table against the growing darkness. A storm was gathering.

"I require tea," Lady Catherine said.

The maid checked the pot in front of Elizabeth. It was half-full and still steaming. She lifted it to pour, but Lady Catherine covered the top of her teacup with her hand.

"I want a fresh pot. And take care that the water is newly drawn.

I will have none of the reboiled sludge you attempted to impose upon me yesterday."

"I swear, ma'am, the tea yesterday—"

"No reused leaves, either."

"Oh, ma'am! We never—"

"Or excuses."

"Yes, ma'am." The poor girl hurried off before Lady Catherine threatened to pour the boiling water over her.

Elizabeth took a pointed sip from her own cup. "The tea here is not the best I have ever been served, but it is not bad."

"That, Mrs. Darcy, illustrates the difference between us. You are accustomed to accepting inferiority. I am not. When I want something, I do not settle for less."

The tea arrived. Fortunately for the serving girl, Meg entered from the outside door just as she started to pour, thus drawing Lady Catherine's derisive gaze to a new target.

"Humph," Lady Catherine said under her breath. "I see the common dining room just became more common."

Meg regarded their party uncertainly, though she did not appear to have overheard Lady Catherine's snub. She went to an empty table in the corner. The sky outside had completely darkened, and the maid brought out another candle for Meg. In the flickering light, she looked lonely sitting there by herself, watching the flame as if she were not sure where else to direct her attention.

Elizabeth called over to her. "Mrs. Garrick, we have nearly finished our own breakfast, but you are welcome to join our table."

Lady Catherine's teacup clanked onto its saucer as a fit of coughing seized her.

Meg jumped up. "Oh, dear!" She hurried over to Lady Catherine and delivered three sharp blows to her back. As she prepared to offer a fourth, Lady Catherine seized her wrist.

"Stop assaulting me!" she sputtered.

"You were choking."

"I merely downed my tea incorrectly, you featherbrain!" She issued a final, deep cough, then drained her teacup to clear her throat. She straightened her spine in an attempt to recapture her dignity.

Meg gave Lady Catherine's back a final, gentle pat. "There, there. My mother had trouble feeding herself too, toward the end. Try eating more slowly."

"The end? The end of what?"

Meg met Elizabeth's gaze and shook her head sympathetically. "They become so irritable when they begin to lose their independence."

A clap of thunder sounded, followed by the fall of rain. It came heavily, sluicing both the ground and Elizabeth's spirits, for it trapped her inside with Lady Catherine.

In the courtyard, the trot of a horse signaled the arrival of a traveler. The animal emitted an unhappy neigh. It was not a traveler, however, but the ostler who hurried in a few moments later. His gaze swept the company, lighting at last on Darcy.

"Beggin' your pardon, sir, for disturbin' your breakfast, but Mr. Crawford's horse is here."

Lady Catherine's teacup clattered a second time. "The scoundrel has returned? Impossible."

"No, ma'am, not him. Just his horse. The saddle's empty."

Lady Catherine scoffed. "Then how do you know the mount is Mr. Crawford's?"

"There's no mistaking the animal, ma'am. Not with a scar like that."

Darcy and Colonel Fitzwilliam left the ladies inside and subjected themselves to the deluge to see the horse for themselves.

By the time they reached the stable, a boy had already unsaddled the mount and was rubbing her down. The horse was disfigured as Anne had described. It was indeed Charleybane.

Darcy inspected the saddle but noted nothing of interest. "Where are Mr. Crawford's saddlebags?" he asked the stable boy.

"The horse didn't return with none, sir."

He exchanged a glance with his cousin. Mr. Crawford had left behind his valise and other luggage, but Darcy assumed he had fled the inn with something more than the clothes on his back. "Did he depart with saddlebags?"

"Don't recollect, sir." The boy finished grooming and moved to another part of the stable.

Colonel Fitzwilliam reached out to stroke the hunter's nose, but the mare shied from his hand. "A noble animal scarred by circumstance," he said. "Does Mr. Crawford spoil everything he touches? I wonder how she came by her injury."

"Anne says Mr. Crawford recently acquired the Thoroughbred from Mr. Sennex as payment for a debt."

"The mare belonged to Neville Sennex? Do not tell me so, for that means I must now consider the horse better off in Mr. Crawford's care, which I find difficult to believe of any feeling creature."

"Including Anne?"

"Especially Anne." Colonel Fitzwilliam shook his head. "What cruel fortune, to escape marriage to a man who is constantly brutal only to wed one who is brutally inconstant. She deserves a happier fate than either Mr. Sennex or Mr. Crawford could ever give her."

"I do not know how she will find one now. Her legal mire is thicker than the mud on my boots."

"Crawford's death would clean up matters quite a bit."

Despite the warm, humid air congesting the stable, the colonel's words chilled Darcy. His cousin was no coward, but he was also no hothead. He had entered the army out of necessity—as a second son, unlikely to inherit unless misfortune struck his elder brother, he had needed a profession, and in his youth had been drawn to the military because it appeared to offer a more stimulating life than would the church or the law. In his years of service he had seen his share of battles and acquitted himself well, earning a reputation as a strong commander undaunted in combat. But his had always been an impersonal aggression, directed at a faceless, collective enemy. Until Henry Crawford crossed his path.

"You expressed a similar sentiment last night," Darcy observed.

"Ease your mind—I have not acted upon it. I merely state a fact: Anne would be far better off with Crawford dead than missing. She would be free to marry whomever she wished while the courts sort out whether her first marriage was valid or not."

"Even could she—or her mother—find a man who is interested, I cannot imagine Anne herself wishes to wed anyone at present. Hymen has not treated her well thus far."

"She may yet find happiness. But before that can happen, we must ascertain Mr. Crawford's fate. Did he abandon his mount voluntarily, or did an accident befall him?"

Darcy had been pondering that very question. "She is a distinctive horse. Mr. Crawford himself presents an average appearance that would not excite notice among strangers, but the animal's scar draws attention and would linger in the memory of anyone he encounters. He might have parted with her in order to travel more inconspicuously. That would help explain why we were all unsuccessful in locating him during our search yesterday evening."

"Surely if he chose to set the mare loose, he did so near a place where he could hire another mount or board a coach. Is there anything distinctive about her shoes? Perhaps we can trace the hoofprints to determine where she became separated from Mr. Crawford."

An enormous crack of thunder satisfied that query. Even if they could have discerned Charleybane's marks from all the others on the road, rain had obliterated them by now. As if to reinforce the point, the shower intensified.

They could not seek Henry Crawford today. The only question remaining was whether they would ever locate him at all.

Sixteen

Henry Crawford, ruined by early independence and bad domestic example, indulged in the freaks of a cold-blooded vanity a little too long.

—Mansfield Park

Darcy turned his head away from the appalling spectacle, grateful that he had come alone despite Elizabeth's offer to accompany him. The servant who had summoned him upon the unfortunate discovery had communicated few details, but something in his manner had forewarned Darcy that the true news lay in what had gone unsaid.

Sir Thomas Bertram muttered something resembling condolences. "You can imagine how surprised I was to learn that Mr. Crawford had been found on my own grounds," he added. "We were still more shocked by his condition. I am sorry to have summoned you so early, but you can see why I do not want him left any longer in his present state."

Sir Thomas's servant had escorted Darcy through the woods of Mansfield Park to a small clearing some distance from the road. It was Darcy's second meeting with Sir Thomas, the first having occurred when the family reported Mr. Crawford's disappearance following the return of his horse. The coroner, a gentleman Sir Thomas had introduced as "my old friend Mr. Stover," was also present, as was Sir Thomas's gamekeeper, who had first come upon the body.

Darcy fought down the bile rising in his throat. As unconscionable as Mr. Crawford's transgressions had been in life, no person deserved to endure such degradation in death as to be reduced to an inhuman mound of torn flesh. Rain had washed away most of the blood, but the body was in an advanced state of decomposition, and prolonged exposure to hungry wildlife and hot, humid weather had rendered what was left of him, particularly his countenance, unrecognizable. Were it not for the dark hair and general build of the remains, Darcy could not have believed it possible that this was a man he knew, let alone had spoken to less than a se'nnight previous. "Are you certain it is Mr. Crawford?"

"That is what we hope you will confirm," said Mr. Stover.

"We identified him by these." Sir Thomas produced a silver snuffbox engraved with the initials *H.C.* and the pair of earrings his daughter Maria had deposited at Henry's feet. "They were in his coat."

Darcy pitied whichever of the men had gotten close enough to the corpse to retrieve Henry's effects. The coat, along with much of Mr. Crawford's other moldering clothing, clung to his damaged body in shreds. The stench was beyond rank, made worse by the fact that the corpse lay in the full sun, just outside what limited shade might have been offered by a nearby cluster of birch trees.

"I saw him pocket those ear-bobs the day he disappeared," Darcy said. "I am afraid this is indeed Henry Crawford." He turned to the gamekeeper. "What sort of animal attacked him?"

The gamekeeper shook his head. "We have no large predators around here. He was dead before the scavengers got to him."

"What killed him, then?"

"That." The coroner pointed to Mr. Crawford's left side. As Darcy stood on the opposite side of the corpse, he had to move to obtain a proper view.

A pistol lay in the grass.

"If you observe the area around what used to be his mouth, you can see black powder burns." Mr. Stover leaned forward and waved away flies to grant a better view. "The shot came from extremely close range."

Darcy would have been content to take his word on the matter, but he looked out of courtesy. There were indeed burns and powder embedded in a vague circle around the mouth, almost like the tattoos one sometimes saw on sailors. The rest of Mr. Crawford's flesh was so discolored and darkened that he had not noticed the burns before—not that he had allowed his gaze to rest on Mr. Crawford's face all that long. "Someone shot him in the mouth?"

"Not just any someone." Mr. Stover exchanged an uneasy glance with Sir Thomas. "I believe we have another Young Werther here."

If the sight and smell of Henry Crawford's corpse had not been enough to turn Darcy's stomach, the coroner's pronouncement was. Darcy had read *The Sorrows of Young Werther* years ago—every one of his schoolfellows had, on the sly. Banned in some countries, the book had been blamed for a spate of imitative deaths.

"Self-murder?" He shook his head. "No—that cannot be."

Yet even as he spoke, he privately admitted the possibility. Goethe's novel appealed to romantic, impulsive young men, and Henry Crawford had proved himself both.

"This would seem to support Mr. Stover's hypothesis." Sir Thomas handed Darcy a water-stained note. "It is the only other item we found on Mr. Crawford's person."

Darcy unfolded the paper. Though the rain that had caused the ink to run had dried, humidity had left the paper damp, and black india stained Darcy's gloves. Most of the words were obscured by smears and blots; Darcy could make out but two: "honor" and "forgiven."

Yes, it could be a suicide message, Mr. Crawford's final apology for his actions before taking his life. But the consequences of self-murder were too severe for the pronouncement to be made without absolute certainty. Suicide was more than just a crime against God; it was a crime against the king. Self-murderers could not be buried in consecrated ground, and their property was forfeited to the Crown. Anne's grief and shame would be compounded, and, were her erstwhile marriage even deemed valid, she would receive nothing for all the misery it had caused her.

Darcy met Sir Thomas's gaze. "This note could have said anything."

"Including farewell."

"There is ample room for doubt."

"Not when considered with the other evidence." The coroner stepped around the body and picked up the pistol. He turned it over in his hands, tracing the escutcheon and other engravings with his fingertip. "This is an expensive firelock. If someone else shot Mr. Crawford, why did he leave it behind?"

"Perhaps to make it appear a case of self-murder. There are many in this village with cause to wish Mr. Crawford ill." Including Sir Thomas. Darcy fervently hoped the magistrate would not allow personal prejudice to influence his actions on so serious an issue. "Perhaps one of the people he wronged decided that depriving Mr. Crawford merely of his life was insufficient retribution. Contriving to have the death ruled a suicide would constitute complete revenge."

"Indeed, it would," Sir Thomas said, "but the fact that there might be others interested in taking Mr. Crawford's life does not eliminate the possibility that he spared them the trouble."

"Where did he obtain the pistol? I do not recall his having one among his possessions."

"Can you say with certainty that he did not? That this is not his weapon?"

Darcy paused. "No. But he traveled here lightly—"

"Following his elopement, Mrs. Norris tells me. Perhaps he anticipated trouble en route to Gretna Green, particularly if he and his bride journeyed by night, and armed himself to ward off highwaymen—or friends of the bride who might pursue them. This is a small weapon, as pistols go, and easily concealed."

"I wonder that Mrs. Norris would happen to share the circumstances of Mr. Crawford's arrival with you, or how she even came into possession of her information," Darcy said.

"She mentioned the news during a visit to my wife earlier this week. My sister-in-law makes it her business to stay informed of goings-on in the village, and to keep us similarly apprised."

The gamekeeper stifled a cough.

The sound drew Sir Thomas's attention. "Have you something to say, Mr. Cobb?"

"No, sir."

Sir Thomas stepped back a few feet from the corpse. "Pray, let us move upwind, or better still, conclude this quickly. Now that the sun has risen above the trees I find the smell overpowering."

Darcy had to concur with Sir Thomas's complaint; the gamekeeper also appeared more than happy to relocate. Only the coroner seemed impervious to the odor as he continued to study the pistol. Darcy wondered how often he was exposed to such gruesome scenes.

Mr. Stover at last left the corpse's side and joined them. "This is certainly a fine weapon. Pierced side plates, gold touch holes, crowned muzzle. Not one I would leave behind, revenge or no. But a dramatic choice for a dramatic act."

"May I?" Darcy asked.

The coroner handed the smoothbore to Darcy. It was indeed a finely crafted weapon, fashioned of a rich brown walnut stock with a curved, deeply chequered grip and carved butt cap. Its case-hardened lock and hammer were engraved with images of a rook—or perhaps it was a crow or raven—and the polished silver escutcheon featured the same. The lock facing carried a London label with the crossed-pistols-and-swords mark of the arm's renowned maker; the top flat of its blued octagonal barrel boasted his name, inlaid in gold: "H. W. Mortimer, Gun Maker to His Majesty."

It was not so much a weapon as a work of art, and it was with reluctance that Darcy surrendered it to Sir Thomas. He privately agreed with Mr. Stover: One would not sacrifice so valuable an arm easily.

His gaze strayed toward the place beside Mr. Crawford where the pistol had lain, but his eye stopped instead on a spot of color in an area of particularly tall grass between him and the deceased. He had not noticed it before, but from his new vantage point upwind he could see something gold caught at the base of overhanging blades. Curious, he walked over to it, nearly tripping over a large rock also hidden in the grass but one stride from his quarry.

It was a circle of silk about two inches in diameter, gold with a pattern of tiny indigo birds lined up like chessmen on a field of or. Its edges were frayed, and three blackened hairline abrasions on its underside radiated out from a scorched bull's-eye perhaps a half-inch round.

"What have you there?" Sir Thomas asked.

"A gun patch," Darcy replied. The circles of fabric were used to load firelocks; the patch was inserted between the powder and the lead ball, and expelled when the weapon was discharged. The shot patch generally fell to the ground a few feet from the muzzle.

The quality of this particular fabric surpassed what one generally used to load weapons. Linen was far more common, and Darcy's choice when hunting. Silks, valued for their strength and sheerness, were sometimes used in critical situations where accuracy was vital, but even then tended to be plain, not employ costly dyes or weaves. This was a singularly expensive gun patch. And Mr. Crawford had been killed by an expensive gun.

Darcy brought the patch to Sir Thomas and the coroner. "If Mr. Crawford indeed shot himself, how did the discharged patch land so far from his body?"

"He has lain here for days," replied Mr. Stover, "with animals coming and going to an extent that one wishes were far less evident. Any number of creatures could have carried it hither."

"Maybe it is not his patch," added Sir Thomas. "Mr. Crawford is hardly the only person ever to fire in these woods. My eldest son and his friends often shoot for sport. The patch could have fallen there on an entirely different occasion, perhaps not even a recent one."

Darcy conceded the possibility, but the fabric did not appear as if it had been tossed about the grove for months. Though the patch had been somewhat sheltered from this week's intermittent rain by the overhanging grass, the area had received such heavy downpours in the days leading up to Mr. Crawford's arrival in Mansfield that had the cloth been exposed to those tempests it would have been muddied or its black powder residue washed out to a much greater extent. If this patch had landed in the grove earlier, it had not preceded the night of Mr. Crawford's disappearance by long.

In addition to the fabric itself being a curious choice for sport shooting, the design was one Darcy had never previously encountered, and the fact that both it and the pistol were ornamented by images of birds heightened his interest. "This is an unusual pattern," Darcy said. "Do you recognize it as one Mr. Bertram uses for his rifle?"

"I cannot say that I do," Sir Thomas admitted. His gamekeeper also denied familiarity.

"And does he typically hunt with silk?"

"Mr. Darcy, difficult as it may be to accept the manner of Mr. Crawford's demise, that scrap of cloth could not have been associated with the shot that caused his death," said Mr. Stover. "You saw how close the range was, and there appears to be no exit wound. I expect that when I complete my examination of the remains, I will find Mr. Crawford's patch lodged with the ball inside his skull."

Darcy was dissatisfied, but saw little value in arguing the point at present. He could not say that he himself was convinced that the patch was related to Henry's shooting, only that the verdict of suicide—though not yet official, almost assuredly forthcoming given the collusion between the magistrate and the coroner—seemed overhasty.

"May I retain it, then? The patch?"

Sir Thomas shrugged. "I see no reason why I or Mr. Stover have need of it. If for some reason it is wanted, I trust you will surrender it?"

"Of course."

"Well, then, as you have no further business here, I suggest you return to the inn and impart the news of Mr. Crawford's demise to his widow—widows—yes, I know of the bigamy allegation; my son informed me of it privately. When Mr. Stover has done with his examination, he will give notice of the inquest."

Darcy knew he had been dismissed, but he was not quite ready to leave. "Might I view Mr. Crawford's remains a final time before I go?" He had no idea what he sought, but something unexplored nagged him.

Sir Thomas's brows rose. "I cannot fathom why you would wish to subject yourself to his corpse again, but do so if you like. For my part, I found Mr. Crawford's company offensive whilst he lived; death has not improved him."

Darcy walked the fifteen paces or so to the body. Mr. Crawford lay on his back, mouth open. Somewhere inside was the ball that had killed him. Had it indeed been self-administered? Despite having found the silk patch suggesting a shot that had come from farther away, despite the repercussions to Anne and, by extension, to the reputation of her entire family, himself included, he could not rationally rule out the possibility of suicide. It was indeed difficult to imagine another scenario that could lead to Mr. Crawford's swallowing a bullet. Not even swallowing—from the coroner's words and the appearance of things, the ball had traveled at an upward angle when it entered. What were the odds of anyone *but* Mr. Crawford himself having aimed so precisely?

If any shooter could, however, it would be the owner of that pistol. Darcy had seen some exquisite weapons in his life, but never one as superior as the firearm he had just held. That piece of craftsmanship had to rival any arm Mr. Mortimer had manufactured for the royal family. As Mr. Stover had said, who would intentionally abandon it? Yet if it indeed belonged to Mr. Crawford, where had he acquired it? It was small, perhaps ten inches long from the grip of its handle to the end of its barrel, a size sometimes called a "traveler's pistol." Had he indeed been traveling with it this whole time?

It might be small, but it was costly—more in price than Darcy would have imagined Mr. Crawford was willing to expend on a pistol. But then, Mr. Crawford was not a man given to sacrifice. He enjoyed everything life offered; enjoyed it rather too much. Reached for it with both hands.

Darcy stared at the spot beside Mr. Crawford where the pistol had lain. And realized what had been prodding the edges of his consciousness.

"Gentlemen, when Mr. Stover picked up the pistol just now, was that the first time any of you handled it?"

They approached. All denied having touched the gun before Darcy's arrival.

"I left it exactly where I found it," the gamekeeper said.

"Did you disturb Mr. Crawford's remains?"

Mr. Cobb regarded Darcy as if he were daft. "Begging your pardon, sir, but would *you* touch a corpse that looked like that? Not without a shovel, I wouldn't, and not without instructions from Sir Thomas."

"And I gave no such order," said Sir Thomas. "Mr. Stover has served as coroner for many years, and I know he prefers to record his observations before anything is moved."

"Why, then, if Mr. Crawford committed suicide, was the pistol lying to the left of his body? Mr. Crawford was right-handed."

Sir Thomas did not immediately reply.

"Perhaps it fell to that side after he fired it," said Mr. Stover.

Darcy did not like that improbable explanation, for the fact that the coroner had offered it increased his doubt over the likelihood of an impartial ruling on the cause of Mr. Crawford's death. Sir Thomas's objectivity was already in question, but Darcy had harbored faint hope that the coroner had had no personal quarrel with the late Mr. Crawford. Could Sir Thomas's "old friend" be relied upon to perform his public duty?

"Perhaps it did fall from his right hand to the opposite side," Darcy said. "Or perhaps Mr. Crawford did not fire the gun."

"Mr. Darcy, I understand and sympathize with your motives. Nobody wants the stigma of suicide associated with his family," said Sir Thomas. "But in taking his own life, Mr. Crawford merely accelerated the process of justice. He was a coward who could not face the shame of a trial. To all appearances, rather than risk hanging, Mr. Crawford chose his own punishment. The consequences of self-murder are indeed severe, but you must admit that Mr. Crawford hardly established for himself a history of considering consequences."

"Then it is particularly incumbent upon you and Mr. Stover to do so before rushing to a judgment that might be erroneous," Darcy replied. "Would you have his heirs deprived of their inheritance and his remains unjustly buried at a crossroads for all eternity?"

"I would have him buried somewhere, and the sooner the better. He is not growing any fresher." Sir Thomas regarded the body with disgust. "Mr. Crawford's corpse has suffered enough indignity, and the people who knew him, enough anguish. There is no reason to prolong both. Let us resolve this matter posthaste. Mr. Stover will complete his examination of the body. If, at its conclusion, he is convinced that Mr. Crawford's death was self-inflicted, then I am, as well."

"What if I am not?"

Sir Thomas was silent. Finally, he turned to the coroner. "Mr. Stover, how soon can you be prepared to hold the formal inquest?"

"I will finish examining the remains today. Then we need only gather any witnesses we want to call. The inquest could be held tomorrow if you wish."

"All right then, Mr. Darcy. If you are not satisfied with the results of Mr. Stover's examination, you have until the inquest to gather evidence of your own."

"I am to solve a murder by the morrow?"

"You need not solve it, simply prove that one occurred."

He had been trying to do so this past half hour with no success. Clearly, Sir Thomas would require Darcy to not merely establish reasonable doubt, but to produce incontrovertible proof. "A single day is hardly sufficient time."

"Something must be done with this rotting corpse."

Seventeen

"Now, be sincere; did you admire me for my impertinence?"

"For the liveliness of your mind, I did."

—Elizabeth and Darcy, Pride and Prejudice

"A gunshot to the face?" Elizabeth shuddered despite the warmth of the air in their chamber.

"I am afraid so." Darcy did his best to force the image of Mr. Crawford's remains from his mind. The day's unpleasantness had only just begun. He not only had a murder investigation to commence, but also still had to break the news of Mr. Crawford's death to Anne and the rest of the family. He had been summoned to Mansfield Wood so early that only Elizabeth knew where he had gone this morning, and upon his return he had proceeded to their room straightaway. He needed some time in her steady companionship before dealing with the others.

"Poor Anne—as if she has not endured enough," she said after he finished narrating the morning's errand. Despite the relative privacy afforded by four walls and a closed door, they nevertheless kept their voices low. Their party nearly filled the inn, and while most of their acquaintances were not wont to eavesdrop, conversations could yet be inadvertently overheard. Too, the subject matter itself dictated somber tones. "Do you believe, as Sir Thomas does, that Mr. Crawford committed self-murder?"

"There is evidence in support of it, but also against. It suits Sir Thomas's interests for Mr. Crawford to have killed himself. It does not suit Anne's. Therefore, I will do what I can to disprove that theory."

"If it is not suicide, then someone not only killed Mr. Crawford but left him to the predations of animals. I dislike thinking anyone capable of that."

He had spared her the most disturbing details of Mr. Crawford's condition, only explained that his remains were not in an appropriate state for visitation by mourners.

If there were any mourners. "Mr. Crawford had no shortage of enemies."

"I daresay our hosts are the only people in town without cause to despise him. Between all his relations-by-marriage occupying the bedchambers and the gossipmongers crowding the dining room every mealtime, business at the Ox and Bull is thriving. But there is a difference between wanting vengeance and actually executing it."

"Yet there is a good chance that someone has—the location of the pistol suggests as much, as does Mr. Crawford's presence in Mansfield Wood in the first place. If Mr. Crawford indeed killed himself, why would he choose to do so on Sir Thomas's estate?"

"Because of its connection to Maria Rushworth?"

"His present difficulties derive from his two marriages, not an affair he ended a year ago without regret. And then there is the matter of the shot patch. I cannot imagine its having come from any weapon but that pistol, yet Sir Thomas quite dismissed it and encouraged his friend to do likewise. I can predict the results of the coroner's examination. Even should Mr. Stover not render an opinion of suicide, Sir Thomas's dislike of Mr. Crawford is so pronounced that I am not confident any official murder investigation would be undertaken in a diligent manner. The magistrate seems content to consider Mr. Crawford's death justice served."

She studied his expression. "Do you?"

It was a difficult question, one he had been pondering since first being summoned to the scene. "I am not exactly overcome by grief," he confessed. "I do, however, believe in the due process of law. To tacitly condone murder, even when justified, sets a dangerous precedent. Regardless of his personal feelings toward Mr. Crawford, as magistrate Sir Thomas ought to uphold his duty, or he risks his district descending into anarchy."

"Mr. Crawford ruined Sir Thomas's daughter. Do you think the magistrate bypassed the courts and sentenced Henry Crawford himself?"

"Before your arrival in the village I heard that Sir Thomas had washed his hands of Maria. But as a father myself, I could see a man who refuses to publicly forgive his daughter nevertheless acting privately to punish her seducer."

"Or, through inaction, protect her if she herself killed her lover. Maria Rushworth was quite warm in her anger the day Mr. Crawford disappeared. She seemed to have just learned of Mr. Rushworth's intentions to divorce her. If her husband's petition succeeds, she will be utterly destroyed in society—divorce is so rare, and it always taints the woman, regardless of individual circumstances. Meanwhile Mr. Crawford, as a man, would have endured a few reproofs and blithely gone on with his life."

"She loses everything, and he, nothing."

"Socially, she will be dead, and might have decided that a literal death for Mr. Crawford would be fair recompense."

"So she lured him to Mansfield Wood to deliver it?" Darcy

pondered the hypothesis a moment. It was not entirely without merit. "The grove in which he was found is rather secluded. Though as unwelcome in her father's house as Mr. Crawford, she would know the grounds, and could have chosen that spot intentionally."

"I wonder, though, where she would have obtained the firearm. Tell me more about the pistol. Was it a gentleman's weapon, or a lady's?"

He looked at her askance. "*Lady's?* What do you know of muff pistols?"

"I have read a novel or two."

"I shall not ask which of them encourage ladies to conceal firearms in their apparel."

"You disapprove? That is unfortunate for me, as I am begun to grow restless in Mansfield and had thought to purchase one as a diversion."

"A muff pistol?"

She laughed. "No, a novel. But now that you have suggested it, perhaps I ought to acquire a pistol along with it. Then, like a proper heroine, I could stop the villain by revealing my weapon and proclaiming, 'Hold, sir—I am armed!' "

He wished they were home, and she reading another novel right now, instead of discussing a very real death. "That is unnecessary. I will protect you from any villains who might be lurking about."

"And who will protect you?"

"I believe it may be safely assumed that the person who shot Mr. Crawford acted out of revenge. So long as I keep my suspicions quiet, he will believe his revenge satisfied and himself safe. I therefore need not fear him, whoever he is."

"You sound certain that the killer is a man."

"Not entirely. Though it was larger than a muff pistol, the weapon found with Mr. Crawford was small enough that it could be comfortably handled by a woman, and a considerable number of women did have motive to harm Mr. Crawford: Maria Rushworth, as we have said, but also two betrayed wives."

"One betrayed wife, for the killer could not possibly be Anne. She is incapacitated. And even were she more ambulatory, she has had nearly constant companionship since the carriage accident, and so could not have been absent long enough to commit the deed."

"I, too, have ruled her out—beyond the impossibility of her circumstances, violence is simply not in her nature. I also consider Mrs. Garrick unlikely. Although she had an opportunity to do away with Mr. Crawford when she rode off in pursuit of him, where on earth would she have obtained a pistol of that quality? Even if she had stolen it, she could not have had it with her when she arrived in Mansfield, for you and I both saw her disembark from the coach with naught but the clothes she wore."

"Ah, but those clothes could have concealed a pistol! Do not regard me so—I only half jest. I rather like Meg, and I do not want to believe her capable of killing anybody. But she did travel all this way unescorted, and before that lived alone with her mother while Mr. Crawford was allegedly sailing the seven seas. It is not unreasonable to suppose she possesses some means of defending herself."

"I do not recall her carrying so much as a reticule in which to keep it."

"That is not the only place a lady might conceal a pistol."

"What *have* you been reading?"

She started to answer, but he shook his head. "Never mind. If indeed the weapon was fired by a woman, I believe Maria Rushworth is the more likely owner. The pistol was manufactured in London, where she lived during her marriage and also during her liaison with Mr. Crawford."

"Do you suppose she purchased it herself?"

"Perhaps, out of her pin money."

Her brows rose. "Apparently, I need to ask for more pin money."

"I wondered how you intend to finance this muff pistol you speak of acquiring."

"By employing my feminine wiles upon you."

"I am impervious to wiles."

"We shall determine that later. Do you think her husband equally resolute? Mr. Rushworth might have purchased the weapon for her, before she left him."

"Do not most women prefer jewelry?"

"We witnessed how highly Maria Rushworth valued gifts of jewelry, at least from Mr. Crawford." Elizabeth was thoughtful a moment. "Maybe the pistol came from him, and those earrings were not the only gift she so dramatically returned to him that day."

"She shot him with the pistol and then dropped it at his side?"

"That would explain why it was left behind. A pistol is not the most romantic gift, though, and Mr. Crawford seems like someone who would be very conscious of creating the proper impression."

"Perhaps it was indeed Mr. Crawford's own pistol, purchased for himself when he and Mrs. Rushworth eloped."

"In anticipation of a duel?"

"What do you know of duels?"

She shrugged. "Someone in a novel has to defend the heroine's honor. And Mr. Crawford has compromised more than his share of ladies."

"More than his share? I did not realize gentlemen received an allowance. 'Tis a shame no one told me while I was still a bachelor. Or does the allotment apply only to rakes?"

"Mr. Crawford was not a rake, precisely. He did not conduct

his life as a gentleman ought, but he was no Mr. Wickham. Though he toyed with women's affections, he did not seem to do so out of predatory intent. He was simply vain and foolish and insensible to the damage he wrought."

"Your defense of him surprises me."

"He is dead; I can afford to be generous. But apparently one of the women he wronged, or a male protector, was less forgiving. Pray describe the pistol further."

"It is smaller than a typical dueling pistol," he said, "but could certainly serve as one. It was made by Mortimer, one of the best gunsmiths in England, and exhibits the finest technical and artistic features of the gunmaker's craft. It is by far the most superior pistol I have ever held."

"Just how many pistols have you held? Perhaps I ought to ask what *you* know of dueling."

"As much as most gentlemen." He had never been called upon to defend his own honor, and hoped he never would. The closest he had come was during his Cambridge years, when a friend who had issued a challenge asked him to serve as his second. Darcy and the defender's second had tried their hardest to mediate the disagreement before the primaries met on the field, but their efforts had been in vain. His friend had died—a pointless waste of a promising life—and all of those involved had been fortunate to escape prosecution.

"An impressive parry," she said, "but I grant you only temporary reprieve from answering my question. Meanwhile, let us return to the matter at hand. You believe the shooting patch you found in the grass came from the pistol beside Mr. Crawford?"

"It is so fine a cloth that I cannot imagine someone's using it to load an ordinary hunting rifle. And it shares a bird motif with the pistol's engravings."

"Might I see it?"

He withdrew the silk from his pocket and handed it to her.

"Damask," she said. "Our gunman has good taste. And it is indeed an interesting pattern—a departure from the more common paisleys and florals." She turned it over and examined the abrasions. "The gunpowder creates an intriguing design of its own—like a black sun, only with few rays. What are these thin black lines coming out from the center?"

"I am curious about them myself. A rifle creates such marks on shot patches, but there are usually more of them—six or seven. They are caused by spiraled cuts within the barrel—rifling—whence the weapon derives its name. But this patch has only three such marks. And if, as I believe, it was fired from the pistol found with Mr. Crawford, that weapon has a smooth bore, and therefore would leave no marks."

"So this patch might not have come from the pistol after all?"

"Please do not dismantle my investigation before it has begun. Sir Thomas is doing a fair enough job of that as it is, and I have little time in which to formulate a plausible theory of events."

"Why not show the patch to Colonel Fitzwilliam? Perhaps Sir Thomas would also allow him to examine the pistol. As a military man, the colonel no doubt possesses extensive knowledge of firearms. And as he carries pistols himself, he is certainly very experienced with them."

He hesitated. "That is my fear."

Her eyes widened as she realized his meaning. "Darcy, surely you do not believe— Oh! But he even spoke of dueling with Mr. Crawford, just before he left in pursuit of him."

That fact troubled Darcy greatly. "He assured me, after the horse returned riderless, that he had not killed Mr. Crawford. I trust his word." A tiny point of doubt yet pricked him, but he did his best to suppress it. "Colonel Fitzwilliam is more than capable of punishing Mr. Crawford on a field of honor, but he would have done it in just that manner—honorably. Gentlemen's duels are not ambushes; they are civilized affairs that adhere to strict protocol. There are rules. There are witnesses in attendance to ensure those rules are followed. Whom would Colonel Fitzwilliam choose as his second, if not me?"

"Dueling is illegal. Perhaps he deliberately excluded you from the proceedings so as not to compromise you."

It would be just like his cousin to take all of the risk upon himself, sparing to whatever extent he could all other family members from any scandal that resulted from his actions. He could have found another, more disinterested, second. But one fact exonerated Colonel Fitzwilliam, in Darcy's mind, as decisively as possible without actually entering another person's thoughts and heart.

"Even had he shot Mr. Crawford in secret, my cousin could not have left his remains exposed for days to the desecration of wildlife and weather. To do so would violate every principle that defines him." Even now, as the body was being examined, the memory of it disgusted Darcy. Whoever had dispatched Mr. Crawford was devoid of conscience. "Formal dueling etiquette dictates the presence of a surgeon to attend to injuries. In the absence of one, Colonel Fitzwilliam would, at the very least, have contrived a means of ensuring the body was discovered before this morning, and would have been unable, in the interim, to look me in the eye and converse with me as freely as he has, knowing that he had left Mr. Crawford in such a state. Though words uttered in a heated moment cast suspicion upon him, his character as demonstrated over the course of three decades exculpates him."

"I am relieved by your conviction of his innocence, for I did not want to consider him capable of such cold-blooded conduct. Yet if we acquit Colonel Fitzwilliam, we are back to Meg, Maria

Rushworth, and Sir Thomas as our chief suspects. Setting aside the women for now, that leaves Sir Thomas. Did he strike you as someone foolish enough to shoot a man, even in a duel, on his own estate, then leave his body lying around for five days until the gamekeeper discovered it?"

"I cannot say that he did."

"Then we need more gentlemen in our pool of candidates. I nominate Mr. Rushworth, the cuckolded husband. Now, there is a man with just cause for retribution. What do we know of him?"

"Very little beyond the fact that he has initiated divorce proceedings against his wife."

"Yes, Maria Rushworth referred to a crim con suit while arguing with Mr. Crawford."

Darcy's brows rose. "'*Crim con*'?" Before petitioning Parliament for a full divorce, the husband of an unfaithful wife first had to win a civil suit against her lover for their adulterous association, legally and euphemistically known as "criminal conversation." Darcy was amused by Elizabeth's use of the abbreviated term employed by members of the legal profession—and also in the salacious newspaper accounts and trial transcripts published to feed the public's appetite for gossip. "I had no idea you were so conversant in legal jargon."

"My reading tastes have not strayed to include sensational trial pamphlets, if that is your concern."

"I should hope not."

"But I have heard enough of such matters to know that crim con trials and divorce petitions are protracted, humiliating processes with uncertain outcomes. Mr. Rushworth might have decided to seek more immediate satisfaction. Perhaps that was the purpose of his call here—to issue a challenge to Mr. Crawford."

"With his mother as his second?"

"Though you tease, you might not be far from the mark. She

could not serve as his official intermediary, of course, but from what you told me of her, the dowager Mrs. Rushworth may well have pushed him to issue the challenge in the first place."

"*That* is entirely possible. I daresay she was irate enough to challenge him herself, were she able. And Mr. Rushworth struck me as a man in the habit of acceding to her will."

"The question is, can he shoot?"

"Once a pistol is loaded—which would not be his responsibility, but that of his second—anybody can shoot; one need only fully cock the hammer and pull the trigger. And as challenger, Mr. Rushworth would have chosen the range." The image of Mr. Crawford's destroyed countenance once more flashed before Darcy, eliciting an involuntary shudder. "The range, however, would not have been as close as Mr. Crawford's wound indicates."

"And when confronting his wife's lover, a gentleman always adheres to form?"

Darcy did not respond. Instead, he regarded the silk patch in Elizabeth's hand and imagined it falling to the ground as the ball carried forward to hit its target. How had it come to land so far away, if the range had been so close?

"I think we need to learn more about Mr. Rushworth," Elizabeth said. "That is, if you want to learn more about Mr. Crawford's death at all."

He regarded her quizzically.

"Your inquiry *could* end right now in this chamber," she said. "Mr. Crawford injured one of your cousins unpardonably. You owe him nothing, and by investigating the circumstances of his demise you risk exposing another cousin to suspicion, for we are not the only witnesses to Colonel Fitzwilliam's hostility toward Mr. Crawford. A suicide ruling would scarcely do Anne's reputation any further damage—it is Meg who stands to lose the most if his estate is forfeited to the Crown. You said earlier that the magistrate seems to consider Mr. Crawford's death justice served. At this moment, I am the only other person, besides his friend the coroner, who knows of your suspicions. They appear only too willing to consider the issue settled, and one word from you will silence me on this subject forever."

Had Mr. Crawford indeed lost his life in a duel or some other honorable manner, Darcy might have been able to leave the matter at rest. But if his execution were simple murder, he could not condone that kind of justice. And he would always wonder which had been the case.

"It would be a heavy silence, for it would carry within it my self-respect. And, I warrant, yours. You are correct in that I have no duty to Mr. Crawford to identify his killer and see him punished. But I have a duty to my own conscience and sense of honor. Believing yours to be as stalwart, I am surprised you made the offer."

"I knew what your reply would be."

She retrieved her bonnet from the top of the chamber's tiny chest of drawers and donned it before the even tinier glass. "Now come—we have little time and much to do, starting with acquainting a good number of people with the news of Mr. Crawford's discovery. I shall be curious as to how each receives it."

"Do you think the murderer might reveal himself?"

"Not intentionally." She tied the bonnet under her chin. "But in the unlikely event that he does, perhaps I should bring a muff pistol."

Eighteen

"Depend upon it I will carry my point."
—*Lady Catherine,* Pride and Prejudice

Anne heard the news in the chamber she had shared with Henry during their brief marriage. She was sitting up in bed, having just finished her breakfast, when Elizabeth and Darcy entered. Colonel Fitzwilliam was seated in a chair at her bedside. The two had been talking, and Anne's countenance reflected more serenity than it had in days. Elizabeth was reluctant to disturb such hard-won peace with the tidings she bore.

She sat down on the edge of the bed, took one of Anne's hands, and delivered the censored version of the morning's events that she and Darcy had agreed upon: Henry's remains had been found with a head wound; the coroner was examining his body to determine its cause.

Anne released a small gasp and an "Oh, poor Henry!" The colonel, upon receiving the news, blinked in momentary, and to all appearances genuine, surprise, but quickly assumed the detachment of a military commander accustomed to hearing reports of death.

After her initial response, the erstwhile Mrs. Crawford assumed an air of dignified composure. Having started grieving the loss of her husband and marriage when she first learned of Henry's duplicity, the permanent bereavement was easier to accept. "So I am a bride and a widow in the span of a fortnight," she said. "Or perhaps neither. It would seem that I am not meant for the marital state."

"No," said Colonel Fitzwilliam, "you simply were not meant for Henry Crawford." He took her other hand. "It may wound you to hear me say this now, but this news frees you. He can no longer wreak havoc with your feelings; his death severs your legal and emotional entanglements with him unquestionably. You need not fear he will come round begging your forgiveness, or torment yourself over whether you should grant it. Mourn him if you must, Anne, but let it not be for long. He does not deserve your tears."

"I have already shed his share. Any remaining ones are for myself and the wreckage I have made of my life."

"Then let those be few, as well."

She nodded and met his eyes. "I am grateful for your friendship through all of this. Were it not for you, I know not how I would bear it." Her gaze quickly shifted to encompass Elizabeth and Darcy. "Were it not for *all* of you." Her gaze strayed back to Colonel Fitzwilliam's countenance, where it lingered before dropping to their hands, which were yet joined.

Elizabeth studied Anne more closely, a notion forming in her mind. Had Anne developed a *tendre* for her cousin? The possibility seemed premature, given that she had been widowed—or whatever one called her current state—so little time, but then again, she had not been married long. Or was this not a new attachment? She recalled Anne's obvious pleasure in dancing with the colonel at the Riveton ball. Had she long harbored feelings for Fitzwilliam, temporarily eclipsed by Henry Crawford's more passionate flirtation?

Her scrutiny moved to the colonel. His solicitude toward Anne was evidenced by the warmth of his expression as he regarded her. Was he beginning to return her sentiments?

With apparent reluctance, Fitzwilliam released Anne's hand, rose, and turned to Darcy. "The sooner Mr. Crawford is laid to rest, the better. What arrangements are being made?"

"He will be interred pending the results of the coroner's examination."

"I expect his family will want him buried at Everingham. Our aunt has the name of his solicitor, who can notify his sister and uncle. Has Lady Catherine been informed?"

"Not yet."

"I anticipate her at any moment. She has requested my assistance with—" Footsteps sounded in the hall. "I believe she comes now."

Lady Catherine burst into the chamber in her usual manner. "Mr. Darcy, I understand you have been on an errand this morning."

"I did not realize my whereabouts held such powerful interest for you."

"They do, insofar as they pertain to the hunt for Mr. Crawford. What have you done to advance the search?"

"I have ended it."

"What? With him yet at large?"

"Mother—"

Lady Catherine ignored her daughter. "I cannot believe this of you, Darcy. How can you so shirk your duty? Until Henry Crawford is found, Anne is at sixes and sevens."

"Mother—"

"I will not tolerate excuses. I want Henry Crawford back here, in this paltry little village, to answer for his conduct. If you cannot bring about—"

"Mother! He is dead!"

At last, Lady Catherine bestowed her attention on Anne. "How do you know he is dead?"

"He was found this morning," Darcy said. "I have seen him myself."

"Well!" For a minute, it seemed that was all her ladyship had to say on the matter. But Elizabeth could see that her mind was hard at work. "Well," she repeated a moment later. "This is the best news I have received in weeks."

"Mother!"

"Anne, do not become sentimental over the man. We have too much to do. What time does the post leave? Never mind—I shall send an express."

"To whom? Mr. Crawford's solicitor?" Elizabeth could not think of any other remote person who required such immediate notification of Mr. Crawford's passing, except perhaps his sister, and she doubted Lady Catherine cared one whit about ensuring that any of his relations were informed in a timely manner of his death.

"No, Mr. Archer can see to that. I must write to Lord Sennex."

"Whatever for?" Darcy asked.

"Anne is a widow. We can renew her betrothal to Mr. Sennex."

"Mother! Henry has not even been laid to rest yet!"

"We must act quickly, lest the existence of that wretched Mrs. Garrick woman come to the viscount's attention." Lady Catherine addressed not Anne, but Darcy and Colonel Fitzwilliam. For all the heed she paid her daughter, Anne might as well not even have been in the room. "At present, the viscount and his son are unaware of Mrs. Garrick, and I intend to keep them in ignorance. They know Anne eloped with Mr. Crawford—revealing that fact was unavoidable when the original betrothal agreement was broken—but no one outside this village knows that the marriage was of questionable legal status. We can yet marry off Anne well, but we cannot risk the bigamy issue becoming public knowledge before such a marriage is achieved. Once the vows have been exchanged, the new bridegroom cannot change his mind. Her place will be secure."

Elizabeth's heart went out to Anne. Widowed but hours, she was already once more subject to her mother's machinations. And what of her possible feelings for Colonel Fitzwilliam? "Would it not be scandalous for Anne to remarry before observing proper mourning?"

"Gossip over an abbreviated mourning period would be nothing compared to that of bigamy. I shall finesse the point with Lord Sennex. His mental faculties are not what they once were, and I have developed proficiency in managing him. I shall put it in his head that the marriage should take place as soon as possible to ensure that he lives to see it. All society knows he is old and frail—if there is talk, it will be little, and the status of a viscount is such that no one will voice disapproval too loudly."

Anne sat up straighter in her bed. "I do not wish to marry Mr. Sennex."

"You *wished* to marry Mr. Crawford, and observe the calamitous consequences of that decision! You have demonstrated all too clearly the soundness of your judgment in such matters. Through selfishness and obstinacy you contrived to marry a man of your own choice; your next marriage shall be to a man of mine. You should consider yourself fortunate if Mr. Sennex will even have you now. As it is, I expect he will demand a much larger settlement from us than that which we negotiated in our previous agreement, one enticing enough for him to overlook your ignominious elopement. Fortunately, Mr. Crawford himself will be funding it."

"How so?" asked Darcy.

"In exchange for Anne's not bringing a suit against him for fraud, Mr. Crawford agreed to a quiet pecuniary transaction as restitution. Mr. Archer handled the matter."

Elizabeth regarded Lady Catherine in amazement. The fact of Mr. Crawford's marriage to Meg had scarcely been revealed before he disappeared, yet in that time, she had managed to exact a financial commitment from him that, while it could not possibly atone for his crimes against Anne, would at least somehow benefit her.

And then Mr. Crawford had died.

In fact, Mr. Archer had most likely been the last person to see Henry Crawford alive. A disturbing thought entered Elizabeth's mind, and she met Darcy's gaze to see if he shared it.

Mr. Archer handled the matter. What other matters had Mr. Archer handled?

Nineteen

Mr. Darcy would never have hazarded such a proposal, if he had not been well assured of his cousin's corroboration.

—Pride and Prejudice

"I may require your assistance," Darcy said as soon as he and Colonel Fitzwilliam extricated themselves from Anne's chamber. Or, more to the point, from Lady Catherine's hearing.

His cousin asked no questions, only answered without hesitation, "Of course."

Darcy glanced about the hall, then decided their conversation was best held elsewhere. Fortunately, they found the small parlor on the main floor unoccupied. Colonel Fitzwilliam regarded Darcy expectantly.

"I believe Henry Crawford has been murdered," Darcy said.

Surprise flashed across Fitzwilliam's countenance. "What raises your suspicion?"

"The lead ball in his brain."

"That would indeed cause quite a head wound. I understand now why you imparted so few details to Anne. Pray continue."

Darcy described the state in which Mr. Crawford had been found. When he finished, he added, "The coroner and Sir Thomas believe it to be a case of suicide."

"And you doubt their judgment?"

"I doubt their objectivity. I also find curious several particulars regarding the pistol. It was found on Mr. Crawford's left side, and this gun patch lay some distance away." He produced the cloth circle and handed it to his cousin.

"Silk. And a fine one at that. His Majesty does not issue patches of this quality to my sharpshooters."

"Nor does he provide firearms such as the one discovered. Among all the weapons you have personally encountered, I defy you to produce a finer example of craftsmanship."

The colonel rubbed his thumb across one of the black rays. A streak of powder smeared onto his skin. "These lines are intriguing."

"I thought so, as well. They suggest the presence of rifling, but the pistol is smoothbore."

"That would seem to indicate that this patch did not come from the pistol you found." Colonel Fitzwilliam frowned in thought. "Are you quite certain it is smoothbore?"

"I held it myself."

"But did you look all the way down the barrel?"

"No."

"Where is the weapon now? I would like to see it if I could."

"Sir Thomas took it into his possession."

Colonel Fitzwilliam consulted his pocketwatch. "The noon hour approaches—early yet for a social visit to Mansfield Park, but our purpose is business. We need to examine that pistol, preferably in strong sunlight. It might contain rifling farther down the barrel—French rifling, it is called, and aptly named, for it is a deceitful practice, but unfortunately one sometimes seen in private firearms. The rifling stops an inch or two from the muzzle, making the pistol appear to be smoothbore—and therefore in compliance with dueling protocol should the need arise—but concealing the improved accuracy of a rifled weapon. It is difficult to detect, and best observed in bright sunlight aimed down the bore."

"If the pistol is so designed, that would account for the marks on the patch. Why, however, are they but three in number?"

"A weapon with hidden rifling is custom made. Its owner may have ordered fewer grooves cut into the bore, to make their presence still less noticeable if the barrel is inspected."

They walked to Mansfield Park directly. Upon being ushered into Sir Thomas's study, they found him in conference with Mr. Stover. The coroner sat in a chair opposite Sir Thomas's desk, holding a small tin in his hands.

"Mr. Stover has completed his examination of Mr. Crawford's remains," Sir Thomas said. "He was just imparting his findings."

"As I anticipated, I found the spent ball embedded in Mr. Crawford's brain matter," the coroner said. "It had carried the fired patch into the wound, verifying that the patch Mr. Darcy discovered did not come from the shot that killed Mr. Crawford."

Darcy received the news with disappointment. He had been so certain that the patch and pistol must share a connection.

Mr. Stover opened the tin he held. "I was, however, surprised by the appearance of the patch." He withdrew a gold circle of the same ornate silk as the one Darcy possessed. It was stained with substances Darcy did not care to contemplate too extensively, but it, too, bore a black "sun" with three evenly spaced rays.

"When I washed the excess matter off the patch, some of the powder came off as well," said the coroner. "But you can see that the fouling pattern, as well as the pattern of the fabric itself, is identical to that of the other patch, indicating that both patches were shot from the same weapon. Yet the pistol found beside Mr. Crawford is a smoothbore."

"Not necessarily," Darcy said. "Colonel Fitzwilliam and I have been discussing the point, and we would like to examine the pistol more closely."

"Outdoors, if we may," the colonel added.

"Outdoors? Whatever for?" Sir Thomas asked.

"To obtain the best view down the barrel. I should also like to clean it beforehand."

Sir Thomas regarded him skeptically, but rose. "Very well." He opened a drawer of his desk and withdrew the pistol. "Let us proceed."

He led them to an open expanse of grass on the south side of the mansion. Colonel Fitzwilliam accepted the pistol from him and stuffed a damp rag, procured by a servant, down the barrel. It emerged blackened by powder residue. The colonel then noted the angle of the sun. He turned so that the axis of the bore was pointed toward the sun and light could penetrate the barrel as deeply as possible. He rotated the weapon slowly, then nodded and handed it to Darcy.

"It is as I suspected."

Darcy held the pistol to the light for himself. At first he saw only darkness. But as he slowly rotated the barrel, the light revealed three spirals deep within.

"This weapon indeed bears rifling." Darcy returned the pistol to Sir Thomas. "If you peer down the shaft as we have done, you will note three grooves."

Both Sir Thomas and the coroner examined the weapon. Afterward, Sir Thomas thanked Darcy for proving the coroner's case for self-murder.

"How have I done so?" Darcy replied. That had hardly been his intent.

"Mr. Crawford's shot obviously came from the pistol found beside him."

"But what of the second patch?"

"What of it?"

"If Mr. Crawford took his own life, why is there evidence of two shots?"

"Perhaps he fired a test shot."

"Unfortunately," said Colonel Fitzwilliam, "the horrors of war sometimes prove too great for young men to bear, so I have experience with suicide. I have never known a man to engage in firing practice beforehand. They are usually confident of succeeding."

"Perhaps in the passion of the moment, he misfired on his first attempt, or the weapon discharged before he took aim."

"Perhaps," the colonel said. "When you discovered the loading materials, were they also near Mr. Crawford's body?"

"We discovered no such materials," Sir Thomas said. "They must have been with his horse."

"His horse returned without anything at all," Darcy said.

"Well, they must be somewhere," said Mr. Stover. "Let us go have another look in the grove."

The clearing appeared unchanged, with the notable exception of Mr. Crawford's absence. The coroner had removed the body to examine it, and it was now being prepared for burial. Though the corpse was gone, its scent yet lingered, as did the impression in the grass from where it had lain so long.

The four gentlemen searched the grove for a powder flask, patch tin, spare balls—anything which would indicate that Mr. Crawford had reloaded his pistol as Sir Thomas insisted must have occurred. Darcy began his part of the quest where he had discovered the second patch, locating the rock over which he had nearly tripped, and working outward in a measured shuffle through the overgrowth. He found nothing.

The coroner circled the area surrounding the body impression while Sir Thomas wandered about halfheartedly kicking through brush that had accumulated at the foot of a wild gooseberry bush along the grove's perimeter. Colonel Fitzwilliam, meanwhile, investigated the bases of a stand of birch trees about ten feet away from where Mr. Crawford had lain. Darcy grew impatient with the futility of their exercise. If reloading apparatus had ever been present, it was long gone.

He walked toward his cousin. Just as he neared, Colonel Fitzwilliam passed his fingertips over a splintered section of bark at approximately eye level on the side of one of the trees. At its center was a small hole.

"Have you found something of interest?" Darcy asked.

"Quite possibly." He produced his folding knife and called for Sir Thomas and Mr. Stover to join them.

Several minutes' application of knife to bark widened the hole sufficiently to pry out a misshapen, dark grey lump.

"It is not a spare ball, but a spent one," the colonel said, "and appears to be of a caliber commensurate with the bore of the pistol. Sir Thomas, if I may?"

The magistrate did not offer the pistol, but his other hand, open and palm up.

Colonel Fitzwilliam surrendered the bullet. Sir Thomas held it to the crown of the muzzle. While impact with the tree had flattened one side, it appeared to be a match. "Mr. Stover, how large was the ball you removed from Mr. Crawford's head?"

"Fifty-four, perhaps fifty-six. It is difficult to measure caliber precisely once a ball has been fired and hit a target. The bore of Mr. Crawford's pistol is fifty-four. I am satisfied the ball that killed him came from this gun."

"We now have both a patch and a ball from a second shot," Darcy said, "yet no loading materials."

"Darcy, would you show me exactly where you found the patch?" his cousin asked.

They paced out the short distance to the rock in the overgrown grass. At Colonel Fitzwilliam's request, Sir Thomas finally handed over the pistol. The colonel sighted the weapon. "There is a direct line from the patch to the point of impact with the tree, at the proper angle to deduce it was fired from here. The body, however, does not fall within this line. It is too far to the side of the tree for the shot to have been aimed at Mr. Crawford where he was found—even if it flew wide, the angle of impact is wrong. Nor could Mr. Crawford have fired this shot into the trunk from his final position—the entry hole in the trunk was nearly opposite him. Either he fired into the tree from here, then moved to kill himself, or—"

"Or the shot that came from here was fired by someone else," Darcy finished. "And most likely it was, because if Mr. Crawford fired both shots, he would have had to reload, and he had no means by which to do so."

"The materials could have been taken from here after the fact," Colonel Fitzwilliam said. "Or a second pistol, loaded at the same time—or at least with the same distinctive patches—was used."

"How can you say there might have been a second pistol?" Sir Thomas said. "Both patches match the unique rifling of Mr. Crawford's weapon."

"It is distinctive but not necessarily unique," said Colonel Fitzwilliam. "Mr. Crawford's pistol could have been commissioned as part of a cased set." It was not uncommon for pistols, particularly custom weapons, to be sold in matched pairs, ostensibly for duels. If a contest of honor was not settled in the first round, the well-prepared owner then had an ancillary pistol at the ready so as not to suspend the duel in the heat of the moment to spend five minutes reloading. Not all cased sets were purchased in anticipation of actual duels; as with other goods collected by the wealthy, if owning one pistol was desirable, owning two was better still, and most pairs were used for improving one's skill at target-shooting rather than defending one's honor, if they were ever fired at all.

"Whether Mr. Crawford's pistol has a twin, or is a single pistol that was fired and reloaded, something—the loading supplies or the second weapon—is missing from this grove that had to have been present at the time of Mr. Crawford's demise," Darcy said. "Which means someone else was in this grove before Mr. Crawford was discovered, and took with him the loading materials or the matching pistol. Either way, this individual was somehow involved in whatever event ended Mr. Crawford's life. I should think that constitutes sufficient evidence to cast reasonable doubt on the probability of suicide."

Sir Thomas stared at Darcy a long moment. At last he turned to the coroner. "What are your thoughts on the matter, Mr. Stover?"

"I am no longer confident in a suicide ruling. I will hold the inquest as planned; if no other information comes to light during it, I shall simply state the cause of death to be a close-range gunshot to the head, and the investigation into how that shot came to be fired can proceed from there."

Sir Thomas appeared disappointed. "I had hoped this matter would be settled by your report. But very well. At least I shall be able to ship Mr. Crawford's rotting remains out of Mansfield and back to Norfolk. Everingham is welcome to them."

Twenty

"Do not deceive yourself into a belief that I will ever recede. I shall not go away, till you have given me the assurance I require."

—*Lady Catherine,* Pride and Prejudice

Mr. Archer had always reminded Elizabeth of an undertaker. However, she had assumed the solicitor's undertakings were aboveboard.

Now she was not quite so certain.

As Elizabeth descended the stairs in search of Meg, who had not yet been informed of her husband's death, she contemplated Lady Catherine's solicitor more seriously. Of all the people she and Darcy had discussed as having motive for Henry Crawford's murder, they had avoided the mention of one who almost certainly had wished him dead.

And Mr. Archer worked for her.

The thought that Lady Catherine had instructed her solicitor to eliminate her daughter's seducer was absurd. Was it not? Darcy's aunt was a titled aristocrat. The daughter of an earl. A landowner in her own right, a patroness of—well, of Mr. Collins, the realm's most obsequious clergyman, but a patroness nevertheless. She might be domineering, she might think herself infallible on the subject of what was best for everybody else, she might be in the habit of bullying everyone around her until she got her own way. But such people as her ladyship—ladies with a capital *L* and the pedigree to support it—did not go round orchestrating assassinations.

Unless they were provoked beyond reason.

And Lady Catherine had every reason. Henry Crawford had not only interfered with what she had considered a very desirable marriage contract, he had destroyed Anne's chances of ever receiving another. Darcy's aunt had been incensed from the moment she learned of the elopement, and her ire had only grown as the magnitude of the damage compounded. Perhaps she had indeed surpassed reason.

Elizabeth suspended her musings for a moment to enquire after Meg. Mrs. Garrick had last been seen heading for the livery. Whatever for, Elizabeth could not imagine, but she followed the direction nonetheless.

She found Meg in the stable, deep in conference with Charleybane. She stood just outside the Thoroughbred's stall, stroking the animal's marred face and speaking in low, lulling tones. The horse leaned its head toward her hand.

Elizabeth was reluctant to interrupt—this was the most content she had ever seen either the mare or the woman, but the news she bore could not be postponed, and Meg deserved to hear it from a sympathetic teller.

"Meg?"

Meg turned. "Mrs. Darcy. I was just—" She glanced back at the Thoroughbred self-consciously. "I was just visiting John's—Mr. Crawford's—horse. I thought she might be missing her owner."

"Are *you* missing her owner?"

"I—" She shook her head and shrugged. "I do not know. I doubt I can ever forgive his betrayal, but all the same, he is my husband, and with each passing day since Charleybane's return, I fear more for his safety."

Elizabeth wished she had a better report to offer. "He has been located."

Relief lit Meg's features, but for only a moment. Then a look of doubt set in. "You have left something unspoken—I can hear it in your voice. Was he found with yet another woman?"

"No. I am afraid he was found dead."

Meg blinked rapidly and swallowed—twice—before speaking. "I feared as much. How?"

"He was shot. The coroner is determining whether by accident or intent."

Charleybane nickered. Meg turned and absently stroked the mare's face while she composed her own. The intelligence had clearly taken her by surprise. So, apparently, had her grief. She wiped her eyes with the back of her hand.

Elizabeth offered her a handkerchief. "I am sorry to be the bearer of such news."

"I am sorry to be the recipient of it." She dabbed the tears and returned the handkerchief. "Now that he is gone, I do not know what I shall do."

"As his widow, you might attempt to petition the courts for dower rights. Even if you receive merely a portion of his personal property, that ought to help support you. This horse alone is worth quite a sum, despite her injury."

"I cannot afford to keep a horse, let alone petition the courts for anything. I cannot afford my room at this inn."

"Do not distress yourself over the room at present."

She shook her head. "That is most generous of you, but I shall find a way to manage for myself." She stroked the horse's mane. "In the meantime, I believe I shall take Charleybane out for some exercise. Perhaps the ride will help organize my thoughts."

Elizabeth left Meg with the mare and went back toward the inn. As she neared the door, Mr. Archer emerged. He nodded brusquely and continued past her, heading for the stables. She followed him with her eyes, her earlier reflections returning to her mind. Where had Mr. Archer gone when he rode off on the night of Mr. Crawford's disappearance? Had he discovered Henry and dispatched him, then returned to report his search unsuccessful?

There was one way to find out. Probably more than one, but today Elizabeth preferred the direct approach. The challenge would be obtaining the information she sought without revealing her suspicions. She retraced her steps to the livery, rapidly inventing and then discarding means of phrasing the questions she wanted to ask, and hoping inspiration would reach her before she reached him. She expected to find him just within, arranging with the ostler the hire of a mount or post-chaise—for what else would take him to the stables?—but he was not immediately inside. Nor were the ostler or his stable hands.

She proceeded toward the rear of the building, where she had left Meg and Charleybane. The Thoroughbred's stall was round a corner, and she slowed at the sound of voices.

". . . her ladyship's interests. His death has not changed that."

"It might have changed mine." The voice was Meg's. The other belonged to Mr. Archer.

"I thought you would see reason. I shall inform her ladyship."

"Do not inform her yet, for I have not made up my mind."

"You are hardly in a position to refuse. Reports already circulate that Mr. Crawford might have been murdered. You were seen riding off after him the night he disappeared."

"So were you."

"I am a respected London solicitor employed by a lady of irreproachable reputation. You are a penniless commoner. Who is more likely to swing from a tree? Come, now, Mrs. Garrick—you need only maintain silence on the subject of your marriage."

The ostler reentered, startling Elizabeth. He asked whether he might be of assistance. She shook her head and departed quickly, hoping Meg and Mr. Archer had not heard him and therefore remained unaware of her presence.

Rather than return to the inn, she strode down the lane, hoping to put enough distance between herself and the livery that when Meg emerged with Charleybane she would not suspect her conversation with Lady Catherine's solicitor had been overheard. Clearly, it had not been their first conversation, nor did it sound like it would be the last.

Elizabeth soon found herself approaching White House, where Maria Rushworth presently resided with her aunt. A curtain fell in one of the front windows, and a moment later Mrs. Norris bustled out.

"Mrs. Darcy, I have seen your husband coming and going from the village all morning. Are there tidings of Mr. Crawford?"

"Why would Mr. Darcy's errands lead you to think of Mr. Crawford?"

"Mr. Crawford has been on my mind since his horse returned without him. Poor, ugly creature."

"Do you refer to Mr. Crawford or the horse?"

"His mount, of course! I have never seen a more frightened animal in all my days. Naturally, one wonders about the fate of its master."

"When there is news of Mr. Crawford that concerns the general public, it will be circulated." No doubt with the aid of Mrs. Norris. Though she had met Mrs. Norris only once before, and that during Maria's argument with Mr. Crawford, Elizabeth knew her well. There was a Mrs. Norris in every village in England.

"But has he been found? However cowardly it was of him to flee, one would not want serious harm to befall him. Not I, at least. He injured my Maria terribly, but never let it be said that I failed in my Christian duty of forgiveness."

"You demonstrate great generosity of spirit."

"I am but a poor widow, yet even one with limited means can afford to be liberal in spirit. I have been telling Maria, and Sir Thomas, too, that if we are to know any peace ourselves we must all of us turn the other cheek. That is what my late husband, the Reverend Mr. Norris, would say were he here."

As Mrs. Norris had hardly seemed moved by the spirit of Christian forgiveness during her last encounter with Henry Crawford, Elizabeth wondered at her change of heart. Had she already heard of the morning's discovery? One such as Mrs. Norris generally managed to be among the first to learn any village news. She could well have been informed of Mr. Crawford's demise by someone at Mansfield Park—perhaps her sister, Lady Bertram—and now angled for more information.

Elizabeth decided to indulge her—or at least, appear to indulge her. In the process she would conduct a fishing expedition of her own.

"I am sure Mr. Crawford would appreciate your magnanimous sentiments. Unfortunately, Mr. Darcy and I were advised this morning that he has passed away."

"It is as I feared! I knew when his horse came back that its return did not bode well. Found him far from here, I expect?"

"No, in fact—in Mansfield Wood."

"Mansfield Wood! Sir Thomas did not say a word. Only imagine—Mr. Crawford's being there all along. Did his horse throw him? It looks a most unsound animal, if you want my opinion."

Elizabeth did not want her opinion, but she did wonder when Mrs. Norris had formed it. "When did you happen to see his horse?"

"I saw it—" She glanced down the lane. "I saw it when he arrived in the village. Everyone passes White House on their way to the Bull."

Indeed, Mrs. Norris could not have a more convenient situation for the gathering of village intelligence. A well-timed peek through her curtains could yield a day's worth of news. Elizabeth decided to offer her a bit more, and see what resulted. "I understand Mr. Crawford died of a gunshot."

"Indeed? How dreadful. Well, I expect his libertine ways must have caught up with him. Died in an argument, no doubt, over some lady or other. One wonders who the other gentleman is."

"Yes," Elizabeth said slowly, "one does." Considering that her niece's husband was such an obvious suspect, Elizabeth would expect Mrs. Norris to be less vocal in her speculations. "I am certain, however, that he will be found."

"Oh!" Mrs. Norris blinked. "Is he still at large?"

"So far as I know."

"Oh, my." She glanced up and down the lane, no doubt hoping to spot a friend to whom she could immediately impart the news.

"How is Mrs. Rushworth?" Elizabeth asked. "Is she at home?"

"Mrs. Rushworth?" she repeated absently, still looking round. At last, she returned her gaze to Elizabeth. "Maria is presently at Sotherton with her husband."

"Oh? I understood she lived with you. I must have been mistaken."

"She has been staying with me—such a good-hearted girl, to keep her poor aunt company. Kindness and thoughtfulness itself, I am sure. But she had matters to discuss with Mr. Rushworth this morning."

"I had hoped to call upon her today. Perhaps I will try again later, after she returns. Is Sotherton far?"

"It is ten miles. I intended to accompany her, but she would not hear of it. I am sure she thought only of my comfort. It will indeed be a long journey—the roads are narrow and toss one about even in the best of weather. But once at Sotherton, all is ease. It is one of the largest and finest estates in England, you know. An ancient manor. Mr. Rushworth is a man of some consequence."

"I did not know. Perhaps Mr. Darcy and I will call upon both Mrs. Rushworth and her husband, to improve our acquaintance with them."

"Perhaps you had better not. As I said, it is a tiresome journey."

"Then maybe we will have an opportunity to converse with Mr. Rushworth the next time he visits Mansfield."

"Mr. Rushworth does not come to the village often. He was a frequent visitor to Mansfield Park whilst courting Maria, but after they wed, they spent all their time in London and other fashionable spots. Of late, however, I believe he has largely been at home."

"With such an estate as you describe, I can well imagine Mr. Rushworth prefers it above any other location—especially now, as hunting season approaches. I have always heard Northamptonshire reputed as fine country for sportsmen."

"Oh, it is. The finest! And Mr. Rushworth loves to hunt and shoot. He is forever talking about his hounds." She glanced up the lane again, focusing on something past Elizabeth's right shoulder. "Oh—there is Jacob Mauston."

Elizabeth turned to see a laborer coming down the road, carrying with him a box of tools.

"If you will excuse me," Mrs. Norris continued, "I must speak with him about some work I would like done."

"By all means."

Mrs. Norris first reentered her house, returned with a key, and locked her door. "One cannot be too cautious," she said as she passed Elizabeth.

Indeed, thought Elizabeth as she watched Mrs. Norris bustle toward Mr. Mauston. In this village, one could not.

Twenty-one

"When my aunt has got a fancy in her head, nothing can stop her."

—*Tom Bertram,* Mansfield Park

"Consider, Darcy, how much Lady Catherine stands to gain from Mr. Crawford's death." Elizabeth lifted the hem of her skirt and picked her way through a particularly muddy patch of road as they walked down the lane past the village green. Overnight rain had made for a damp, slow walk to Mrs. Norris's house, where they hoped to find Maria Rushworth at home following her previous day's journey to Sotherton. "As she said, she now can pass off Anne as a widow. Provided Meg does not draw attention to herself, no one in society need ever know that Anne's first marriage was invalid, whereas if Mr. Crawford were still alive, the scandal would have inevitably been exposed. Even if she fails to complete the alliance with the Sennex family, Anne's reputation is partially preserved. In fact, she looks like a romantic heroine—her windswept courtship and elopement brought to a premature, tragic end by her groom's sudden death. She will be a figure of sympathy, not scorn."

"His death is a fortunate coincidence for my aunt, nothing more."

"Are you entirely certain? Mr. Archer went off in pursuit of Mr. Crawford that night. And, I recall the following morning, observing a streak of golden residue on the lower leg of his trousers. Perhaps it was pollen from some plant in the grove."

"Or anywhere in the village. The rain has been so abundant that the weeds are, as well."

"Why are you so quick to eliminate him as a suspect?"

"Mr. Archer is a highly reputable London solicitor. He deals exclusively with the aristocracy, and charges fees that render him immune to the temptation of increasing his coffers by dirtying his hands with anything so tawdry—not to mention risky—as murder."

"Could he not have hired a third party to complete the business?"

Darcy released an exasperated sigh. "I suppose he could have. But there are other individuals who are far more likely to have committed the deed." They had arrived at the gate of White House. "Including a certain discarded mistress who lives here."

They passed through the gate to the front door, which appeared to have recently been worked upon. Elizabeth noted that a second lock had been installed.

"Have you the earrings?" Darcy asked. The jewelry formed the pretext of their call.

"In my reticule." She glanced at him archly. "In the absence of a muff pistol."

They knocked on the door and were greeted by the maid, who bade them wait in the entry while she announced them. Voices carried from the morning room.

"Well, you simply must try again." The tones belonged unmistakably to Mrs. Norris.

"Perhaps I do not want to try again." Petulance. Definitely Maria.

"Do not be ridiculous. Anything is better than divorce, and now that Mr. Crawford is dead, it will be easier to persuade Mr. Rushworth to reconcile. You should have tried harder yesterday. Why did you not?"

"Because he was as stupid and dull as ever, and the whole visit only reminded me of why I left him for Mr. Crawford in the first place. Also, his mother was in the room the entire time, standing watch—the old dragon. We could not have a private word. Even could I tolerate living with Mr. Rushworth again, she would never allow it. I do not think he uses the necessary without her permission."

"Next time I shall come with you to divert her. I ought to have gone yesterday and never should have let you persuade me otherwise."

"There will be no next time."

"Maria, I managed matters once with Mr. Rushworth; I will manage them again."

A break in their conversation suggested that the maid had at last won Mrs. Norris's attention. Darcy and Elizabeth heard their names announced; they were the next minute ushered into the morning room.

Maria picked indifferently at a piece of needlework as Mrs. Norris greeted them. After the requisite exchange of empty pleasantries, Elizabeth addressed Mrs. Rushworth.

"We are happy to find you at home," she said. "I do wish this were merely a social call, but I am afraid my husband and I must beg your assistance. As Mrs. Norris has no doubt told you, Mr. Crawford was discovered dead yesterday. His injuries were such that his remains were identified by his personal effects—among them, these earrings." She withdrew the baubles from her reticule and held them toward Maria. "Mr. Darcy and I are fairly certain these are the ear-bobs you returned to Mr. Crawford on the day of his disappearance, but we hope you will confirm our identification. As you surely understand, this is too important a matter to risk error."

Maria set aside her needlework to take the ear-bobs from Elizabeth's hand. She outlined one of the pendant gems with her forefinger, her expression impassive. "Yes, these are the earrings."

"We are trying to trace Mr. Crawford's movements that day. Did you happen to see him again after you left the inn?"

"No. I came back to White House and did not go out again."

"I can vouch for her on that account," said Mrs. Norris.

"But you left here for a time to visit my mother."

Mrs. Norris regarded Maria with annoyance. Elizabeth wondered whether she had been trying to reinforce her niece's alibi out of suspicion—or knowledge—that she had not in fact been where she claimed.

"So I did," Mrs. Norris said. "But you were in your chamber when I departed, and still there when I returned."

"I have nowhere else to go in this deplorable village. As if I care whether anybody in Mansfield receives me." She closed her hand around the earrings and reached out to return them to Elizabeth. "Here. I have answered your questions."

Mrs. Norris intercepted. "Allow me to see those, Maria."

Mrs. Rushworth surrendered them to her aunt, who held them up to catch the light. Sunlight glinted off the sapphires. "You ought to keep these. Mr. Crawford no longer has any use for them."

"Neither do I."

"Well—I shall retain them lest you change your mind."

Before Elizabeth could issue a startled protest, Mrs. Norris deposited the earrings in her own workbag. Elizabeth decided to let the presumptuousness go for now, as she and Darcy had yet more information they hoped to obtain.

"Mrs. Rushworth, I realize that speaking of Mr. Crawford might cause you distress, but may I ask you to indulge me in a few more queries?"

"It depends upon what they are."

"Another item was found with Mr. Crawford's remains—a pistol. Do you recall his having possessed one?"

"Not whilst we were in London. I have never seen Everingham, however, and so do not know what possessions he might keep there."

The sound of a carriage drew their attention to the window. A chaise had come up the lane and stopped in front of White House. Elizabeth recognized the livery.

"Mr. Rushworth has come to call!" Mrs. Norris exclaimed. "See, Maria—it is not too late. Matters between you might yet be patched up." She crossed to the window to obtain a better view. "He has just alighted. Smooth your hair, child—remind him why he married you."

"But I—"

"Oh, why did *she* have to accompany him?" Mrs. Norris scowled as Mr. Rushworth handed his mother out of the carriage. "Well, no matter. I will manage her, as I said I would. Do not you fret, Maria—your Aunt Norris will have you living back at Sotherton Court within a fortnight."

Maria stood and stomped. "You are not listening! I—"

"Maria, I am the only remaining friend you have. Who but your Aunt Norris stepped forward to take you in when your own father would not? You must heed my counsel. Divorce is an evil to be avoided at all costs. Mr. Rushworth may be thick-witted, but he is the only chance you have at salvaging your respectability." Mrs. Norris turned from the window and glanced at the Darcys with an almost startled expression. Apparently in her exultation over Mr. Rushworth's arrival, she had forgotten their presence. "If you will excuse us, we have done speaking about Mr. Crawford."

"We were just about to take leave," Darcy said. They rose.

A knock on the door was quickly followed by the maid's announcing the Rushworths' arrival. Mother and son entered, the dowager responding to the Darcys' presence with disdain.

"You are Mr. Crawford's friend, are you not?"

Darcy offered his name and acknowledged the association. "Mr. Crawford was a recent acquaintance, a relation by marriage." Elizabeth supposed that was as accurate a description of their connection as ought to be attempted. Darcy then introduced Elizabeth, who received a cool nod. Mr. Rushworth bowed, his expression warmer, though not by much.

"Maria, there is a matter of business we need to discuss," said Mr. Rushworth. "Is there another room in which we could—"

"No, no!" Mrs. Norris interjected. "Stay right here. The Darcys were just departing."

She instructed the maid to show them out, and dismissed them with scarcely a glance. "Now, Mrs. Rushworth, let us move to the drawing room while your son and my niece converse. May I offer you some tea? Cook prepared Bath cakes this morning, and I have a very fine wild gooseberry jam—my only remaining jar from last year, as I have not yet had time to put up any this season. I know a spot with superior berries—"

"We shall not stay long."

Elizabeth and Darcy followed the maid to the front door. The servant opened it, startling a man on the other side who had been about to knock. He was a large, burly fellow, and had with him a large, burly dog. Elizabeth had never seen such an enormous mastiff, and was thankful the man held it on a leash.

The man and maid greeted each other. "And who is this?" the maid asked, nodding toward the animal.

"Wolfgang. Mrs. Norris told me to bring him round today."

"Well, bring him round to the back door and we'll get him familiar with the place."

Elizabeth held her tongue until she and Darcy were beyond the gate. "I dislike that woman more with every meeting."

"Which one?"

"Mrs.—" She had been about to say "Norris," but stopped herself. "All of them, actually. Maria reminds me too much of my youngest sister, and the two older matrons are at least as dictatorial as Lady Catherine."

"Mrs. Norris and the dowager do seem to share some common traits with my aunt."

"The three of them are insufferable—so certain that they know what is best for everybody else." Though their power was confined to the domestic sphere, they wielded it with divine self-righteousness. "They could model for a portrait of the Fates."

"Mrs. Norris spinning the thread, Mrs. Rushworth measuring it, and Lady Catherine cutting it off?"

"A sanctimonious triumvirate that rules through intimidation." She took his arm to steady herself as she negotiated another muddy patch of road.

"Surely they do not intimidate *you*? Why, you have been standing up to my aunt since before we were engaged, and after a few more years as mistress of Pemberley I fully expect you will be as capable as they of commanding everybody around you."

She halted abruptly. "Are you quite serious?" Images of herself ten, fifteen years into the future flashed in her mind. She saw herself arranging a betrothal for Lily-Anne without her knowledge, manipulating her neighbors, lecturing her guests. She did not like what she saw. Did Darcy truly think her capable of such behavior? "No one knows what is best for everybody else, including me," she said. "And I do not want to become the sort of person who thinks she does."

"I did but jest," he said. "I could never have married you if I thought you inclined to my aunt's propensities. One Lady Catherine in our family is more than enough."

They reached the inn and elected to partake of an early dinner. They were startled when their server appeared.

"Meg? Whatever are you doing?"

"One of the girls quit after Lady Catherine yelled at her again, and I have taken her job. I told you I would find a means of supporting myself."

"But—do you want to work as a servant?"

"I worked at an inn before my marriage; I can work in one again."

Within ten minutes, another pair of patrons had taken a table in the dining room: Mr. Rushworth and his mother. Meg greeted them with a smile. Mr. Rushworth returned it with a polite nod. The dowager scowled.

"Welcome," Meg said. "Have you dined at the Ox and Bull before?"

"On a few occasions," Mr. Rushworth replied. "Though when last we were here, we did not linger to eat."

"Had places to be, did you?"

"Yes, we were on our way to London."

"Well, I am glad you have returned. What can I bring you?"

Elizabeth glanced at Darcy. Had Mr. Rushworth gone to London to purchase a pistol after his discussion with Henry Crawford? He could not have returned quickly enough to have killed Mr. Crawford that night, but Mr. Crawford had been missing for days before his discovery—perhaps the murder had not taken place on the evening of his disappearance, but some time later.

On the other hand, perhaps Mr. Rushworth had been far to the south when the murder occurred.

Darcy answered her unspoken question in muted tones shielded from the Rushworths' hearing by Meg's cheerful chatter. "We can probably verify how long he was in London. If it was any length of time, he likely would have been seen at one of his clubs. Or perhaps he filed court papers related to the crim con trial. I will ask Mr. Harper to make some enquiries."

Elizabeth knew their solicitor could be relied upon to conduct his investigation discreetly.

They finished their meal and headed for their chamber. As they reached the base of the stairs, the front door opened. An old man with a cane shuffled in, followed by his sullen son.

"Why, Mr. Darcy—it is Mr. Darcy, is it not?—how good to see you again."

Lord Sennex had arrived.

Twenty-two

"Younger sons cannot marry where they like . . . there are not many in my rank of life who can afford to marry without some attention to money."

—*Colonel Fitzwilliam,* Pride and Prejudice

Lady Catherine gripped the top of the chair back, too impatient to sit down. "Whatever is taking his lordship so long?"

"Doubtless he requires more time than you or I to cope with the stairs," Darcy replied. "I am sure he will be down as soon as he is able."

The only room available for Lord Sennex's use had been the upper-level chamber vacated by Mr. Lautus some days ago. That gentleman apparently had grown so weary of the Crawford–de Bourgh entourage occupying all the attention of the Bull's employees that he had departed without so much as informing his host of his intention of never returning. Darcy was beginning to wish he could flee the inn himself. He had trouble tolerating his aunt for more than a se'nnight when he had all of Pemberley or

Rosings in which to lose himself; the inn's close quarters were becoming closer with each passing day.

As their party now comprised the whole of the inn's guest list, Lady Catherine had commandeered the small parlor for their use in holding the imminent meeting. Colonel Fitzwilliam paced restlessly while Mr. Archer sat in front of the empty fireplace.

"This is *not* how I intended to conduct these negotiations," his aunt said. "I had planned to send Mr. Archer to Hawthorn Manor. I certainly did not want Mr. Sennex and his lordship to come here, where they might encounter that Garrick woman flitting about and learn that Anne might never have been truly married." She drummed her fingers on the chair. "I can manage Lord Sennex. It is Neville Sennex and their solicitor who concern me. Fortunately the solicitor is not expected for a day or two."

Colonel Fitzwilliam halted his agitated movements. "I must again express my conviction that this betrothal is not in Anne's best interest. I spoke with her not twenty minutes ago and she dreads the very thought of it. Indeed, I harbor reservations of my own about Mr. Sennex's suitability. Anne's cooperation is coerced by her contrition over the Crawford debacle and her reluctance to defy you."

"So long as she cooperates, I do not care what her motivation is."

"But in my opinion—"

"I have not solicited your opinion."

"Then why have you asked me to this meeting?"

"For the same reason I invited Mr. Darcy to attend. I want your help in persuading Mr. Sennex to accept terms most advantageous to Anne."

"Anne's inheritance of Rosings is secure whether she marries or not," Darcy said. "Why pressure her to wed at all?"

"To preserve her reputation. To ennoble our family line. To

create another generation . . . if she has not begun *that* already." She emitted a sound of disgust. "I pray she does not carry Mr. Crawford's child. As it is, Mr. Sennex will almost certainly insist the wedding be postponed until that fact is determined."

A moment later, Lord Sennex and his son entered. Lady Catherine greeted them warmly—as warm as conversation with her ladyship ever became—and invited them to sit.

Neville shook his head. "I am not staying. I only escorted my father down at his insistence."

Lady Catherine frowned. "Surely you want a voice in these proceedings?"

"The only thing I have to say about the matter is that I refuse to participate. Your daughter's elopement humiliated me beyond restitution. Henry Crawford might have managed to get himself killed before I had an opportunity to seek satisfaction, but I will not take his widow on any terms. No fortune in the world is worth lowering myself to accept used goods."

Lady Catherine gasped.

"Neville," the viscount said in a even tone, "you must reconsider—"

"No. As I told you the entire length of our journey, I am decided. If you remain determined to bring Miss de Bourgh—pardon me, *Mrs. Crawford*—into this family, you will have to marry her yourself."

With that, he abruptly departed. All stared in silence at the door Mr. Sennex had closed behind him with force that echoed in the walls.

"I . . . er, I believe I need to sit down." The viscount leaned heavily on his cane. Darcy went to him and assisted him into a chair.

Lady Catherine eyed him appraisingly.

"I—I am afraid I must apologize for my son. I had hoped

that once we arrived . . . Perhaps if he could meet with Mrs. Crawford . . ."

"Given his present disposition, I do not think that advisable," said Colonel Fitzwilliam.

Lord Sennex released a sigh so heavy that it seemed to deflate his entire carriage. "I had so hoped to see him settled. Hawthorn Manor has been a lonely place since my wife passed away. I looked forward to a young bride cheering its halls again."

Lady Catherine took the chair next to him. "How long have you been a widower?"

"Oh, it has been . . . now let me see . . ." His wrinkles deepened as he concentrated. He issued another sigh. "A score of years, at least."

"That is a long time to be alone," she said in the most sympathetic voice Darcy had ever heard issue from her lips.

"Have you ever considered remarrying?"

"Anne will never agree to it."

"Of course she will," Lady Catherine told Colonel Fitzwilliam after Lord Sennex left the parlor. "This is an even better arrangement than her marrying the son. She will become a viscountess immediately. With that title, no one will dare criticize her elopement. And Lord Sennex was in favor of the special license, so we need not worry about the reading of the banns—the wedding can take place immediately. He is too addled to even think about waiting long enough to ensure Anne is not in a family way. If she is, it will be an easy matter to dupe him into believing the child is his. Mr. Archer, go draft the marriage agreement directly. I want his lordship to sign it before his solicitor arrives."

As Mr. Archer departed to do her bidding, Darcy exchanged glances with his cousin.

"Have you considered," Darcy said to his aunt, "that the viscountcy will pass to Neville Sennex and his children, not to any children of Anne's?"

"If Neville Sennex produces children."

"You do not think he will eventually wed?"

"It is a chance I am willing to take to preserve Anne's respectability."

"She need not marry a man more than twice her age to do so," said Colonel Fitzwilliam.

"Who else is there? She is almost thirty years old. Suitors were hardly lining up on the steps of Rosings before her elopement. You heard what Neville Sennex said. His own humiliation aside, he is correct in that Anne's association with Mr. Crawford has tainted her. What man of consequence will have her now? What gentleman at all?"

"I will."

Lady Catherine stared at the colonel. "What are you saying, Fitzwilliam?"

"I am offering my hand—if Anne herself is willing to accept it."

"Despite the fact that Henry Crawford compromised her? And that she could be carrying his child?"

"Yes."

Lady Catherine's brows rose. "That is very noble of you. But entirely unnecessary. We have just achieved an understanding with Viscount Sennex, and he offers a superior situation. Marrying Anne to her own cousin, a younger son with no land or title of his own, would make the marriage look like a patched-up business. I will not have Society thinking that the daughter of Sir Lewis de Bourgh could do no better than an army officer bought by her fortune and pressured by duty to restore the family name."

Colonel Fitzwilliam's jaw tightened. "Why do we not allow

Anne to determine that? She is over one-and-twenty. She can decide for herself which offer she prefers to accept, if she wants to accept one at all."

"I forbid you to mention this to Anne."

"You *forbid* me?"

Lady Catherine released a heavy breath. "I can see how the alliance you propose will materially benefit you, and make worthwhile the sacrifice of overlooking her compromised state. But if she defies me in this matter, she will not receive a shilling of her trust funds—the other trustees will side with me and refuse to release her annual income. If, however, you are patient, you can still gain. Wait until she is widowed again to marry her. The viscount is old and frail; his passing will not take long. Then she will have a restored reputation and the handsome jointure I just negotiated with him, as well as Rosings, to bring to your marriage."

"My offer was not about money."

Lady Catherine laughed coldly. "I thought you were more worldly, Fitzwilliam. Marriages are always about money, whether that fact is acknowledged or not."

Their aunt left to oversee Mr. Archer's progress in drafting the agreement with Sennex. Colonel Fitzwilliam was silent; Darcy could tell he struggled to subdue his resentment toward Lady Catherine.

"For my part," Darcy said, "I believe Anne would be fortunate in a marriage to you."

"It is gratifying to know that you, at least, think so."

"I was, however, as surprised as Lady Catherine by your offer."

Colonel Fitzwilliam became very busy with a button on the cuff of his coat. "It is not about money."

Twenty-three

"Now, seriously, what have you ever known of self-denial and dependence? When have you been prevented by want of money from going wherever you chose, or procuring any thing you had a fancy for?"

—Elizabeth to Colonel Fitzwilliam, Pride and Prejudice

"Colonel Fitzwilliam made an offer for Anne's hand?" Elizabeth found the news delightful. A slow smile spread across her countenance, unrepressed by the jostling of the carriage as she and Darcy made their way to Thornton Lacey. Eager to escape the inn for a while, they had decided to visit the village where Edmund Bertram resided in hopes of learning more from the clergyman about Mr. Crawford's history with the Bertram and Rushworth families.

"Yes. And Lady Catherine rejected it."

The smile immediately transformed into a frown. "Whatever is she thinking?"

"That she would rather see Anne attached to a doddering but wealthy and titled old man, than to a soldier with far less to recommend him."

"Oh, come, now—Colonel Fitzwilliam has plenty to recommend him. He is the son of an earl."

"A younger son, and Anne is the niece of that same earl. He would bring no new connections to the marriage."

"Even so, he is hardly impoverished. He did not inherit the earldom from his father, but he inherited *something*—he must have a substantial portion to call his own."

"Not substantial enough by Lady Catherine's standards. To her mind, the only thing he offers is respectability, which the viscount, as a peer, trumps."

Confound Lady Catherine. Elizabeth had witnessed quite enough of her rank pretensions. "What about affection? Does that count for nothing?"

"We are speaking of my aunt."

"Oh, yes: 'Affection has no place in such an important decision as marriage.' How could I forget?"

"What *has* affection to do with this particular instance? Do you believe Anne and Colonel Fitzwilliam would in time grow to feel about each other as we do?"

"I suspect they already might."

"Indeed?" He appeared surprised, and somewhat doubtful.

"Did you not observe the way she looked at him yesterday morning? Or how long he held her hand?"

"No, I did not."

Was that not just like a man? Elizabeth rolled her eyes and glanced out the window as the carriage rounded a curve. "Has it also escaped your notice how attentive he has been toward her since the accident? One must almost drag him away from her bedside."

"He is her cousin, and she is injured."

She turned her gaze back upon him. "You are her cousin."

"I would much rather be at your bedside."

"My point precisely! When you left him just now, where did he go?"

"To Anne's chamber."

"Aha!"

"But only to assist her down the stairs. He said she is feeling improved enough today that she wanted to take her dinner in the dining room."

She laughed.

"What is so amusing?"

"That assistance will require a bit of hand-holding and other contact, I warrant."

"Of what are you accusing Colonel Fitzwilliam?"

"Not a thing. I have no doubt of his behaving as a perfect gentleman, and she a perfect lady, and nothing untoward occurring between them." She deliberately looked out the window once more. "At least, not on the staircase."

"Elizabeth!"

She laughed again. "I do not even accuse either of them of being ardently in love—not yet. Whatever one or both of them might be feeling, I think is undeclared even within their own hearts, let alone to each other. And perhaps I am seeing what does not exist. But I have my suspicions, and I would much rather entertain happy ones involving your cousins than the more grave suspicions we have lately contemplated regarding Mr. Crawford's murder."

"Their being in love is not a happy scenario if my aunt has her way with this marriage between Anne and Lord Sennex."

"Indeed not. And although Anne is of age, and cannot be forced to wed anybody, she is so remorseful about her elopement and the evil it has brought upon her that I do not think she has the confidence to resist her mother a second time. The first instance was difficult enough." Her expression grew pensive. "Perhaps your aunt can be worked upon?"

"And perhaps Mr. Crawford will rise from the dead." He shook his head. "No, she is determined to effect an alliance with the Sennex family one way or another. I suppose we should simply give thanks that her sights have shifted from Mr. Sennex to the viscount himself. At least he is benign."

"Neville Sennex did not inherit his violent nature from his father?"

"I have heard that his lordship was a bit of a hothead in his youth—he had a rather inflated sense of honor, and heaven help anyone who might challenge it. Time, however, has tempered him. He still prizes honor, but demonstrates it in a dignified manner. At least, with as much dignity as the weaknesses of advancing age allow him."

"Then I suppose Anne is indeed better off wed to him than to his son. Though I am somewhat surprised that Lady Catherine relinquished her designs on Mr. Sennex so easily. I rather imagined she had aspirations of a future grandson of hers inheriting the viscountcy."

Darcy was silent for a moment. A vague feeling of dread had been hovering at the edges of his consciousness since the meeting with Lady Catherine, and it had been aggravated by an exchange he had overheard afterward. "I begin to wonder whether my aunt may yet harbor such aspirations."

"How can she? Neville Sennex is the viscount's eldest son. Anne could bear his lordship a dozen boys and it would make no difference—the title will pass to Neville, and to his son afterward."

"Unless Neville never has a son." He lowered his voice, disliking the thought of articulating his apprehension, even to Elizabeth. "While securing this chaise for our use, I encountered Neville Sennex. He was wanting to hire a horse to pay a call at Mansfield Park—apparently Sir Thomas's eldest son is an acquaintance of his from one of the London clubs—Boodle's, I believe. Lady Catherine, who had followed me to the livery to continue a conversation begun inside, overheard Mr. Sennex's request and offered him the use of Charleybane."

"That was exceedingly generous of her, considering the mare is not hers to lend."

"Mr. Sennex is Charleybane's previous owner. But in view of how offended my aunt was by Neville's rejection of Anne, I was entirely taken aback by her having made the offer at all. I attributed it to her wanting to maintain favorable relations with Lord Sennex, who was wandering about the courtyard. But then Mrs. Garrick happened by, which brought to mind Lady Catherine's having hired her a horse the evening of Mr. Crawford's disappearance."

"When she was hoping Meg might come to harm."

"Charleybane is skittish and unpredictable. And, I suspect, not fond of the former master who abused her."

"Now, Darcy, not one day ago you utterly dismissed my hypothesis about the involvement of your aunt's solicitor in Henry Crawford's death, and now here you have Lady Catherine plotting an assassination with a skittish horse as the murder weapon."

"I merely say that I begin to have misgivings about my aunt's motives in a number of transactions since her arrival in Mansfield."

"And what will you do if those misgivings take root and blossom into full-grown convictions? If you find evidence that she was involved in Mr. Crawford's death, will you bring it to Sir Thomas? She is your aunt, after all, and I know your sense of family loyalty to be as strong as your veneration for justice."

Darcy had been wrestling with that very dilemma. He quite honestly did not know what he would do, and was almost tempted to abandon his investigative efforts so that he would not have to face that decision. "Let us hope that I need not make that choice."

The carriage slowed. Darcy glanced out the window. They had not reached the village yet, but neared a crossroads. A man on horseback approached from another direction and hailed their driver.

Darcy studied the rider as well as he could from this distance. Highwaymen were a constant concern for travelers, and one should always be on his guard. The gentleman in question, however, appeared harmless. In fact, he appeared familiar.

Darcy leaned forward and peered more intently. Elizabeth, too, now looked out the window. And gasped.

"Darcy, is that truly . . . ?"

It could not be. Yet it was.

Henry Crawford.

Twenty-four

"There seems something more speakingly incomprehensible in the powers, the failures, the inequalities of memory, than in any other of our intelligences."

—Fanny Price, Mansfield Park

Elizabeth could not believe her eyes. "How?"

"I cannot explain it." Darcy instructed the driver to stop. They alighted just as Mr. Crawford reached the chaise.

"Pardon me—I did not mean to trouble you so far as to leave your carriage. I merely sought confirmation that this is the London road, as I am not familiar with the area and there is no signpost."

Elizabeth was the first to recover herself. "Mr. Crawford, how ever did you come to be here?"

"I beg your pardon?"

"We believed you dead."

"Madam, I happily offer my assurance that you are mistaken on that point. As you can see, I am quite alive. But as I am not the Mr. Crawford for whom you apparently take me, perhaps that gentleman is indeed less fortunate."

"You most certainly *are* Mr. Henry Crawford," Darcy said. "I would know you anywhere."

"I am not, sir. My name is John Garrick."

Now Elizabeth could not believe her ears. Not only was Mr. Crawford alive, but insistent upon continuing the fraud he had perpetrated against Meg. What could he possibly hope to accomplish by behaving so?

Darcy had adopted a stance so rigid that Elizabeth had seen it only a few times before—on occasions when he was beyond incensed. "Mr. Crawford, kindly spare us the insult of subjecting us to this charade any longer."

"I give you my word, sir, I am not Mr. Crawford, but John Garrick."

"John Garrick is a fiction you invented."

"My wife would tell you otherwise, were she here. Now if you will excuse me, I have a great distance to travel before reaching home. I am sorry I am not the person you believe me to be—though if he is dead, I am not that sorry." He signaled his horse to trot.

"Is your wife's name Meg?" Elizabeth called after him.

He brought the bay to a halt and turned around. "How did you know that?"

"She is in Mansfield. She has been looking for you."

"Meg is here in Northamptonshire? How did she get here?"

"You know perfectly well how she came to be here." Darcy clipped his words. "You saw her arrive."

"When?"

"A se'nnight ago."

"A se'nnight ago I was—" He abruptly stopped speaking.

"You were what?"

"A se'nnight ago I was injured," he said. "I have no memory of events leading up to that night."

"How very convenient."

"It was a head injury—a wound along my temple." He dismounted and removed his hat. "See—it has not fully healed."

Elizabeth and Darcy both looked at the side of his head. The gentleman indeed sported a stripe of damaged flesh above his ear. The wound garnered no sympathy from Darcy. His tone did not soften in the least as he asked what had caused the injury.

"I . . ." Mr. Crawford turned away from the impassive Darcy and instead addressed Elizabeth. "I need to see my wife."

"Which one?" Darcy asked.

Mr. Crawford regarded him with confusion, then turned back to Elizabeth. "Please—you said you know where Meg is. Will you take me to her?"

Elizabeth could not determine what Mr. Crawford was about. "Do you also wish to see Anne?"

"Who is Anne?"

At that, Darcy's ire flared. "We will take you to see Meg, but only if you answer some questions first."

Mr. Crawford glanced between them, as if trying to determine whether they could be trusted. How absurd—considering that he was the one with a record of betrayal.

"I . . . I believe a bullet caused my injury," he told Elizabeth.

"Whence did this bullet come?" Darcy asked.

"As I told you, I do not recall what happened. I woke up Thursday morning to the sensation of rain falling upon me. I was lying in a grove. It was dawn, or shortly thereafter—I could not be sure, clouds so darkened the sky. I had no idea where I was or how I came to be there. My head ached beyond anything, and I had trouble holding a thought. The side of my face was sticky with my own blood. It was agony to lift my head from the ground but I managed to push myself into a sitting position. That is when I noticed a pistol lying beside me."

"And when did you notice the body?" Darcy asked.

Mr. Crawford started. "How do you know about the body?"

"It was still there days later, when it was mistaken for you. Whose body is it, Mr. Crawford, and why did you kill him?"

"I do not know!" He ran a shaking hand through his hair. "I do not know what happened, or who he was. I left the pistol where it lay—I wanted no part of it—and stumbled over to him, but he was past any assistance this world could offer. My mind was so cloudy that I could scarcely stand. A whinny drew my attention to a cluster of trees. This horse was tied there. I know not whether it was his horse or mine. I untied her, somehow managed to climb into the saddle, and nudged her forward.

"I must have lost consciousness again shortly afterward, for I remember nothing else until I woke up again in a crofter's cottage. The farmer told me he had seen the horse pass his home with me slumped over her neck, and so had stopped the animal and brought me inside. His daughter nursed me until today, when I at last felt myself strong enough to attempt getting home to Meg. But you tell me she is near. I have revealed all I know—will you take me to her now?"

Elizabeth looked to Darcy. He was clearly unconvinced by Mr. Crawford's story, but he assented. Their driver turned the chaise around and they headed back to Mansfield with Mr. Crawford accompanying on horseback.

"Just when one thinks Henry Crawford's affairs could not become more knotty . . ." Elizabeth shook her head in amazement. "You are quite certain this gentleman is indeed Mr. Crawford?"

"Yes. Are not you?"

"Almost certain. He looks like Henry Crawford, but we have been mistaken in the past about the true identities of other individuals. And if this gentleman is indeed Mr. Crawford, that means you erred in identifying the corpse discovered in Mansfield Wood."

"I am well aware of that," he said tersely.

The defensive response took her aback. "I did not mean that as a criticism of you, only a statement of fact. Sir Thomas and the coroner also bear responsibility. I wonder who the unfortunate gentleman is, if not Mr. Crawford?"

"I cannot speculate. Whoever the deceased might be, Henry Crawford's reappearance absolves us of any interest in the matter. From the sound of things, Mr. Crawford himself is most likely responsible for the man's death, and even if he is not, I happily relinquish to Sir Thomas the charge of determining what occurred."

"Our lives have indeed become simpler this half hour. Though Anne's life, however, has not. I wonder what Lady Catherine will do when she catches sight of Mr. Crawford? Anne cannot marry the viscount now without first fully disclosing the details of her first marriage. As it is, he might not live long enough for the courts to sort out the matter."

"My aunt will be most seriously displeased."

"Poor Mr. Crawford—to return from the dead, only to have all his acquaintance wish he would go back." She looked out the window at the gentleman in question riding beside them. "Do you suppose he truly believes himself to be Mr. Garrick?"

"The man has either lost the ability to distinguish his real existence from playacting, or he hopes to somehow use the ruse to win pardon for his crimes. I speculate the latter."

"Do you think his head injury might have muddled his memory?"

"We shall see how he behaves in the presence of his wife."

"Which wife?"

"Both of them."

When they neared the village, Darcy suggested to Mr. Crawford that he ride in the chaise and allow his mount to follow. "Everyone in the village believes you dead. It will not do to have you parade through the streets. The shock would cause ladies to swoon."

Mr. Crawford readily complied. As they rode the remaining mile, he spoke little of himself, providing no new information about his present circumstances. From the time the farmer found him until the present morning, he claimed, he had been confined to the cottage as he recovered and come into contact with no one save the crofter and his daughter. At last today he had believed himself restored enough to attempt the journey home.

He made repeated inquiries about Meg. Elizabeth and Darcy volunteered few details.

"When did you last see your wife?" Elizabeth asked.

"I cannot recall. I am a merchant marine, and thus do not enjoy opportunities enough to spend time at home with her."

Darcy regarded him with impatience. "If you are a marine, why do you not speak more like a sailor?"

"I . . ." Mr. Crawford appeared confused and lapsed into contemplative silence.

Upon reaching the inn, they ushered Mr. Crawford into the small parlor as quickly as they could. His arrival, however, was noted by several patrons in the dining room, who then swallowed the remainder of their meals at an indigestion-courting rate so as to be the first to circulate the news abroad.

Mr. Crawford's arrival was also noticed by Meg, who nearly dropped a tray full of food in her shock. Her struggle to keep its entire contents from tumbling to the floor drew his attention.

"Meg!" Happy expectation, coupled with relief, overcame his countenance.

Her breath caught in her throat. She turned to Elizabeth, her wide eyes begging an explanation.

Elizabeth took the tray from her hands, set it down, and led her toward the parlor. "We are as astonished as you are. Come, he has been asking for you."

They shut the parlor door against intrusive eyes. Darcy stood in one corner, arms folded across his chest. Mr. Crawford took a step toward Meg.

"Meg, why do you regard me so? It is as if you do not recognize me. It is I—John."

"John?" The name prodded Meg from her disbelieving daze. "John! How dare you use that name?"

"What do you mean? That is my name. What other am I supposed to use?"

"Henry Crawford—the name you revealed to me before you disappeared. We thought you were dead, you know."

"*Who* is this Henry Crawford fellow? I heard his name whispered even as we entered."

Meg looked as if she wanted to strike him, but restrained herself. "Where have you been this past week?"

"I suffered an injury and have been recovering at a farm several miles hence. A crofter and his daughter took me in."

"A crofter with a daughter? And you've been there a week. Have you married *her* yet?"

"I do not understand you."

"I do not understand *you*! After everything you did to me, now you come back here calling yourself John Garrick? What do you want from me?"

He took another step toward her. "I want my wife."

"Do not come near me!" She kicked him in the shin.

"Ouch!" He doubled over and reached for his leg. Suddenly, he shifted his hands to his head. "I am dizzy."

He hobbled to a chair and sat down. He shut his eyes tightly for a minute, then opened them and regarded Meg in wonderment. "You have done that before."

"I have done what?"

"Kicked me that way."

"Yes. Once."

"Here, at this inn. Outside."

"Yes."

"I am remembering . . . We argued—I do not recall the subject—but we argued . . . and afterward I went to my chamber. I found a note there—an unsigned note. Its author invited me to meet at the grove in Mansfield Wood, there to discuss a matter of honor that could not be forgiven."

He rubbed his brow and turned to Darcy. "I kept the appointment. When I arrived, I was met by a man with a pistol. I recognized him as another guest at this inn—he had the room next to mine. He said I had behaved dishonorably, and that he had been hired to punish my conduct. I said, would he kindly name his employer? He refused, just handed me a pistol that matched his own and ordered me to walk fifteen paces. He took his shot as I was yet turning around. A searing pain seized my temple, and I fell to the ground, believing myself dying."

"What occurred afterward?" Darcy asked.

"It is as I told you earlier. I recollect nothing more. Except . . ."

"Except what?"

"The body. When I awoke, the body that was lying nearby—it was his."

Darcy opened the door and summoned Mr. Gower. Though surely he had heard the news of Mr. Crawford's return as it circulated the inn, their host nevertheless regarded Henry in amazement upon entering.

"What can you tell us about the gentleman who occupied the room next to Mr. Crawford's?"

"Mr. Lautus? He arrived just after you did; gave an address in Birmingham when he signed the register. Settled his account in full each day and kept to himself, mostly. I last saw him the day your wife and all the others arrived. He said he would be moving on soon, though at the time I did not understand him to mean that day. But Mrs. Garrick's coach arrived while we were speaking and in the confusion I must have mistook him."

"Mr. Crawford has information pertaining to him that will be of interest to the magistrate. Kindly send someone for Sir Thomas."

No sooner had Mr. Gower left the parlor than Lady Catherine entered it. Upon sighting Mr. Crawford in the chair, her expression turned stony.

"So, the report is true. You are yet among the living."

"Yes, madam."

"Is there no end to the damage you wreak? Your very existence causes me tribulation and grief."

Henry turned to Elizabeth. "Do I know her?"

"She is your mother-in-law."

"You are mistaken. She is not Meg's mother."

"Henry Crawford's mother-in-law."

"Oh. Perhaps he is happier dead."

"What is this you are saying?" Lady Catherine snapped. "What is this pretense? *You* are Henry Crawford! And because of you, my plans for Anne's future have once more come undone."

"What? What do you say about Anne?" Viscount Sennex shuffled into the room. "Oh, here you are, Lady Catherine. I have been looking for you this hour. I have questions about the agreement we discussed—"

"I am afraid we must discuss it further, my lord, before it can be finalized."

"Further? Very well. But what has this gentleman to do with my bride?"

"Nothing, my lord. Nothing that need trouble you. He is only—only a Mr. Garrick."

He blinked and scratched his head. "But I thought I heard you call him Henry Crawford."

"You did. I should not have addressed him so."

"Well, is he Mr. Crawford or Mr. Garrick?"

"The matter is complicated."

The viscount rubbed his chin, which appeared in need of shaving. "If he is Mr. Crawford, is he Miss de Bourgh's Mr. Crawford?"

"Anne no longer has a Mr. Crawford."

The elderly gentleman appeared so confused that he looked as if he could not at once absorb Lady Catherine's words and remain standing. He leaned heavily on his cane. "This is all most perplexing . . ."

"Indeed, it is, my lord. Allow me to escort you back to your chamber whilst I explain everything you need to know." With a final glare at Mr. Crawford, Lady Catherine led the viscount from the room.

Elizabeth wondered just how Lady Catherine planned to "explain" the present situation in a way that would enable her plan to proceed. As sorry as Elizabeth felt for Anne, she experienced equal sympathy for Lord Sennex. It vexed her to witness Lady Catherine taking advantage of his age and mental frailty to advance her own selfish interests.

She excused herself from the parlor temporarily. To her knowledge, no one had yet informed Anne or Colonel Fitzwilliam of Mr. Crawford's return from the dead, an omission she undertook to rectify. She was stopped on her way to the staircase by Mrs. Norris, who apparently had come to the inn solely for the purpose of being among the first in the village to obtain particulars about Mr. Crawford's miraculous resurrection.

"Mrs. Darcy, is it true? Is Henry Crawford indeed alive?"

Elizabeth lacked the patience to deal with the busybody at present. The day would soon turn to evening, yet there seemed to be no end of it in sight.

"Yes, he is. Would you care to join the queue of persons who have business with him?"

Her eyes widened. "No—no, indeed! I merely wanted to know—for Maria's sake. I have no wish to see that scoundrel."

Now that Henry Crawford was alive once more, he was again a scoundrel. So much for Christian forgiveness.

"But if Mr. Crawford is alive," Mrs. Norris pressed, "who was found in Mansfield Wood?"

"A traveler."

"Does anyone know who killed him?"

"That is perhaps a question best directed to Sir Thomas. Now, if you will excuse me . . ."

Elizabeth left Mrs. Norris and headed upstairs, restraining herself from physically throwing back her shoulders to shake off the encounter. She found the old gossip more disagreeable with every conversation.

On the landing, she met Colonel Fitzwilliam and quickly apprised him of the day's extraordinary events. His jaw settled into the same rigid set as Darcy's did when aggravated, and she was struck by the resemblance between the cousins. They both carried within them a strong sense of honor, and a subsequent disdain for those who so profoundly lacked one of their own. Both were highly conscious of duty; just as Darcy upheld his responsibility to his tenants and others who depended upon him for their livelihood, so, too, did Colonel Fitzwilliam take seriously his responsibility to the men under his command. They also shared a commitment to family, particularly the protection of those in their charge. He was a good man, Colonel Fitzwilliam, and could make a fine husband to Anne if only Lady Catherine and Henry Crawford would leave them be.

He muttered something under his breath. Elizabeth could not quite make it out, but from the hard expression of his eyes she suspected it was not the most gentlemanly of sentiments.

"I was on my way to acquaint Anne with this turn of events," she said. "Though perhaps you would do me the favor of delivering the news? You have been a steadfast companion to her these many days; she might hear it better from you."

"I would that there was no such news to impart," he said. "But yes, I shall tell her directly."

As she left him, she wondered whether Henry's return would prove a blessing in the end. Perhaps Lady Catherine's grand designs would at last crumble, and she would be forced to give them up and accept Anne's wishes.

She reached the main floor in time to see Viscount Sennex coming in the front door with Mrs. Norris, of all people. Whatever had the two of them to do with each other?

"I thought you were conversing with Lady Catherine, my lord?"

"Indeed, yes. Then I stepped outside for a moment and became a bit turned around. This kind lady took pity on me and led me back."

"He was returning from the necessary," Mrs. Norris offered in a too-loud whisper. "You might want to keep a watch on him, lest he wander off and be unable to find his way back." She tapped her head meaningfully. Fortunately, the viscount did not seem to notice her less-than-subtle reference to his mental state. He was busy shuffling back out the door.

"I shall bear that in mind, thank you." She hastily excused herself from Mrs. Norris and caught up with the viscount just outside.

"My lord, I believe your room is this way—within the building?"

"What? Oh! Yes—yes, of course. I was merely on an errand"—he glanced in the direction of the necessary—"of a personal nature."

Had he not just attended to such an errand? Pity entered her heart as she regarded the elderly man. He did not appear *that* feeble, but looks could be deceiving, as evidenced by his frequent trips to the privy. It was, she supposed, one of the indignities of old age. Poor Viscount Sennex.

Poor Anne!

"Do not you worry about me, young lady. I shall return to my chamber in a few minutes."

Elizabeth forced a cheerful smile to her lips. "Of course."

She felt, as she watched him walk off, that she ought to wait to ensure that he actually made it back to his room safely. He looked so frail—his posture stooped, his clothes hanging loosely on a frame that no longer filled them. But she did not want to subject the viscount to the embarrassment of being treated like a toddler whose nurse stood outside the privy door. Why was his valet not more attentive? Surely he had brought a personal servant, had he not? Come to think on it, she had not seen one with him—perhaps he and Neville had brought only one to attend them both, and Neville commanded more of his service.

She spotted Nat, the innkeeper's son, and pressed a penny into his hand. Nodding toward the viscount, she asked Nat to discreetly help him back to his room if need be. "And here is a sixpence to remain watchful of the viscount's future visits out of doors."

"Yes, ma'am!"

By the time she returned to the parlor, Sir Thomas had arrived and heard Mr. Crawford's tale. The magistrate addressed Darcy. "If Mr. Crawford is speaking truthfully, it would seem that you and Colonel Fitzwilliam were correct about the existence of a second pistol. Where is it now, Mr. Crawford?"

"I know not. I recall seeing only one when I awoke, and that I left behind. I was, however, extremely disoriented and could well have overlooked it, especially in the dismal light."

"And you do not recall shooting Mr. Lautus with either pistol?"

"Not at all."

With an air and expression of dissatisfaction, Sir Thomas rose from his seat. "That will do for now, I suppose. I shall repeat your story to the coroner. He might have additional questions for you, as might I whilst I verify what you have related and attempt to learn more about Mr. Lautus. Are you lodging here at the Bull?"

"I have no idea. I have not even considered the matter of tonight's lodging. I suppose I shall indeed stay here, if there is a room."

Mr. Gower was again summoned, and regretfully informed them that the Ox and Bull had not a single vacant chamber. Mr. Crawford's former room had been assigned to Neville Sennex. Sir Thomas himself, however, struck upon a solution.

"Mr. Sennex is an acquaintance of my son's," he said. "I met him this afternoon—in fact, I believe he is yet at Mansfield Park. We shall simply invite him to stay with us. His lordship is welcome too, if the viscount is inclined."

"The viscount is fatigued from the journey from Buckinghamshire and has only just settled into his chamber here," Elizabeth said. "Let us not uproot him at this hour."

All was arranged. Neville Sennex returned to the inn long enough to supervise the transportation of his belongings and take cursory leave of the viscount. He then made continued use of Henry's horse to hie himself to Mansfield Park, where he reveled in freedom from any care over his father's happiness or comfort, while Henry Crawford took possession of his former chamber.

It was the last time either gentleman was seen alive.

Twenty-five

He was entangled by his own vanity.

—Mansfield Park

"Not again?"

Darcy signaled to Elizabeth to keep her voice hushed. Though the inn bustled below with sounds of breakfast being prepared, he was not certain whether others were yet awake, and he did not want to be overheard. "I am afraid so," he said. "That horse is a bad omen."

"The horse has nothing to do with it. She is merely an innocent victim of circumstances."

Charleybane had once again returned riderless to the Ox and Bull. Upon her arrival, Mr. Gower had looked in on his newest guest—and then summoned Darcy. Mr. Crawford's chamber was empty. The bed had been slept in, but otherwise the room exhibited no sign of disturbance. Nor any indication that Mr. Crawford—or John Garrick, or whoever he claimed to be today—ever planned to return. Though he had once again left behind his valise, as Garrick he had insisted it was not his.

Darcy, who had hastily donned breeches and a shirt to accompany Mr. Gower to Henry's room, had returned to his own chamber to finish dressing and field questions from Elizabeth to which he had no answers.

"Perhaps he remembered who he was and fled," she suggested.

"Perhaps he never forgot." Darcy had not been fully convinced of Mr. Crawford's claim of amnesia, and now was even more suspicious of its having been yet another one of his theatrical performances, this one enacted to escape prosecution for having killed Mr. Lautus.

He struggled to tie his cravat in the tiny glass. The effort went poorly, as he had not patience for it. The sooner Sir Thomas was informed of Henry Crawford's latest disappearance, the sooner Darcy could have done with the entire matter.

Elizabeth crossed to him, took hold of the ends of the cloth, and tried to lend assistance. "It is still unfair to accuse the horse of complicity. Besides, I thought you told me last night that the Thoroughbred was in Neville Sennex's possession."

He frowned. "You are correct—she was. I had forgotten."

"Well, then we cannot malign her for returning here. Were I her, I would escape Neville Sennex at first opportunity, too." She loosened the uneven knot she had made and started over. "One wonders, though, how she was able to simply wander off from Mansfield Park's stables. I would expect the groom to exercise better guardianship over the horses of guests."

"As would I."

She chuckled. "Perhaps Mr. Sennex went out for an early-morning ride and Lady Catherine's fondest hopes have indeed come to fruition." Her hands suddenly stilled, and her expression lost its mirth. "Darcy, you do not suppose—"

"That the horse threw him?" The possibility was not an outrageous one, considering how Mr. Sennex had treated the mare during his ownership. Until he had confirmation of any such accident, however, he would reassure Elizabeth. "I doubt anything unfortunate has befallen Mr. Sennex. I doubt he has even stirred from his bed at this hour." He settled his hands on her waist. "I wish I could say the same."

She awarded him a mischievous smile. "I see my wiles are working after all."

"Quite well."

" 'Tis a relief. I had begun to fear that motherhood had diminished them. Perhaps I shall win that muff pistol yet."

She released the ends of his cravat and stepped back. "Not, however, if I am judged by my skill with gentlemen's neckcloths. I seem to have made an even greater tangle of this than before I attempted to help."

Darcy retrieved a fresh neckcloth. In so doing, he spied the shot patch from the grove. Sir Thomas had not yet asked for its return for use in investigating Mr. Lautus's death, but surely he would want it. He tucked the patch into one of his pockets.

Elizabeth's observation about the horse prompted him to greater haste in calling upon Sir Thomas, despite the uncivilized hour. He did not believe in coincidences, and Charleybane's unexpected appearance at the same time as Mr. Crawford's disappearance raised questions in his mind that he preferred to settle without delay.

He would call on Sir Thomas before even breaking his fast. And he wanted Colonel Fitzwilliam to accompany him.

"Not again?" Sir Thomas stared at his gamekeeper incredulously.

Darcy and Colonel Fitzwilliam had no sooner been shown

into the study than Mr. Cobb had entered to report another discovery in the now infamous grove.

"Yes, sir. Though found in a more timely manner, at least." The gamekeeper conveyed the particulars, each one causing Sir Thomas increasing agitation. "Do you and the gentlemen want to come see for yourselves?"

Sir Thomas rubbed his temples. In the space of a minute he seemed to have aged a decade. "Of course. Tell Badderley to summon Mr. Stover."

They arrived in the grove to a scene very much like the one they had found a se'nnight previous. Mr. Crawford sprawled lifeless in the grass.

This time there could be no mistake. The body was definitely his, and he was definitely dead. A scarlet hole in his chest and the blood soaking his clothing announced that a pistol had once more been aimed at him, this time with greater accuracy.

Upon the present occasion, however, Mr. Crawford was joined in death by a person familiar to them all: Neville Sennex. The viscount's son lay in a heap about twenty paces away. He had not been thrown from his horse. Riding accidents generally did not leave a bullet hole through one's heart.

Darcy observed Sir Thomas's pale countenance with sympathy. Any death was a serious matter, but to have the son of a viscount discovered slain on one's property, where he had been staying as a guest, was an event no one wanted to experience.

"I ought to inform Viscount Sennex immediately," Sir Thomas said. "I understand his lordship is in failing health. I hope his heart can survive the news."

"I have known the viscount for many years," said Colonel Fitzwilliam. "I will accompany you when you deliver the tidings, if you like; they might be easier to bear coming from a familiar person."

"I would be most obliged."

For a field that had seen so much death in recent days, the scene appeared oddly peaceful. Darcy observed no sign that the two men had engaged in any sort of physical struggle or pursuit that had led to the exchange of gunfire. Their bodies lay on their sides, more or less facing each other. Though the pistols themselves were absent, spent patches—two near Mr. Sennex, one near Mr. Crawford—littered the ground between them. Their deaths had been an orderly affair.

The colonel glanced from one body to the other. "Two gentlemen of means, one of whom eloped with the other's betrothed. I have seen the results of more than a few duels during my career, and this certainly has the appearance of one."

"Neville Sennex complained last night that he had been denied satisfaction in the matter of Miss de Bourgh's elopement," Darcy said. "The Sennex family takes honor seriously, and you and I both knew Neville Sennex to be a man of incendiary temperament. I would not be surprised if he called out Mr. Crawford and made him defend his actions."

"Nor would I," Fitzwilliam said. "In fact, the Sennex family is so honor-driven that it might bring the viscount some small comfort to know his son died in a contest of honor."

"Small indeed," said Sir Thomas. "He has lost his only heir."

Darcy glanced at Colonel Fitzwilliam. With Neville dead, a son born to his lordship and Anne would inherit the viscountcy. There would be no dissuading Lady Catherine from effecting the marriage now. And, now that he needed to produce another heir posthaste, the viscount himself would likely press as hard for a timely wedding—provided he even had the mental clarity to realize what was at stake.

Colonel Fitzwilliam did not meet Darcy's gaze, but rather, swept the grove with his own, frowning. "A proper duel involves a veritable entourage of participants—not only the primaries and seconds, but also the presiding officer, four officer seconds, and a surgeon—at a minimum."

Darcy quickly took his meaning. "It does not appear that ten or more men were tramping about here this morning. Much of the grass remains untrodden, and the shot patches seem to be lying where they fell." He recalled Elizabeth's words about whether a gentleman confronting a rival lover always adhered to form. He also remembered Neville's confrontation with Sir John Trauth in the card room at the Riveton ball. "Perhaps Neville Sennex felt it unnecessary to heed all the precepts of the Code Duello. He is quicker to talk about honor than to practice it."

Colonel Fitzwilliam nodded. "A duel between Mr. Sennex and Mr. Crawford might well have been of a more . . . informal nature."

"I wonder whether their unconventional duel began in an even more unorthodox manner," said Darcy. "If Henry Crawford can be believed, Mr. Lautus claimed to have been hired by someone to teach him a lesson about honor. Perhaps that 'someone' was Mr. Sennex."

"I deem it possible," Colonel Fitzwilliam said. "Inasmuch as I believe Mr. Sennex likely to have issued a challenge to Mr. Crawford, I believe him equally likely to have delegated the first attempt to mete out punishment. Neville was probably the least honorable Sennex to have been born into that family in generations; very good at spouting off about honor but poor in his own demonstration of it. I warrant he would have had no qualms about letting someone else perform the dangerous work of defending his honor from foes."

"And then when Mr. Lautus failed, he was forced to complete the business himself," Darcy said.

"It would be just like him to arrange a less-than-proper means of settling their contest, with as few witnesses as possible."

"There might not have been a crowd of observers here," said Darcy, "but there was at least one other person—the individual who took their pistols afterward."

"I dislike all these missing weapons," Sir Thomas declared. "We still have not located the matching pistol to the Mortimer found with Mr. Lautus. If Neville Sennex *did* hire Mr. Lautus, I wonder, then, whether he knew anything regarding the whereabouts of the missing Mortimer pistol, or perhaps used it himself this morning."

"That might prove easy enough to determine," Darcy said. He walked to one of the patches near Mr. Sennex. It was a golden silk circle with the same bird pattern and three rifling marks surrounding a black center circle.

"You would seem to have your answer." Darcy handed the patch to the magistrate. "This patch matches the two already in our possession. Somehow the missing pistol found its way into Mr. Sennex's hands after the encounter between Mr. Crawford and Mr. Lautus."

"Did Mr. Sennex retrieve it himself?" Sir Thomas asked.

"He had five days in which to do so before Mr. Lautus's body was discovered—plenty of time to travel from Buckinghamshire and back," Darcy said. "Though he would have had to know where to come. Was he ever a guest in your home before last night?"

"I am not certain. I had never met him before, but my son Tom frequently has friends to visit while I am traveling on business."

Another patch lay nearby. Darcy picked it up. Same fabric, same rifling marks.

Bigger black bull's-eye at the center.

Darcy asked Sir Thomas to hand back the patch he had just surrendered. He held it next to this new one. Not only the black powder circle, but the fabric itself, was of a larger diameter. "These two patches differ in size."

Colonel Fitzwilliam took them from him while Darcy reached into his pocket for the one he had brought from the previous shootings. "The larger center circle suggests that a larger ball was used," said the colonel.

Darcy unfolded the old patch and compared it to those just found. It matched the smaller of the two. "Unless the evidentiary pistol left your custody, Sir Thomas, the shot seated with the smaller of these new patches was fired from the missing Mortimer."

"It has not left my custody."

"Forgive me, but are you quite certain? Mr. Sennex was a guest in your home last night."

Sir Thomas's expression indicated that he did not appreciate the suggestion that he had failed to exercise proper stewardship over the pistol. "I am certain."

Colonel Fitzwilliam walked toward Mr. Crawford and retrieved the patch that lay about five feet in front of the corpse. "It is of the same silk," he said as he walked back, "in the larger size." All four patches shared the three black rifling lines.

"Were this a proper duel," Darcy said, "I would have expected Mr. Crawford to provide his own pistols, but it appears that all the shots were fired by weapons with similar rifling, and loaded by the same individual."

"Were this a proper duel, the weapons would not bear rifling at all," Colonel Fitzwilliam reminded them. "And it is consistent with what we know of Neville Sennex's character to believe he might have owned a pair of pistols with hidden rifling."

"Or two sets," Darcy said. "It would seem we are now also seeking at least one larger pistol."

"The size of the spent balls will be able to confirm that, assuming they can be found." Colonel Fitzwilliam approached Mr. Sennex's remains.

"Pray do not disturb him," said Sir Thomas. "Mr. Stover will want to see the bodies as we found them. He is rather particular."

Darcy would have liked very much to disturb Mr. Sennex just enough to close his eyelids and shield them all from his lifeless gaze. The expression of astonishment that yet dominated his countenance disturbed Darcy every time he accidentally glanced in his direction. Neville must not have expected Henry Crawford to prove so accurate a marksman.

Colonel Fitzwilliam, however, seemed entirely untroubled by the open eyes. Darcy imagined his cousin had seen the glassy stare of death often enough on the battlefield to have become oblivious to its unsettling effects.

Mr. Sennex had landed on his side, and Colonel Fitzwilliam circled round him. "I do not see a wound that would indicate the ball passed clear through him. We may be fortunate enough to find it lodged inside, as with Mr. Lautus. Mr. Crawford sprawls at a more difficult angle to judge, but we can be hopeful that he, too, exhibits no exit wound."

Mr. Stover himself arrived but minutes later. Upon being apprised of the latest developments, he promised to complete his examinations with all possible haste. While the coroner conducted his work, Darcy and the others had work of their own to perform.

Starting with visiting the viscount. They not only needed to advise him of Neville's death, but also to question him about whether his son had owned a pair of dueling pistols.

A rather dishonorable pair of dueling pistols.

Twenty-six

There is nothing like employment, active, indispensable employment, for relieving sorrow.

—Mansfield Park

"Pray forgive me." Elizabeth leaned across the table so that Anne could hear her lowered voice. "When I suggested breakfasting together in the dining room now that you are recovered, I forgot about the fact that Meg has become employed here."

Anne shook her head. "You need not apologize. I was bound to encounter her eventually."

Meg, who had been hovering near the kitchen door, came over and offered an awkward greeting. Anne returned it with all the decorum one could be expected to muster toward a woman with whom one shared a husband—that is to say, with equal awkwardness. Fortunately, no one else was in the room to observe the meeting.

Meg went to retrieve their tea. She returned with a pot and

two cups. As she set Anne's teacup before her, she offered Anne a self-conscious half-smile, then turned to go.

"Mrs. Garrick?" Anne said.

She paused. "I cannot bear to hear that name. Call me Meg."

"Meg, I—" Anne glanced at Elizabeth, who encouraged her to continue. "I want you to know—I had no idea. That he was married."

A short, mirthless laugh escaped Meg. "Apparently, neither did he." She shook her head. "We are in a fine mess, are we not? But I do not blame you for it, Mrs. Crawford."

"Do call me Anne, for I cannot bear *that* name."

Nat came into the room just then. As Elizabeth had not yet seen Lord Sennex that morning, she excused herself and went to speak with the boy.

"How are you this morning, Nat?"

"Very well, ma'am. I have been watching out for Lord Sennex as you asked."

"I am glad to hear it. The task has not interfered with your other duties, I hope?"

"Not greatly, though I can see why you want me to do it. He was about his business so long last night that I started to worry. But when I got closer to the privy, he was no longer within—I found him poking around the bushes to one side of it. Said he had lost something, but found it, and all was well. I think he dropped his cane and then accidentally kicked it under a bush, for he was stooping when I came upon him. I led him back to his room—tried to take him by the arm to help him a bit, but he wanted no part of that. A proud man, he is, even if his mind is not quite sharp."

"He is, indeed. Have you seen him yet this morning?"

"I have. He got past me somehow, for I didn't notice him leave the inn, but not long after sun-up I saw him come back inside.

He was moving slowly—the walk to the privy must have tired him, or maybe he forgot where it was and wandered about for a while before he found it. Why he does not simply use the chamber pot, I don't know. Maybe he forgets it's there."

Elizabeth did not care to speculate on the matter. Apparently, she had been well justified in her concern for the viscount's welfare.

By the time she finished with Nat, Meg was seated at the table with Anne, and the two were talking over tea as if they had known each other for years. Apparently, their mutual betrayal by Henry had united them. Meg had a gift for putting people at ease; Elizabeth could see why Henry had been drawn to her.

She decided to leave them to their conversation while she checked on Lord Sennex. Receiving no immediate response to her initial rap on the viscount's door, she knocked a second time. "Lord Sennex? It is Mrs. Darcy."

Her latter attempt elicited sounds of movement. "Just a moment," he called. She heard something small fall to the floor, followed by muttering. A minute later he opened the door.

"What can I do for you, Mrs. Darcy?"

"I came to make that very enquiry of your lordship. With your son gone, I wanted to ensure that you were properly attended. Do you require anything this morning?"

He stared at her, uncomprehending, for a moment.

"My lord?"

"What? Oh! I—no, I do not believe I need anything. Kind of you to enquire, however. You must have been a very dutiful daughter to your father."

"I like to believe so. I thought I heard something fall. Is all well?"

"Oh, indeed. I only dropped something. It was a—now, what was it?" He turned to look back into his chamber. "Yes—oh, yes."

He opened the door wider so that she could see into the room. Unlike her chamber, his had a small table, and upon it was a chess set. "I was just setting up the game, moving everything into position. I knocked down a black knight unexpectedly, but all is fine now."

"Your lordship brings a chess set along when traveling?"

"Very often. It provides occupation. I had this one designed for travel. The board folds into a case, you see." He gestured her inside. "Would you care to have a look?"

She followed him to the table. It was a lovely set, each piece carved in intricate detail. The knights appeared ready to charge, the pawns to march, the kings to command. The castles hosted small rooks roosting at the top of each tower.

"It is a fine set," she said. "With whom do you play? Your son?"

"No. Neville—" He cleared his throat. "Neville never showed much interest in the game. I play—well, never mind. You indulge me by enquiring, but the amusements of an old man cannot be of interest to a young person."

She pitied the viscount. A sadness seemed to envelop him. How lonely he must often be, with an impatient, self-absorbed son and scarcely anyone else to pay attention to him. "They are of great interest to me. Do go on."

"I play against myself, mostly. White Sennex versus Black." He lifted the white king, his hand betraying a slight tremor. "It has been years since I faced a truly worthy opponent."

"Mr. Darcy plays chess. Perhaps he may provide your lordship a challenge."

"Perhaps." He replaced the piece and steered her toward the door. "I thank you for enquiring after me, Mrs. Darcy, but as you can see, I am fine." He yawned. "Though perhaps less lively than I was at your age. I believe I will have a bit of a nap."

She returned to the dining room to discover Anne's company

considerably expanded. Darcy, Colonel Fitzwilliam, and Sir Thomas had joined her and Meg. All bore grave expressions. The colonel sat in a chair beside Anne, talking to both women in a low voice, while the other two gentlemen stood nearby. Upon sighting Elizabeth, Darcy came to her.

"You have unfortunate news, I take it?" Elizabeth asked.

"Mr. Crawford is dead."

"For certain this time?"

"Yes. And so is Neville Sennex."

"Oh, my." Her thoughts immediately went to the frail old man she had just left upstairs. "This will be a terrible blow to the viscount."

Lord Sennex swayed, his cane proving insufficient to steady him. Darcy and Colonel Fitzwilliam helped him to a chair.

"Oh!" The viscount's hands quivered. He gripped his knees as if trying to still the tremors. "Oh . . ."

"My lord—"

He closed his eyes and slowly moved his head from side to side. "Oh, Neville . . ."

"The coroner believes he died quickly," said Colonel Fitzwilliam. "And honorably. It appears he dueled with Mr. Henry Crawford."

"Mr. Crawford? I thought Mr. Crawford was dead?"

"He is now," said Sir Thomas.

A chessboard sat on the small table beside the viscount, and he took up one of the pieces. He turned the black knight over in his hands, at last setting it down to one side of the set. "At least Neville settled that business properly."

As Sir Thomas spoke with Lord Sennex, Darcy surreptitiously scanned the viscount's room. In the far corner stood a wardrobe, one door slightly ajar. Within, Darcy could see two hanging frock coats and a large mahogany case inlaid with a gold chess castle. His lordship's trunk rested in another corner of the chamber, its lid closed. Against its side rested a valise.

The viscount tried to stand. "I must make arrangements to have him transported back to Buckinghamshire."

"The coroner is still examining him," said Sir Thomas. "In the meantime, I have a few questions for your lordship about the pistols he might have used."

"My son is dead. What does it matter which pistols he used?"

Sir Thomas produced the small pistol they had found with Mr. Lautus. "Have you seen this before?"

"I—I have never seen that pistol in Neville's possession." He glanced from one man to the next. "Must we do this now? My son will be just as dead tomorrow."

"My lord—"

The viscount stood, leaning on his cane. "I am not familiar with every belonging of my son's." His voice trembled, and he rocked slightly.

Sir Thomas caught his elbow. "Perhaps this might be easier if you sat back down."

"I do not want to sit down!"

"My lord, I do not mean to further distress you," said Sir Thomas. "Please understand that I am merely discharging my duty as an agent of the Crown to ensure justice is served in the matter of your son's death. And that of Mr. Crawford."

"I do not give a damn about Mr. Crawford." He raised his right arm and shook a finger at Sir Thomas. Actually, his arm might have shaken of its own accord—the viscount grew more agitated with each passing minute. "As for my son, if he died defending his honor, then I am satisfied that justice was served."

"My lord—"

"Cease *my lord*-ing me! If you wish to show respect, end this interview altogether and leave me in peace."

Darcy interceded. "If you will but allow us a couple questions more, we shall not have to disturb you further."

The viscount sighed heavily. "What are your questions?" He sounded exhausted, and somehow looked smaller and more frail than he had when they arrived.

"There was a guest registered here by the name of Mr. Lautus," Darcy said. "Do you know him?"

"Should I know him?" He turned to the colonel, his expression all confusion. "Colonel Fitzwilliam, is Mr. Lautus one of our neighbors? Pray, help me remember. His name is not familiar to me, but I—from time to time I forget things . . ."

"No, my lord. He is not one of our neighbors. But he did occupy this room before you arrived. Did you by chance find anything he might have left behind?"

"The only items in this chamber are my own possessions."

Darcy could listen to the interrogation no longer. The viscount was obviously overwhelmed; to prolong the questioning was to torture an old man who had not been given even a minute in which to grieve for his son. "Perhaps, Sir Thomas, we can continue this later?"

"We are done."

Sir Thomas apologized to the viscount for the necessity of having to so question him. Lord Sennex merely nodded and sank into his chair once more.

As they left, he swept the pieces off the chessboard with a single motion. And put his head in his hands.

Twenty-seven

The scheme advanced. Opposition was vain.

—Mansfield Park

"When a man dies, it seems that someone ought to mourn him," Elizabeth said as they retired to their room that evening.

It had been a long day, and Darcy anticipated the next several would prove still longer. "To which man do you refer?"

She did not immediately answer. "All three of them, I suppose," she finally said. "Mr. Crawford's actual demise has inspired far more gossip than grief—I expect because anyone inclined to regret his passing got an early start when he died the first time. Though Neville Sennex's death has deeply saddened his lordship, Lady Catherine is jubilant, for it has opened the way for Anne to give birth to a future viscount. Mr. Lautus, nobody here knew, although perhaps there might be someone in Birmingham who will miss him."

"Sir Thomas travels there tomorrow to determine that. He hopes to learn who might have hired him to kill Mr. Crawford."

She sat down on the bed. "Perhaps Sir Thomas will also learn more about the pistol found with him."

Darcy hesitated. "That, it seems, has fallen to me."

"Oh?"

"The coroner's examination confirms that Henry Crawford was shot either with the same pistol that killed Mr. Lautus, or a matching one. Mr. Stover compared the bullets found in both bodies, borrowing Mr. Dawson's apothecary scales to weigh them, and marks on the gun patches indicate the same distinctive rifling of the barrels for both shots. Meanwhile, the bullet found in Neville Sennex was larger, as were the other two patches found this morning, indicating that his killing shot came from a bigger pistol. Yet the patches from those shots share the same fabric and rifling as those from the smaller pistols. Somehow, the pistols are related, and we need to determine the connection."

"How will you do so?"

"I am bringing the one pistol in our possession to the gunmaker himself. The gun's furniture—its engravings and so forth—is distinctive, and Mr. Mortimer will have records. He should be able to tell me for whom it was made, and whether others were produced for the same purchaser." He retrieved the portmanteau he had used on his journey to Scotland and opened it on the bed beside her.

"Why does Sir Thomas not undertake the errand himself?"

"He has contacts in Birmingham that will make that aspect of the investigation easier for him to complete than if someone else attempted it, and he does not want to delay pursuing one lead for another. So he has asked me to go to London bearing a request with his official seal as magistrate, which should be sufficient to obtain Mr. Mortimer's full cooperation."

Her expression was wistful as she watched him pack a few essentials. "Do you expect to be long in London?"

"I shall depart at first light. I hope one or two days will prove sufficient to obtain the information we need, plus a day's travel there and another back. Mortimer produces a high volume of arms, however, so if the pistol is not a recent purchase it might take some time to locate it in his records."

She removed one of his shirts and refolded it. "I would offer to accompany you, but I do not want to leave Anne. Lady Catherine is now pressing her harder than ever to marry Lord Sennex with all possible haste, and since Colonel Fitzwilliam made his offer your aunt looks upon him almost as an adversary. She thwarts any opportunity for private conversation between your cousins. I have hopes that Anne may yet muster the courage to stand up to her mother, but in any event, she needs the support of a friend." She returned the shirt to the travel bag, her hand lingering upon it.

He wished she *could* accompany him. He had grown weary some time ago of this inn and its company, and wanted nothing more than to steal away with his wife to someplace—anyplace—far removed from the murders and machinations with which they had been surrounded. He most desired to go home to Pemberley, but barring that, London would do. However, as much as duty called him forth, it required her to stay.

"It is just as well," he said sportively. "You would only slow me down."

"Oh?"

"Indeed. Journeys always take twice as long when you accompany me."

"I see." She returned his lighthearted tone. "And are there no advantages to my companionship?"

"There are definite advantages." He lifted her hand and kissed it. "That is why they take twice as long."

Elizabeth shifted in her chair and stole what she hoped was a discreet glimpse at the case clock in the parlor. Noon—a mere six minutes since her last covert glance. Her suspicions were confirmed.

She would die at this card table.

Against her better instincts, she had consented to participate in a game of quadrille with Anne, Lady Catherine, and Lord Sennex. Her ladyship had proposed it as a means of diverting the viscount. Ostensibly, they were distracting him from his heartache over the loss of Neville; in reality, Lady Catherine sought to distract him from what remained of his judgment.

Before the game was over, Anne and Lord Sennex would have all but exchanged vows. Lady Catherine's campaign for the marriage to occur by special license had already met with success; she now forged ahead to secure a date. Her blatant manipulation of a man weakened by age and debilitated by grief made Elizabeth recoil. It also so distracted her from game play that she was in danger of losing enough pin money to purchase three muff pistols.

"As the special license enables us to hold the wedding at any convenient location, you could wed at Hawthorn Manor. We need not even return to Rosings after Mr. Sennex's funeral; the marriage could take place shortly thereafter."

"An efficient proposal," the viscount said. "The guests could come for one event and stay for the other. We could even serve the leftover funeral meats at the wedding breakfast."

Elizabeth studied him instead of her cards, trying to determine whether he had offered the outrageous suggestion out of sarcasm or senility.

"Now, what is trump?" he asked.

"Hearts, my lord," Lady Catherine said. "You named them."

"I took the bid? Oh, yes—I suppose I did."

Senility.

He selected a card from his hand and captured the trick, his third straight. Somehow, despite the dual impairment of his mental state and Lady Catherine's conversation, he was managing to retain the lead.

"I did not mean to propose that the wedding should follow quite that hard upon," Lady Catherine said.

"No, no—it is a capital idea. I am glad you suggested it."

"Surely no one in Society would look askance at someone of your lordship's years assuaging his sorrow with a bride. Perhaps it will not be long before you have a new heir to cheer you."

Anne colored and occupied herself in rearranging her cards.

The viscount selected another lead from his hand. "Kindly remind me, Lady Catherine, when is Neville's funeral?"

"Three days' time." Lady Catherine frowned as he captured another trick. "Mr. Sennex's body is being transported to Buckinghamshire tomorrow morning. Your lordship planned to accompany it, with the rest of us making the journey the following day."

"Ah, yes." Lord Sennex became lost in thought so long that Elizabeth began to wonder whether he would ever return. At last, he played a card. "It will be a lonely journey home, I am afraid." He turned to Anne. "I wonder whether you would consent to ride with me."

"She would be delighted," Lady Catherine declared.

Anne, her felicity apparently too great for expression, merely nodded her assent.

"Excellent. And would you, Mrs. Darcy, accompany us? After all, we must maintain decorum."

Elizabeth agreed, far more for Anne's sake than for the sake of propriety. She looked at Anne, willing her to assert herself. But Anne offered no objection to the travel arrangements or the marriage, only a low card already defeated by her mother's and the viscount's plays.

Lady Catherine was so satisfied with herself that she did not even scowl when the viscount captured his sixth trick, and the pool.

Twenty-eight

"It raises my spleen more than any thing, to have the pretence of being asked, of being given a choice, and at the same time addressed in such a way as to oblige one to do the very thing—whatever it be!"

—*Tom Bertram,* Mansfield Park

Anne walked slowly but confidently round the common with Elizabeth, her recovery all but complete. The two of them had sought a few minutes' exercise before the journey to Buckinghamshire. The coach with Neville's remains had already departed; his lordship's carriage was presently being prepared and would depart soon.

Uncertain when to anticipate her husband's return, Elizabeth had sent word to him at their London townhouse, and also left a note for him with Mr. Gower, explaining her removal to Buckinghamshire. She hoped it would not be long before he could meet her there. Or better still, before they could go home altogether. She missed Lily-Anne exceedingly. She was glad, however, that her child was safe at Pemberley, and not with her in Mansfield amid death and mayhem. She prayed Darcy had met with success on his errand so that the investigation he felt honor-bound to assist could come to a close.

Elizabeth had thought that getting Anne out of the inn for a while would do her good, and the prescription appeared to be having the desired effect. Not only was the exercise strengthening her body, but the distance from Lady Catherine was strengthening her spirit. Elizabeth regretted that they must now turn their steps back toward the inn.

"I expect the viscount is anxious to reach Hawthorn Manor." Anne's voice held little enthusiasm.

"You seem not quite eager to go there yourself."

"An alliance with a feebleminded, elderly man is hardly the marriage most women dream about," she said. "But then, neither is discovering that one's dashing young husband is married to someone else."

"You do not have to marry Lord Sennex, you know."

An unseasonably cool breeze marshaled the air, an early reminder of the coming autumn. Anne shivered and crossed her arms. "I signed the betrothal agreement last night. I could not defy my mother a second time, and I have no superior prospects on the horizon."

"Do not you?"

Anne looked at her sharply. "I am doubtful as to your meaning."

"I am doubtful of it myself. But I did notice how your gaze followed a certain mutual acquaintance of ours when he left for Mansfield Park this morning to learn whether Sir Thomas had returned from Birmingham."

She hesitated. "Nothing more than friendship shall ever come from that quarter."

Apparently, Anne was unaware of the offer Colonel Fitzwilliam had made. "And if it did?"

A soft smile, meant only for herself, played upon her lips for the shortest of moments before fading. "It is impossible."

"It is impossible only if you wed someone else." Elizabeth stopped walking and faced her. "Do not make a decision about marriage to Lord Sennex based on what Colonel Fitzwilliam might feel, or what your mother wants, or what Society will say. Just know that, should you decide that you cannot honor your betrothal to the viscount while also honoring your responsibility to yourself and your own happiness, you will not find yourself friendless. In fact, I will stand directly beside you if you wish."

Anne broke off eye contact and looked at the ground some distance away. "May I ask you something terribly . . . delicate?"

"Yes."

"How did you know you were with child?"

Elizabeth studied her. A flush started at Anne's neck and crept up to her cheeks. "Is this why you feel unable to resist the marriage to Lord Sennex?"

Anne raised her eyes and nodded.

Elizabeth responded frankly, and asked Anne some equally frank questions in return. She wished Mrs. Godwin, her midwife, were in Mansfield to consult, but she was able to offer Anne some reassurance: Though only time would reveal her state with certainty, none of what Anne told her corresponded to her own experience.

They had nearly reached the inn, and Anne looked toward the waiting carriage. The viscount, his cane in one hand, his chess case in the other, wandered about the courtyard. The once-proud figure was nearly swallowed by the loose folds of his greatcoat. He created an almost endearing image—but endearing in a grandfatherly, not matrimonial, way.

Anne turned to Elizabeth. "Will you come stand by me now?"

Darcy returned to Number 89 Fleet Street precisely on time. Yesterday, the younger H. W. Mortimer had identified the pistol as having been made a score or more years ago, and asked for a day to review his father's older records. Darcy hoped the gunsmith had found what he sought. He was anxious to finish his errand and commence his journey north. He was also anxious to regain possession of the pistol, which he had felt uneasy leaving behind. If there were anybody in London, however, with whom he was comfortable leaving the weapon, it was the family of artisans who had crafted it.

Mr. Mortimer greeted him warmly. "I found the record. Though I was but a boy when my father made this set, I thought I remembered it, for it was an unusual one, but I wanted to be certain." He showed Darcy the description. "My father made this pistol thirty years ago as part of a quad set of duelers—two primary pistols, and two second-sized pistols, all in a single case. This pistol is one of the smaller; the larger guns have eight-inch barrels. All four bear the rifling you enquired about, and all four have a rook image engraved into their locks, hammers, and escutcheons. The description also notes a rook on the case lid."

"On the case lid?" Darcy repeated.

"Indeed—there is a small illustration." The renowned gunsmith showed the record to Darcy, then pointed to the name of the purchaser. But he need not have bothered.

Darcy already knew.

"Lord Sennex?"

The viscount broke off from his reverie and offered them a gentle smile. "Mrs. Crawford! Mrs. Darcy! Are you ready to depart?"

"I hoped we might have a word with you first," Anne said. "A private word?"

"Of course." He drew his brows together. "But will we not have ample opportunity for conversation in the carriage?"

"I beg your indulgence. Shall we step over here?"

They moved to an area on one side of the inn where a tall hedge shielded them from the view of employees and passers-by. Elizabeth offered to carry the chess set for him, so that he might better handle his cane, but he politely declined.

"Now, what have you to say, my dear lady?"

Anne glanced at Elizabeth and took a deep breath. "I am afraid, my lord, that I cannot marry you."

Lord Sennex blinked. "I do not understand."

"I cannot marry you. I believe that a marriage between us, particularly one entered into in such a hasty manner, can only lead to unhappiness. I beg your forgiveness . . ."

"But—" He looked like a confused child. "We have an agreement. I saw you sign it yester eve—I am certain I did."

"I did, my lord. And, again, I am deeply sorry. But I must break our engagement."

Lord Sennex stared at her in befuddlement. "I must have misheard you."

"No, my lord—"

"Yes, yes—that must be the case. For I have something, you see, something certain to change your mind—" He allowed his cane to fall to the ground so that he could reach into an inner fold of his greatcoat. "Ah, yes—here it is." He withdrew his hand.

It held a pistol, which he cocked and aimed at Anne.

"Now, my dear . . . would you care to reconsider?"

Twenty-nine

"A man in distressed circumstances has not time for all those elegant decorums which other people may observe."

—*Elizabeth*, Pride and Prejudice

Darcy did not notice the approaching sunset as he rode into Mansfield. His mind was too preoccupied with the need to lay eyes on Elizabeth. Once he ascertained her whereabouts and safety, he would go to Mansfield Park to tell Sir Thomas that Lord Sennex was their man.

A gnawing fear had seized him the entire distance from London to Buckinghamshire. He had received her note, informing him of her travel plans, just before leaving town, and had prayed that the viscount's murderous inclinations did not include ladies.

When he had arrived at Hawthorn Manor and been told that the viscount's carriage had never appeared as expected, and when a stop at Riveton had also yielded no Elizabeth or Anne, the fear turned to dread. All the way to Mansfield village, he hoped that their travel plans had merely been delayed, that he would walk into the Ox and Bull to find Elizabeth and Anne at supper in the dining room. Instead, he discovered only Colonel Fitzwilliam.

"Please tell me that Elizabeth and Anne are still here."

Colonel Fitzwilliam regarded Darcy with a mixture of surprise and alarm. "They are not—they went to Buckinghamshire this morning. Why do you appear here in such a state of apprehension?"

"I have just come from Hawthorn Manor. The viscount and his carriage never arrived. I rode straight there from London—after Mr. Mortimer told me that Lord Sennex owns a quad set of dueling pistols with rook engravings and French rifling."

Colonel Fitzwilliam leapt to his feet. "They departed some ten hours ago. He could have taken them anywhere."

Elizabeth studied Lord Sennex as the carriage jostled its way north, still stunned that she had so utterly underestimated the crafty old man. Upon drawing his pistol, he had rapidly proved himself in full possession of his faculties.

"Perhaps, Mrs. Crawford, you simply prefer your weddings over the anvil?" he had said. "Very well. Anything to accommodate my bride."

Walking easily without the discarded cane, he had commanded the two shocked ladies into his carriage under threat of harm if they called attention to themselves. His manservant, a tall, dark, wiry fellow, waited within, his forbidding countenance an effective mute to any impulse they might have felt to cry out.

Once outside the village proper, he had informed the postilion of their new destination. Then he had handed his pistol to his servant and opened the chess case—or what Elizabeth had presumed to be the case for his chess set. It instead was a large gun case with molded compartments for four pistols—two large and two small—and various items Elizabeth took for loading equipment and other accessories. The two small pistol compartments were empty. One of those pistols was now in the servant's hand.

The other was in Darcy's—so far distant that he might as well be in Antigua.

Lord Sennex removed one of the larger pistols. Noting Elizabeth's observation, he spoke. "Yes, it is loaded, if you are wondering. They all are—Mr. Lautus might have been an incompetent fool, but it was good of him to leave my second set of loading materials behind in his room at the inn. Else I would have had no bullets for the smaller pistol, and it is such a convenient size for carrying on one's person."

Elizabeth found his refined manner more menacing than would have been open threats.

"I suppose I should be equally grateful to that odious Mrs. Norris for discarding the pistol while I happened to be nearby," he continued, "though how she came by it after Lautus managed to get himself killed, I still have not determined."

He closed the case and set it on the seat between him and the servant. "It is a long journey to Scotland, so we might as well all be acquainted." He gestured toward the servant. "This is Antonio. He will help me keep an eye on you. Antonio, this is Mrs. Darcy and my fiancée, Mrs. Crawford. Or, I suppose I should call you Miss de Bourgh, should I not, since your marriage to Mr. Crawford was of questionable status?"

"I did not realize your lordship was aware of that fact. I thought my mother managed to keep the particulars from you."

"One has only to listen to the right conversations to learn all manner of interesting information. And nobody pays attention to senile old men."

"Is that why you perpetrated the charade?" Elizabeth asked. "To spy upon people?"

"Not at all, my dear lady. The pretense began for Neville's benefit. He did not, however, appreciate it." The viscount's expression hardened. "My son did not appreciate much."

Elizabeth could hear the barely restrained hostility beneath his words. "You appeared to be mourning him deeply these two days past."

"I have been mourning the man he could have been. Ought to have been." He regarded the pistol in his hand. "Neville was the greatest disappointment of my life. Dying was the most honorable thing he ever did."

Elizabeth had not been particularly impressed by Mr. Sennex, but the depth of the viscount's acrimony surprised her. "That is a harsh thing to say about your only son."

"He was not my son."

Darcy and Colonel Fitzwilliam questioned everyone, searched everywhere. Those who had witnessed Elizabeth and Anne depart saw only that they had climbed into the carriage willingly. Lady Catherine had been vexed that Anne went without taking proper leave of her mother, but had attributed the neglect to pique over her engagement to the viscount. The note Elizabeth had left for Darcy offered no clues.

Darcy's heart pressed against his rib cage as he and Colonel Fitzwilliam entered the viscount's chamber. He had begun to doubt their finding any indication of where Lord Sennex might have taken Elizabeth and Anne.

"What chafes my conscience the most is that I *saw* the deuced pistol case," Darcy said. "Right there, in the wardrobe, while we questioned him. I saw the rook—the chessman—on its lid and took it for a game case."

"Why would you have thought anything else? Quad sets are so rare that we certainly were not seeking a gun case of that size—perhaps two smaller ones, if anything—and he had a chessboard set up on this table. I am certain the double entendre of the 'rook' was intentional. The viscount has always preferred the challenge of intellectual games to the sports his son favored." He frowned and ran his hand over the table upon which the chessboard had rested. Fine black particles clung to his fingers.

"Priming powder. He loaded the pistols in here."

At Elizabeth's startled reaction, Lord Sennex clarified. "Do not mistake my meaning—Neville was of my blood. I do not cast aspersions upon my late wife. But he had no understanding of the legacy he inherited along with his name, and the responsibility that comes along with it. He did not take care to protect his reputation or our fortune. He squandered both through gaming and intemperate living, and never considered the consequences. Nor did he develop a gentleman's control over his temper.

"For years I followed behind him, tidying his messes as best I could, trying to salvage our family's dignity and prevent him from spending us into bankruptcy or humiliating us out of good society. But my efforts had the opposite effect—he came to take me for granted along with everything else, and assumed that whatever scrape he got himself into, his father the viscount would repair the damage. I wondered if by my own actions I had inadvertently encouraged his irresponsibility.

"And so my ruse began. I pretended to fail, both in mind and body, in hopes that my perceived decline would bring about greater consciousness of duty on his part. But it only worsened his conduct. In his mind, my frailty removed me as an obstacle to his selfish pursuits. Any words I spoke about honoring one's birthright he dismissed as the ramblings of an old man."

"And this is the man I would have wed?" Anne said. "He sounds no better than Mr. Crawford. I cannot believe my mother initiated the match."

The viscount chuckled, a hollow sound, devoid of mirth. "Your mother only thinks she initiated the match. By the time she arrived at Riveton, anxious to preserve her daughter from spinsterhood, Neville had depleted our estate. We needed a rapid infusion of funds, and marriage to an heiress was the ideal solution. When she began calling upon every family in the neighborhood with an unattached son, I was ready. She thought she was taking advantage of my weakness, but without even realizing it, she advanced my scheme. We both would have emerged from the church doors satisfied, were it not for Mr. Crawford's interference."

The venom in his voice as he pronounced the name "Crawford" was potent. He gripped his pistol so tightly that Elizabeth thought he would bruise his leg with the butt cap.

"Was it you who hired Mr. Lautus to kill Henry Crawford?" she asked.

The viscount emitted a derisive noise. "Certainly not. Hired assassins are for cravens. Mr. Crawford's elopement with Neville's betrothed insulted my son's honor, and he was eager for revenge. Their dispute should have been settled in a gentlemanly manner—civilized, prearranged combat—a dignified contest such as the ones I fought in my own youth. I told Neville as much, and lent him these pistols, which had served me so well.

"But Neville was lazy and cowardly, and did not want to face Mr. Crawford himself. Without my knowledge, he hired Mr.

Lautus—where he found such a character, I do not know. He instructed the buffoon to stage a duel of sorts, and equipped him with two of my pistols. My pistols! The very weapons I had used to defend our family honor in years past were given to a stranger to make a mockery of a sacred gentlemen's rite.

"When I learned the truth, I was furious. My senile ruse prevented me from giving full vent to my anger, but my son had disappointed me. In a way that could not be forgiven."

Having nowhere else to seek hints of the viscount's destination, Darcy and Colonel Fitzwilliam searched the courtyard and perimeter of the inn. The ostler had said he saw Lord Sennex and the two ladies approach the carriage from one side, near a large hedge. A look about produced the viscount's cane lying forgotten on the ground.

Darcy examined it closely. It was an ordinary cane—no blades on the end or hidden compartments at the top. What was extraordinary about it was that they should find it at all.

"I do not believe I have seen the viscount walk without aid these several years, at least," Colonel Fitzwilliam said. "I wonder how he is getting around without it."

"Quite well, if I might say so," declared a young voice on the other side of the hedge. Nat Gower came around. "I saw him walk with the ladies from here to the carriage, and he appeared to have no trouble."

"Did you see him drop the cane?" Darcy asked.

"No, sir. I was on the other side of the hedge. Mrs. Darcy had asked me to keep a lookout for the viscount so he wouldn't wander off, so whenever he went outside I stuck close but stayed where he wouldn't notice me."

Faint hope began to flicker inside Darcy. Perhaps this boy had observed something no one else had. "Did you hear anything he said to Mrs. Darcy or Mrs. Crawford?"

"I didn't follow Lord Sennex when he first came over here with the ladies—I figured if Mrs. Darcy was with him, all was well, and I didn't want to eavesdrop. But they were out of my sight for a while, and I got to worrying that maybe they had parted and the viscount had wandered off some other way. So I came closer. Didn't hear much—the viscount said something about weddings and anvils and accommodating his bride—and then they started walking so I ducked out of sight."

Darcy gave the boy a shilling. "If you remember anything else, come tell me."

"I will, sir!"

As the boy ran off, Darcy looked at Colonel Fitzwilliam. His cousin read his thoughts.

"Weddings and anvils," the colonel said. "Do you think they are bound for Scotland?"

"It is a long journey. If we are wrong, we lose days chasing false hope." Darcy did not want to contemplate how much worse the situation would be if they raced all the way to Gretna Green only to discover they had erred. "We cannot even be certain they head for Gretna—the viscount could take them to any Scottish village."

"We could divide. One of us could stay here."

"And do what?"

"Feel impotent and torment himself over what might be occurring two hundred fifty miles away."

His cousin's response elicited a grim half-smile from Darcy. It was in neither of their natures to remain idle while others acted. "The viscount has a case full of pistols. I think we should both go. And given their advance start, we cannot afford another moment's delay."

Darcy did not know what they would find, or what would unfold, when they reached their destination. But based on previous experience, of one thing he was convinced.

Nothing good came of elopements to Scotland.

"I have reached a decision," Anne announced as she and Elizabeth reentered the carriage after another all-too-brief stop. She spoke in a low voice so as not to be overheard by Antonio, who followed behind, his pistol ever-present but concealed from spectators. "If we survive this, I shall happily spend the rest of my life as a spinster."

They would survive this. In that, Elizabeth was determined. "No more elopements? I cannot imagine why. This one has been so agreeable that I begin to regret my own mundane nuptials at Longbourn."

This had been the most grueling journey of Elizabeth's life. Anxious to reach Scotland before any pursuers caught up with them, and equally anxious lest an opportunity present itself for his abductees to escape, the viscount had traveled through the night and all the next day with only the most abbreviated of stops to change horses. They were even denied meals at the posting inns; to prevent any conversation with employees or other guests, the viscount bought only portable food such as bread and cheese that could be consumed in the carriage. After more than four-and-twenty hours of cramped seating and ceaseless jostling, every muscle of Elizabeth's body ached.

Yet other than the hardship of prolonged, involuntary travel, the viscount's treatment of them in general had been fair. He demonstrated the respect due them as ladies, expected his servant to do the same, and himself behaved as a gentleman. He yet considered himself a man of honor; indeed, a great deal of his conversation seemed to derive from a desire to defend his conduct as honorable and prove himself to be yet upholding the tenets by which he had lived his life. That men of honor did not generally kidnap ladies at gunpoint and subject them to an arduous journey with the end purpose of a forced marriage did not seem to trouble him.

The paradox intrigued Elizabeth.

Though more lucid than he had appeared during the period of his deception, the viscount had definitely lost some of his ability to reason. He might not be senile, but he was not altogether sane. And so as they rode, she kept him talking as much as she could—in part to learn more about the events that had been transpiring around them, in part to tire him, and in part to better understand how his mind worked.

Once more on the road, it was an easy matter to bring Lord Sennex back to his tale. She had only to enquire about the viscount's cherished pistols. "After Mr. Lautus failed in his commission, how did you retrieve the weapons Mr. Sennex had given him?"

"One is in the custody of Sir Thomas; Neville was to have recovered it while staying at Mansfield Park. My useless son, however, could not even succeed at that, and so it remains in Sir Thomas's possession. I did not know what had become of the other, until entirely by chance I happened upon that loathsome Mrs. Norris prowling around the inn's privy. It was occupied, and she waited outside. I startled her and she dropped the pistol. I pretended not to notice her kick it under the bushes—a facile deception, when one is already thought to be addled. As she then left without using the privy, I can only presume she planned to discard the pistol down it. A *Mortimer* pistol! One of the finest he ever made! And she would have dropped it into a hole of—" He emitted a sound of utter disgust. "Stupid, reprehensible woman! I wanted to shoot *her* with it.

"But I had more important matters at Mansfield. By then,

Henry Crawford had returned, providing an opportunity for Neville to finally satisfy his honor. This time, I was present to ensure everything proceeded properly. Because of the previous mishandled duel, secrecy was even more critical, and so participants were minimal. No seconds, no surgeon—only the two primaries and myself, the presiding officer."

"How did you persuade Mr. Sennex to involve himself directly this time?" Elizabeth asked.

"Upon my instructions, Antonio led Neville to the grove, where he impatiently awaited my arrival, not knowing why he had been summoned. Mr. Crawford required more persuasion. The muzzle of my pistol, however, proved sufficient motivation for him to leave the inn with me and return to the grove.

"When we arrived and I announced what we were gathered there to do, Neville at first dismissed the duel as the scheme of a senile old man. I could see, however, that he indeed wanted satisfaction from Mr. Crawford—he was simply too cowardly to jeopardize his own person to achieve it. But when Mr. Crawford continued to maintain that he was someone named John Garrick and that he had no knowledge of any offense against Neville, his denials so enraged Neville that at last my son was spurred to defend his honor as a gentleman ought.

"Mr. Crawford had no weapon of his own, so I armed him with one of mine—the match to the one I handed to Neville. I retained the small pistol for myself. They stood at a measured distance and were to fire at my word of command.

"As I was about to voice the order, Neville fired. His shot flew so wide that I know not what shamed me more—his premature fire or his pathetic aim. I stared at him, unable to believe my own son capable of such dishonorable conduct.

"But the worst was yet to come. He regarded Mr. Crawford, still holding his cocked pistol, and fear entered Neville's eyes. My son was so lily-livered that he backed away, looking as if he might run. His cravenness disgusted me. I ordered him to stand his ground and take Mr. Crawford's fire like a man.

"The sudden realization that I was in full possession of my faculties stunned Neville into submission. Mr. Crawford, however, would not finish the proceedings. He yet claimed that he had no knowledge of the business that had brought us there. His lies to me were nearly as great an insult to my honor as had been his offense against Neville's. I issued the command to fire; he not only refused, he mocked the gravity of the trial, thereby insulting me further. I ordered him once more to fire or be fired upon. He laughed and ridiculed me. So I brought up my own pistol and silenced him.

"He died quickly—took his final breath just as I reached him to retrieve the pistol from his hand. Neville called over to me, asking whether Mr. Crawford were dead, and I nodded. 'Capital,' he said, bravado once more taking hold of him. 'I am glad to have this ridiculous affair ended.' Ridiculous, he called it—when minutes before, he could not stand steady for cowardice.

"I did not recognize him as my son any longer. He, who had dissipated our family fortune, whose conduct had blackened a name that had stood proud for generations, who held his honor so cheap he would not defend it. I wanted no part of him.

"I raised the undischarged pistol and fired."

Thirty

"We met by appointment, he to defend, I to punish his conduct."
—Colonel Brandon, Sense and Sensibility

The viscount's chaise, horses still harnessed, sat outside the same Gretna Green inn where Darcy and Colonel Fitzwilliam had found Anne after her first elopement. The viscount's post-boy attempted to stop them from entering, but backed off when he saw the colonel remove a pistol from one of his bucket holsters.

Darcy dismounted, never more grateful to have reached the end of a journey. They had ridden so hard and so long, stopping only when absolutely necessary to change horses or indulge in brief rests, that he was beyond exhausted. Colonel Fitzwilliam, whose military life better prepared him for tests of endurance, also showed signs of extreme fatigue.

"Is the viscount inside?" the colonel asked.

The post-boy took in Colonel Fitzwilliam's red coat, then the pistol, and nodded. Though the pistol was untrained and but half-cocked, his gaze stayed upon it.

"Does he have two ladies with him?" Darcy asked.

"He does, sir. Not sure which of them he was in such a hurry to get here with. Just arrived a few minutes ago."

Colonel Fitzwilliam removed his other pistol from its holster and handed it to Darcy. "I hope we are not too late."

They entered to hear the opening words of the wedding ceremony, interrupted by their sudden entrance. Darcy had no sooner laid eyes on Elizabeth and saw to his relief that she appeared unharmed than the viscount grabbed Anne and thrust the muzzle of a pistol under her chin.

"The wedding will continue."

The unanticipated movement startled Darcy but he quickly recovered. "No, my lord, it will not." He trained his own pistol on the viscount, as did Colonel Fitzwilliam.

From behind them came the sound of a hammer being cocked. A tall, dark-haired man in servant's livery held a pistol that looked very similar to the empty Mortimer gun Darcy still carried in the pocket of his greatcoat.

Lord Sennex addressed the astonished innkeeper-turned-parson. "Do continue with the nuptials."

"Surely your lordship would not harm a lady?" Darcy asked.

"Not if she cooperates."

"She does not appear inclined toward this marriage."

The viscount's expression shifted from civilized to sinister. "Then she should not have signed the betrothal agreement when her mother put it in front of her. I, on the other hand, am very inclined toward the marriage, for I need her fortune to restore the family honor my son worked so hard to tarnish."

"Lord Sennex, is it honorable to force a lady into marriage?" Darcy asked. "To threaten her life?"

"She signed the agreement herself. It is she who acts dishonorably by refusing to fulfill that obligation—after committing the same offense against my son by running off with Mr. Crawford."

Lord Sennex trembled. The journey which had worn Darcy out had utterly drained the older man, who was now so overwrought that he was in danger of accidentally discharging the weapon. "Is *anybody* governed by honor these days? Miss de Bourgh is not. My son was not. Mr. Crawford certainly was not. The world has become a place where disgraceful conduct is not only tolerated but encouraged." He shook his head forcefully. "No! Miss de Bourgh made a commitment to me, and she will see it through."

"Miss de Bourgh has the right to break an engagement."

"Miss de Bourgh made a promise! Now she retracts, and you encourage her! No one understands honor anymore, let alone values it. No one stands up to defend it!"

"I will defend it," Colonel Fitzwilliam calmly declared.

"And just how, Colonel, do you intend to do that?"

"In abducting Miss de Bourgh, your lordship has committed a grave offense against my cousin, a lady under my protection." He lowered his weapon. "Let us resolve this as gentlemen."

Lord Sennex regarded the colonel with surprise. Followed by respect.

"I should have known a military man would yet understand." A smile of satisfaction twisted the corners of his mouth. "We passed a field along the road, just before entering the village, with enough surrounding trees to afford privacy. We can conduct our business there."

"Pistols or swords?"

The viscount cackled. "Does my preference not go without saying?"

"Very well, then. Pistols. At fifteen paces."

Fitzwilliam drew Darcy aside. His visage—nay, his entire carriage—held grim determination. This was not James Fitzwilliam, the cousin with whom Darcy had grown up, the dependent younger son who had been born into privilege without any responsibilities to justify it. This was Colonel Fitzwilliam, the commander who had entered battle unflinchingly to champion Crown and country. And now to champion Anne.

"Will you serve as my second?"

"You need not even ask," Darcy said. "Of course I shall. But you realize that my first order of business will be to attempt a peaceful reconciliation?"

"There is no other way to resolve this—he is half mad with desperation and rage, and talks of nothing but restoring the family honor. And even were his lordship to apologize, words are insufficient atonement for his crimes against Anne." He looked toward her. The viscount's hold on Anne had relaxed, but she nevertheless appeared frightened—now as much for Colonel Fitzwilliam as for herself. Remorse clouded his expression. "She has been surrounded by scoundrels trying to use her for their own gain—from the Sennexes to her own mother. I should have stepped forward to defend her long before now."

Darcy approached Lord Sennex. "Colonel Fitzwilliam has appointed me as his second. Who will serve as yours?" He glanced at the servant. That would not do.

"I shall act as my own."

"Your lordship cannot do that."

"I can and I will! I heard what the colonel said just now. I might be old, but I am not mad, and I am not incapable. I have felled more opponents than you have ever faced, including two this very week. No one here is qualified to serve as my second—no one shares my rank in society. So I shall take on that role myself."

"A second's role is chiefly to mediate arrangements with a

cooler head than the primary participants are likely to possess. Your lordship cannot possibly discharge that portion of the second's duty."

"I will act as my own second."

As there was no dissuading him on the matter, Darcy moved on to the next point of negotiation. "At what time do you want to meet?"

"Immediately."

"My lord, you know that is not advisable. We are all of us exhausted from traveling here, and the Code discourages hot-headed proceedings."

"The honor of the Sennex name has waited long enough to be restored. I want to resolve this business without further delay."

Apparently, there was no reasoning with the viscount on any particular. "I shall convey your wishes to Colonel Fitzwilliam. And the terms of firing?"

"Two shots each. And as the challenged party," he said loudly enough for the colonel to hear him, "I demand the first shot."

Alternate fire was an outmoded practice, replaced in current dueling protocol by simultaneous fire at signal or at pleasure. But it was the method the viscount had likely used in his younger days.

"You may have it," Colonel Fitzwilliam said.

Darcy strode back to his cousin and looked at him sharply. "By consenting to alternate fire, you might never have an opportunity to take your own shot."

"I know."

"Do you intend to let him use his own pistols? Recall that his weapons are rifled."

"I have not forgotten." His gaze was on the viscount, who was becoming increasingly agitated. "However, if we demand to inspect the barrels, he will consider that an insult to *his* honor, and *he* will then call *me* out, or you, or perhaps us both, and there will never be an end to this until all of us end up like Henry Crawford." He shook his head. "No—let him use his pistols, and take the first shot, and let us proceed directly to the field as he has asked. He is so distraught that perhaps his aim will be hindered, and we can end this affair with no one getting injured."

"No one? Do you intend to delope?"

"If his shot misses, I will. My purpose is justice for Anne, not the slaying of an old man."

The arrangements were settled. As there was no presiding officer, Darcy took on that role as well, insofar as asking the innkeeper to send the village surgeon, or quack, or whatever passed for a medical man there, to attend them at the field.

At long last he found an opportunity to embrace Elizabeth and determine with certainty that she was well. The strength of his hold expressed more than he had words to say. When he finally released her, the pistol in the pocket of his greatcoat swung forward, striking against her.

"Ouch," she said with surprise. "What is that?"

"The viscount's fourth pistol," he said in a voice low enough so that others would not hear. "I am still carrying it since going to London. It is of no use to me, as it is unloaded, but I am certainly not going to return it to him."

"He seems to have quite enough weaponry as it is."

They all proceeded to the field. The ladies and the viscount's servant stood to one side. They were soon joined by the village surgeon. As Edinburgh boasted a Royal College of Surgeons superior to London's, Darcy hoped for his cousin's sake that Gretna Green's medical man knew what he was about should the need for his services arise.

The gentlemen removed their greatcoats; Colonel Fitzwilliam and Lord Sennex also stripped down to their shirtsleeves to prove that neither wore any manner of concealed armor. Darcy handed his greatcoat to Elizabeth, pressed her hand, and went to dispatch his duties.

Before the duel could commence, the weapons needed to be loaded by the seconds in each other's presence to ensure they were charged smooth and single. Though Darcy and the colonel knew perfectly well that the viscount's bores were not smooth, protocol must nonetheless be followed. Colonel Fitzwilliam handed Darcy his pistol, along with two powder flasks, the powder measure, a pouch of balls, and a patch tin.

Under the supervision of Lord Sennex, Darcy took one of Colonel Fitzwilliam's military pistols and dumped the existing charge by firing it into the ground. He then removed the ramrod from the underside of the barrel, half-cocked the hammer, and poured black powder from the larger flask into the measure. Thirty grains would propel the ball with sufficient force at the agreed-upon firing range. He sent the powder down the barrel.

He next withdrew a lead ball from the pouch and opened the tin. Instead of the linen patches he expected to find, the tin held circles of silk. He regarded his cousin in question.

The colonel shrugged. "I visited Hardwick's shop while you were in London."

Darcy took one of the oiled patches and centered it on the end of the muzzle. He placed the ball over it, then rammed the load down the bore, firmly seating the patch and ball atop the powder. He secured the ramrod back onto the pistol.

One step remained.

From the other flask, he poured a small amount of fine priming powder into the pan. He then snapped the frizzen into place and presented the pistol to Lord Sennex for inspection.

The viscount took the weapon, looked into the bore, and returned it to Darcy.

"I am satisfied that the bore is smooth and the charge fairly loaded."

Darcy handed the pistol to Colonel Fitzwilliam, then emptied and reloaded his cousin's other pistol.

Lord Sennex next discharged and loaded his weapons, following the same process as had Darcy. When he presented the large pistols for inspection, Darcy looked into the bores. From this angle, the tops of the bores indeed appeared smooth, but he knew better. He met his cousin's gaze.

Colonel Fitzwilliam remained resolute. "We are satisfied," he said.

Once the viscount finished charging his two primary pistols, he reloaded the second-sized gun, though no one anticipated its use. Darcy watched him place the priming powder into the pan and close the frizzen.

With all the pistols charged, Colonel Fitzwilliam took the field with one while Darcy held the other in reserve to give to his cousin after the first round of fire. Lord Sennex retained one of his large pistols, placing the other and the smaller pistol in the open case off to the side of the field, near the spectators.

The principals met in the center of the field, fully cocked their pistols, and pointed them skyward. At Darcy's word, they counted their paces.

Lord Sennex moved slowly, the ordeal of the past several days having taken an obvious toll. Though Colonel Fitzwilliam carried himself with military bearing, Darcy knew that he, too, was not at his best.

They turned and faced each other. Colonel Fitzwilliam stood steady as Lord Sennex lowered his weapon and took his shot.

It hit.

The ball struck Colonel Fitzwilliam's right arm, causing him to nearly drop his weapon. He gripped his elbow. Blood seeped past his fingers.

Thankfully, the viscount's aim was not as accurate as it had been when he had settled the duel between Mr. Crawford and Neville. Darcy moved toward his cousin, but the colonel motioned him away. He refused the surgeon's attention, as well.

After a minute or two, he recovered himself. Though his arm trembled, Colonel Fitzwilliam stood firm. He raised his weapon.

And fired into the air.

Lord Sennex released an outraged cry. "You insult me by deloping? Do you think that because I am old, I cannot submit to your fire like a man?"

Now that the colonel had fired, Darcy approached his cousin. His left hand was slick with blood. His shirtsleeve was ripped, the fabric stained crimson.

"The wound is not serious," Colonel Fitzwilliam said. "The ball passed straight through the flesh and did not hit bone. But my hand shakes so much that even had I not planned to delope, I would have been unable to hit him."

"Then that ends the business for today."

The viscount strode over to them. "Is the colonel injured or is he not?"

"He is injured enough that his hand shakes," Darcy said. "We will have to continue this on the morrow."

"Why?" he barked. "What difference makes impaired aim if he is only going to shoot into the air?"

"We all know the rules of the Code. A wound sufficient to make the hand shake postpones completion of the duel."

"The Code also forbids firing into the air. If Colonel Fitzwilliam is not courageous enough to kill me, he should not have issued the challenge."

"Deloping is common practice, despite that prohibition."

"If the colonel will not acknowledge that rule, I do not acknowledge the other. We will finish this today."

"Yes," said Colonel Fitzwilliam. "Let us."

Lord Sennex stormed off to exchange his used pistol for the loaded one. Colonel Fitzwilliam handed Darcy his discharged weapon. His hand trembled so badly that he could hardly raise it.

Darcy took the weapon from him, but did not give him the reserve pistol. "You cannot face him in this condition. If his shot does not hit you, your own might."

"The viscount insists on settling the matter this day."

"It *will* end today. I shall stand in for you."

"No," he said vehemently. "I am the one who issued the challenge."

"And I agreed to serve as your second knowing full well that I might be required to take your place."

Colonel Fitzwilliam looked over at Anne. Her face was pale, her expression grave. "This is my fight."

"You have fought it bravely and honorably. Now stand down."

After some minutes' further argument, the colonel finally agreed. Darcy deliberately avoided looking in Elizabeth's direction. Likely she was so displeased by this turn of events that if the viscount did not kill him, she might. Colonel Fitzwilliam remained on the field but out of firing range.

Darcy stripped to his shirtsleeves and met the viscount in the center of the field to count new paces. Lord Sennex nearly spat with rage. "Now the colonel will not face me at all? Very well. We shall see whether his second is more manly than he is."

Darcy cocked his pistol and counted his paces.

And turned to face the viscount's fire.

Thirty-one

"I could meet him in no other way."

—*Colonel Brandon,* Sense and Sensibility

Lord Sennex's shot missed.

Darcy heard the ball whistle past. Then he lowered his pistol, pointing it at the ground.

The viscount stared at him, at first uncomprehending. Then he exploded.

"You refuse to fire *at all*? What is the meaning of this? You call this a duel? This is a farce! I command you to fire!"

Darcy stood still. "My lord, I decline."

"I said fire, damn you!"

Darcy bowed to his lordship and started to leave the field.

"This is not to be countenanced! How *dare* you insult me in this manner? This is supposed to be a contest of *honor*!"

Darcy met Colonel Fitzwilliam and they continued walking together toward the others. The viscount walked faster. He rushed over to the open case, threw down his discharged gun, and grabbed the small pistol.

"Stop!"

Darcy halted. The viscount had the pistol aimed straight at Darcy's chest.

He had not foreseen this, and regretted that he had moved so near the spectators. Elizabeth was somewhere behind Lord Sennex—he could not quite see her—but Anne and Colonel Fitzwilliam both stood within the viscount's range. As, of course, did he.

"Put the weapon down, Lord Sennex," he said calmly. "The duel is over."

The viscount was so angry that tremors seized him. He reached up and fully cocked the pistol.

"There were to be *four* shots fired today." His hoarse voice quavered. "If you will not take the fourth, I shall."

"My lord, I will not."

"Very well, then."

The viscount pulled the trigger. There was a spark as flint struck frizzen, snapping open the pan.

But no explosion.

The pan was empty.

The viscount's astonished expression rapidly transformed to one of rage. He looked from the useless weapon to Darcy accusingly. With a cry, he advanced, raising the pistol as if to strike Darcy with it.

He stopped suddenly at two sounds from behind him.

A hammer being cocked. And Elizabeth's voice.

"Hold, sir! I am armed."

Thirty-two

Let no one presume to give the feelings of a young woman on receiving the assurance of that affection of which she has scarcely allowed herself to entertain a hope.

—Mansfield Park

While Darcy dealt with the viscount, Anne hurried to Colonel Fitzwilliam.

"Are you—" Anne extended a hand toward the colonel, but stopped short of actually touching him. "Are you seriously injured?"

"I am not."

She released a shaky breath. "Good—that is—that is good. I was so . . ." A soft cry escaped her. She looked away, struggling to regain her composure.

The surgeon came over to assess Colonel Fitzwilliam, insisting that he sit down. Anne knelt beside him. As the doctor cut away the colonel's sleeve to better access the injury, the patient had attention only for Anne.

"Are *you* well? Please tell me that Lord Sennex did not—"

"I was quite frightened, but he did not harm me."

At her assurance, he relaxed, making it easier for the surgeon to tend him. With Anne's assistance, the doctor staunched the flow of blood and wrapped the arm in a bandage. The wound was in need of stitching, which he preferred to do in his office if the colonel felt himself capable of walking there. Fitzwilliam sent him ahead, saying he would meet him presently.

When the surgeon had gone, he searched Anne's face. "If any harm had come to you . . ."

"If significant harm had come to *you* . . ." She lowered her gaze. "I—I do not know how I . . ." Her hands moved nervously in her lap, gripping, then releasing, the fabric of her gown.

He regarded her in silence for a long moment.

"Marry me."

She drew in a sharp breath and raised her head. "Oh, James, you cannot mean that."

"I most certainly mean it. Marry me."

She blinked and brought one hand to her chest. "I am so astonished, I do not know what to say."

He reached for her hand and took it into his own. "Say 'yes.' "

Emotion played across her features as she looked into his face. She nodded. "Yes." A smile formed, and spread until her eyes were alight. "Yes," she repeated.

Delight overtaking his own countenance, he gathered her to him and held her tightly with his good arm. "You should know that I already sought your mother's permission, and she refused it. But now that marriage to the viscount is impossible, perhaps—"

"It does not matter. I am over one-and-twenty. I can make my own choice, and I choose you."

"She threatened to withhold your funds."

"I am content to live without them, if you are."

"I would much rather live with you." He reluctantly released her. "We will not starve, you know. My father hardly left me destitute. But it is a smaller income than you likely looked forward to."

"The only person disappointed will be my mother."

"Can you be happy as a soldier's wife?"

Another smile overcame her countenance. "I do not deserve this much happiness."

"Why not?"

Her expression became more sober. "The terrible mistake I made."

"It is in the past."

"You say that now."

"I say it for ever."

"But Mr. Crawford and I lived together as man and wife, and that cannot be undone. What if I am—"

"Anne." He took both of her hands in his. "I hope we have a house full of children. And every one of them—*every* one—shall bear the name Fitzwilliam." He paused. "In fact, marry me now."

"Before we know?"

"Right here. Today. Unless you would rather not have another Scottish wedding?"

She laughed. "My mother will be furious."

"I shall defend you. I am now in practice."

Elizabeth, certain the couple had utterly forgotten the presence of everyone else, tried to discreetly leave the field. Colonel Fitzwilliam, however, stopped her.

"Where are you going?"

"I thought to grant you some privacy in which to continue making your plans."

"Do not stray far," Anne said. "It seems that I, too, require a second this day."

Thirty-three

Let other pens dwell on guilt and misery. I quit such odious subjects as soon as I can, impatient to restore everybody, not greatly in fault themselves, to tolerable comfort, and to have done with all the rest.

—Mansfield Park

Lady Catherine was indeed furious about Anne's second Scottish marriage, but her ire was short-lived. Upon reflection, and a hint from Mr. Archer, she came to consider herself fortunate that any respectable gentleman, let alone one so honorable as Colonel Fitzwilliam, still wanted her daughter. She approved the match, pending solemnization in a proper English church, and within hours convinced herself—and began putting word about—that a marriage between the cousins was entirely her idea. She even recanted her threat to withhold Anne's trust income. By the day of their "real" (i.e., English) wedding, the couple's happiness was increased by the knowledge that Anne carried no child of Henry's, and therefore no reminders or questions to trouble their future. The church bells tolled a fresh start to their life together.

Though the law tacitly overlooked the duel between Colonel Fitzwilliam and Lord Sennex, it could not ignore the viscount's abduction of Anne, nor the two duels that took place at Mansfield Park. Lord Sennex was charged with kidnapping and the murders of Henry Crawford and Neville Sennex. Before he could stand trial, however, his lordship suffered an apoplectic fit that truly did muddle his mind. He spent the remainder of his days in a world of the past where he was still a vital young man capable of defending his honor against all challenges, insensible to most of the present world around him.

While the Sennexes were responsible for both attacks on Mr. Crawford, it was Mrs. Norris and her propensities for inserting herself into everyone else's affairs and making free with Sir Thomas's bounty that led to Mr. Lautus's demise. The agent's assassination attempt against Mr. Crawford had an unanticipated witness when Mrs. Norris, walking home from a visit to Mansfield Park, decided to relieve a few favorite wild gooseberry bushes of their harvest. She heard the shot and, exalting in the belief that she was about to catch a poacher, came upon the scene as the agent set down his pistol to rifle Henry's body. Observing Mr. Lautus from behind, she mistook him for Henry and approached him to demand an explanation of what he was doing. When he turned around, she realized her mistake. He instinctively grabbed the pistol he had just set down, but then, recalling that it was no longer loaded, looked past Mrs. Norris to the cocked but undischarged pistol that had flown from Henry's hand when he fell.

Mrs. Norris, following his gaze and realizing his intent, reached the weapon first. She shot Mr. Lautus and fled, taking the incriminating pistol with her to dispose of elsewhere. In her terror and the gathering darkness she did not pause to retrieve the other pistol, nor, she claimed, did she realize Henry was still alive. When only one body was found, and it was mistaken for Mr. Crawford,

Mrs. Norris thought the man she had shot yet lived and lay in wait to finish her off. She dared not reveal what she knew. Upon Henry's unexpected return from the dead, she realized she was indeed a murderess after all and tried to dispose of the gun in a location wholly unconnected to her.

Mrs. Norris's involvement in Mr. Lautus's death was deemed by Sir Thomas to be an act of self-defense. But the incident so haunted her—or at least, so she told her sister—constantly—that she persuaded herself that only her removal to another country ("preferably one with an agreeable climate, such as Italy") could quell her unease. Sir Thomas responded favorably to her none-too-subtle hints that he ought to finance said relocation, but only on the condition that she take Maria with her. To the relief of all those left behind, they departed forthwith for the Continent, where living together in exile became mutual punishment for aunt and niece.

Meg continued her employment at the Ox and Bull, her amiable nature helping to draw even more customers, which in turn led to the addition of yet another wing to the sprawling structure. Among the inn's frequent patrons was Mr. Rushworth. Being sympathetic to the burdens of living with an elderly and oft-times difficult parent, Meg encouraged Mr. Rushworth to dine at the inn whenever business brought him near the village, upon which occasions she distinguished herself as the first person in his life to patiently listen to him. Though Mr. Rushworth had no difficulty obtaining a divorce from Maria, it was nevertheless a protracted process, and during the interval he found increasingly frequent cause to pass through the village, particularly at mealtime.

Eventually, after years of believing herself a sailor's wife, Meg's ship came in: She married Mr. Rushworth. What to all the world might seem a highly improbable alliance between a lively but poor girl and a wealthy but proud gentleman was in fact the most sensible match imaginable to the two parties most concerned. Mr. Rushworth had experienced enough of high-born debutantes; what Meg lacked in pedigree and education was more than compensated for by her common sense, unselfish nature, and appreciation for the gift of his regard. For Meg's part, Mr. Rushworth might not be sharp or witty, but he was steadfast and forthright, and she had experienced enough of charming, silver-tongued gentlemen. Theirs was a felicitous marriage, each valuing in the other the traits so opposite those of their previous spouses.

The dowager Mrs. Rushworth vehemently objected, of course, to Meg's common origins. But her son was resolute, and after the marriage, the mother's continued observation of her new daughter-in-law's prudence, loyalty, and genuine solicitude toward her son eventually won her over. Meg was everything Maria Bertram was not, and in the end fulfilled her domestic duties more capably and faithfully than her predecessor ever had.

Epilogue

"My good qualities are under your protection, and you are to exaggerate them as much as possible."

—Elizabeth to Darcy, Pride and Prejudice

Mr. and Mrs. Darcy returned home from their Mansfield misadventure to a joyful reunion with their daughter. They had missed her in the weeks of their absence, and now, free of the confining inn and its confining company, indulged in long walks in Pemberley's gardens with Lily-Anne and rambles through its woods with each other as autumn arrived to paint the landscape. Within doors, Mama and Papa spoiled Lily-Anne quite shamelessly, and were rewarded by the sight of not one, but two teeth every time she smiled.

They had been home little more than a fortnight when Darcy surprised Elizabeth one evening with a parcel. He entered her dressing room and offered it to her with a mysterious air.

She set aside her needlework. "What is this?"

"A present."

"Whatever for?"

"Do I require a reason?"

"A dutiful husband never requires a reason." She accepted the parcel and motioned for him to sit beside her. "In fact, perhaps you ought to impart that advice to Colonel Fitzwilliam to ensure his domestic felicity."

"I doubt he needs counsel from me. He and Anne seem well in the way of happiness, despite the precarious path that brought them to it."

She thought of Anne, and of her sister Kitty, whose own path to marital happiness had not been smooth. And of Darcy's sister, Georgiana, whose destination had yet to be determined but who, under the influence of Mr. Wickham, had almost taken a fatal misstep along the way. "It seems that many a proper young lady must negotiate a precarious path to happiness, past the bounders and Lady Catherines in their lives."

"That is why many a proper lady herself *becomes* a Lady Catherine, attempting to reduce the peril by directing the affairs of others in the manner she determines best."

Elizabeth considered her own daughter, asleep in the nursery. Every impulse drove her to protect Lily-Anne from tears and tumbles and childhood ills, and eventually from the Henry Crawfords of the world. But there were other ways of protecting one's children, and oneself, without using the guise of civility to manipulate others in a manner that was in truth not at all civilized.

"I will never evolve into such a 'lady,' " she declared.

"No, you shan't, for it is not in your nature." In a lighter tone, he added, "And you have other means of defense."

He gestured toward the parcel. "Now—deny no longer my pleasure in giving that to you."

She studied his expression, trying to make out his intent. Failing, she offered him an arch look of her own. "I am all curiosity."

She removed the wrapping paper to discover a small rosewood case engraved with her initials. She could not imagine what it might contain. "The case alone is lovely," she said.

"Open it."

She did—and laughed. "It is a most romantic gift."

"I thought you would like it."

"I do indeed," she said earnestly. "It is absolutely exquisite, and my mere possession of it shall make me the envy of all the other ladies of my acquaintance."

She lifted it out of the box, turned it over in her hands, and raised her eyes to meet his. "But whatever shall I do with it?"

"Your shooting lessons commence tomorrow."

CPSIA information can be obtained at www.ICGtesting.com
Printed in the USA
LVOW070254290313

326624LV00001B/18/P